ONE-EYED WILLY

The Jewel of the Spanish Main

PART ONE

LAWRENCE PHILIP

Charleston, SC
www.PalmettoPublishing.com

One Eyed Willy
Copyright © 2021 by Lawrence Philip

All rights reserved

Hardcover ISBN: 978-1-68515-366-3
Paperback ISBN: 978-1-68515-367-0
eBook ISBN: 978-1-68515-368-7

G rowing up isn't easy. Now close your eyes and then open one. Now open two. You already see the world fifty percent better than me. My names Lawrence Phillip I'm here to tell you a story....

Keep your head down hopefully they don't say something, that's me on the bus. Eight periods and six hours later my mother was right the day was over.

The realities of tomorrow were inescapable, they continued to repeat themselves. And It was then, I said goodbye to reality, picked my head up and said hello to imagination. Welcome to the story of One Eyed Willy.

CHAPTER ONE

The Caribbean was once home to a vast array of people from all corners of the earth. The islands were surrounded by light-blue waters that imitated the sky and the sands on the shoreline—just as in an hourglass—turning back the hands of time to an era that pioneered a new world.

Here, empires fought ferocious battles for control over new, undiscovered lands filled with riches such as gold and silver. Civilizations that had existed for millennia were annihilated in the name of King and country. These empires, along with their business of cultivating the fertile land with the blood of slaves for profit, ran rampant in this new world.

During these conflicts, able men were hired and trained to disrupt trade routes and hijack ships loaded with an unimaginable value in cargo, and were given the name of privateers. However, and rightly so, some became so addicted to the rewards, they decided to venture out on their own without the approval of the Crown. These men were ruthless, daring, heartless and without doubt, intelligent. These were known as pirates, and this is the story of the most famous pirate of his time.

One-Eyed Willy was born William James Walsh on August 10th, 1632, to James and Teresa Walsh of London, England, and most notably, he was born blind in his left eye.

His father, James, at one time one of the wealthiest men in the city, worked for the East India Company in the south of the City of London. James would often frequent Windsor Castle to speak with King Charles

I, discussing and negotiating fine trade agreements with territories and other countries. He would often travel for weeks, sometimes months.

There, he went about bartering these agreements both for the company and the Crown.

However, it was not during one of these trips that James had met Teresa Pordobel. He was a high-ranking officer in the King's Army, and whilst accompanying the King on an official visit with the Spanish monarchy in Madrid, Spain, *that* was where he met Teresa—the rest was history.

William would be an only child, and growing up with the use of only one eye was going to pose an obvious challenge for any young boy, and it was not any different for William.

As a rather unassuming and shy boy, anyway, having such an obvious deformity and disadvantage only made him even less confident. His father wanted to ensure this would not have a significant adverse effect on William's schooling, especially not impeding his progress.

And so it came to be that young William was duly enrolled in the King's School in Canterbury, England, quite some distance away from his parents. Some of the brightest young heirs from the wealthiest families in the land were enrolled into these prestigious walls of academia, and one of these privileged young boys was Oliver Hamilton, the son of Sir George Hamilton of New Castle.

Like King Charles I, Sir George was also a Scot and loyal to the Crown during the Bishops' Wars in which the Scots were in occupation of northern England. And in return for his loyalty, he was given land and official recognition, so he sent his eldest son Oliver away to study at King's.

Outside of the St. Martin's Church on a cloudy April afternoon in 1644, William was sitting on the church steps with his friend, Prince Charles II, reading his Bible.

He was resting there, just minding his own business as he usually did.

He liked to stay out of the limelight, as little noticed by the other boys as possible.

Plus, William wasn't a big lad at all; in fact, you could say he was rather underdeveloped, and he stood no higher than the back of a chair.

He had black shoulder-length hair, wore a white shirt, black pants and a patch over his useless eye—which was still there to be seen, but was glassy and opaque, and good for nothing whatsoever. Charles, slightly taller and more slender than William, was royalty, and both their fathers were close friends.

It was on this afternoon as young William sat minding his own business that Oliver Hamilton and a few of his friends approached the two boys on the church steps, striding up full of themselves.

"Well, if it isn't the Cyclops. Hey, Cyclops, what are you reading?"

"Why don't you bugger off, Oliver, and just leave William be?" Charles replied. "Hmm, now, was I speaking to the son of a traitor, or was I speaking to the Cyclops?" "I'll have you know I'm next in line to be King," replied Charles.

"Ha! I doubt it! You're next in line for the guillotine!" Oliver said loudly, and laughed.

"Don't worry, it's no bother, Charles. If you must know, Oliver, I'm reading verses from Job," said William. "I can read some to you if you like?"

Oliver was much taller and broader than William, and walked up one step and rested his elbow on his knee. "Hmm, *read* it to me?" he asked, laughing loudly to make a show of himself to his friends. "He asked if he could *read it* to me! Did you all hear that, boys?" He eyed his group of friends who also burst into a raucous laughter. Then he turned back to William who looked confused.

"You mean you can really read?" Oliver went on, pressing the point home. "Well, pardon me— then I'm surprised. I always thought you were dumb as well as blind. And anyway," he added, "I'm not particularly sure if God wants someone like you in his kingdom."

He looked around to the other boys, glancing one to the next, and sought approval from them for his own joke at which he was laughing copiously and slapping his knee.

Everyone joined in, staring and pointing at poor William whose face was a deep red.

"Right, Oliver, now that's enough," Charles intervened. "Job 34:5. *Did not he who made me in the womb make him and the same one fashion us in the womb.*"

"Prince Charles the Traitor, do you intend do something or would you like to sit back down and be quiet like a good chap?" said Oliver. Charles sat back down and Oliver continued.

"Now, do not be fooled, William. Understand it thus. *We* were created in God's image," Oliver said sternly, pointing at his friends. "And even *this* traitor, again, fashioned after God."

He pointed at Charles, then back at William. "*You,* on the other hand, are simply a deformity, spawned by the hideous fornication of a demon and a witch. You will *never* be one of us, Walsh." "Are you at all familiar with Greek mythology. About the Cyclops, Oliver?" said William.

"No, Willy. May I call you Willy? I do not concentrate my thoughts on heathens that may or may not have ever existed," Oliver responded.

"Giants, Oliver! They were human-eating giants! It is believed they aided Zeus in defeating the Titans and that they forged the very thunderbolts he used to do so," William said sarcastically.

Forks of lightning appeared overhead, followed by a loud rumble of thunder that startled even Oliver and his friends. William remained calm and unshaken by the noise.

"Well, since you fancy Cyclops, then maybe we should call you *eyeless Willy* instead? *No-eyed Willy?* No, wait; that's not it. Hmm, let me think. I've got it," said Oliver.

One of Oliver's friends chimed in. "What? What is it? What shall we call him, Oliver?"

"We shall call you *One-Eyed Willy.*"

Oliver proclaimed it as though it was a mandate, a done deal, no more to be discussed.

William closed his Bible angrily and wiped away a single, lonely tear from his eye. "No, you may not call me Willy," he replied, and ran off.

Oliver and his friends started shouting *One-Eyed Willy* and laughed as William made his escape. Charles shook his head, stood up and walked down the steps. "Someday, Oliver, your sins will catch up with you like the time Guy Fawkes was executed for his treasonous plot against my grandfather, James I. You'll see, Oliver, and on that day, William and I will also celebrate." He turned and ran off in the direction of William, crying out, "William, wait! Wait for me!"

For the next few months, and with his new nickname, William was the subject of laughter at the whim of Oliver Hamilton. The brutality of words was difficult at times for William, but he never lost the focus of his studies despite it all. He yearned to do well at school, to become someone, to excel and to leave school and get a job. Not just any job either, but a really good one.

One to be proud of. And so, he was like a sponge, absorbing and retaining as much information as he could, paying vigilant attention in all of his lessons.

Even though his best friend, Charles II, ironically was removed from King's School by his father the King—because it was too dangerous for Charles to remain—William stayed committed to his education, dearly wanting to soak up as much knowledge as he could.

Young William was fascinated by every aspect of the school itself and its broad curriculum on offer, also loving every single thing it offered to him as an opportunity, especially the studies involving swordsmanship and footwork. Despite his visual disadvantage, he was determined to grasp the skills involved in swordsmanship. And things were only going to get even better for him since early in the summer of the year of Our Lord, 1644, a young teacher by the name of Rupert came to King's. He was both a man of honor and a scholar.

And his primary class was all about the Art of War, and Sun Tzu.

William was fascinated by everything to do with the sword and would practice with a wooden replica at every opportunity he had. One day, when the sun was bursting its fire across the campus and the grass was brown and parched from thirst, William took shade under a large apple tree and began banging his sword against it in frustration. He was bored that day. Bored and sad.

The young apples, not yet ripe, were falling but this was no bother to William.

There was a depth of irritation behind his swings, and smoke in his eye.

Professor Rupert noticed William all by himself under the apple tree and proceeded to greet him. The pale-faced, future Prince of the Rhine approached—Rupert indeed walked like royalty and wore a long, refined brown wig just past his shoulders—and in a very astute German accent, asked, "So, what say you, young William? Why are you here alone? What is troubling you?"

"I am angry, Sir Rupert, and I am taking it out on this tree. I try so hard, Sir Rupert. Every day of my life, Sir <u>Rupert</u>, I try with all my might not to let my differences bother me, yet they do." William continued to swing his sword against the tree, only faster and harder.

"I know I'm not like the other children, I know I'm different," William said.

"And what makes you think you are different from the other children?" replied Rupert.

William stopped releasing his anger upon the tree that, after all, had not done a single thing to hurt him, and yelled, "Well, it's obvious, isn't it? Because *I'm blind*, Sir Rupert, blind. And I am ugly because of my dead eye too. Can't you see that? Can't you see any of it? Well, if you cannot, you are the only one—because they all remind me of it every day, calling me One-Eyed Willy." William threw the sword down, folded his arms and leaned his head against the tree.

"Why can't I be like all the other children? Why did this have to happen to me?" His voice grew plaintive and teary but he was determined not to cry.

He turned his head away so that Rupert could not see his show of emotion.

He would never cry. Never, ever, ever because he was used to being bullied and had learned the more he cried, the harder things became for him, drawing in more and more mean boys.

"You're right, William," Rupert said in a soft voice and put his hand on William's shoulder.

"You're right, you're not like the other children. You are, in my opinion, far more unique in ambition. You have a reservoir of intelligence in that mind of yours and a heart made of gold and silver. We haven't even had the chance to speak of the special talents you have yet to unlock." "Um. What? You think I'm talented?" questioned William.

"No, William. I don't think so. I *know* so, and I am going to make it my personal mission to give you the key to those abilities. See, William, when the Lord takes something away, he also gives something back far greater and I'm very eager to see exactly what he has given you. How would you like to learn how to use a real sword and become the best swordsman here at King's?" Rupert asked in a serious tone.

"Oh, boy, would I! But *how* can I?" William asked.

"Well, you see, I'm going to teach you," said Rupert.

William spent the next two-and-a-half years learning the intricate ways of the sword.

He also studied the Art of War.

For almost thirty months, he was able to use what he was learning to pay no further mind to the brutal attacks by Oliver Hamilton and his gang of taunting troublemakers. Now, he still minded his own business, not worrying or getting involved in what any of the other stupid boys were doing to cause mischief and to draw attention to themselves. But now, when they did still pick on him, he felt more self-assured, more certain he could defend himself if he needed to. Even just knowing that meant he did not get emotional anymore, and did not let anyone affect him the way they used to. Now, they could tease and taunt him all they liked; his nose still remained in his book.

They still tried, of course, but they found it dull and hard work trying to get an emotional response from William, who seemed to have grown up in so many ways.

It was simply not much fun these days to torment him. Most frequently, William would just laugh along with it or ignore their vile words completely, more immersed in what he was learning. In time, they found other more gullible boys to torment and harass.

The attention given to William by Mr. Rupert had indeed been welcomed on a number of fronts, for life was also far different than it used to be whenever he had returned home.

James, William's father, was overwhelmed with so many difficult choices, and working to keep a happy wife was proving to be the most challenging. He was so engrossed in this that he barely had time to cast his eye or his mind over anything else.

His attention was torn—torn between the demanding affairs of both home and abroad.

Europe was entangled in a long war, and preserving trade agreements between feuding nations wasn't easy but was expected by both the company and the King. The relationship between the King and parliament was not in good standing.

Decisions that favored King and country, which cemented James in his position, would also be his downfall. The King and parliament were in the midst of a civil war, yet the trading company did not take sides; it naturally sold to the highest bidder. Whoever held the most coin in his purse was the one to whom any good trading company would sell. That was just business. William's father took a gamble on going against parliament with regard to a new alcohol coming out of the Caribbean. Shamefully, he heavily invested funds in rum, and they were not even the King's.

King Charles was financially decimated and desperately in need of the coin, so William's father went to Spain to negotiate a trade agreement.

In the days before his journey to Madrid, he had spoken to the Earl of Essex who was in control of parliament and opposition to the King. James spoke about having his wife's portrait painted as a gift to her for their anniversary, since he would be unable to celebrate due to his business affairs.

The Earl not only agreed, but he also invited Teresa and young William to the celebration of

Guy Fawkes 'night at Windsor Castle.

Teresa was to become the focus of a painting by none other than Rembrandt van Rijn.

The great painter's exact words were, "The canvas would be fortuitous to have such beauty fill the abandonment of color."

The intention was for this fine painting to later be hung in the House of Lords. Unfortunately for William, the Earl had other intentions for Teresa.

Since William's father would not be in attendance, and seduced as she was with wine and halls of grandeur, the Earl easily took Teresa into his bed. Young William, still standing outside enjoying the fires, food, and fireworks with all the other children, had not the slightest clue.

He was too busy and engrossed looking out over the city of London in a courtyard made for a king. William was astonished. Servants were serving food and drink, and the grass perfectly cut.

Somehow, they could even make it appear wonderfully sunny outside during the nighttime, with all the many brightly colored candles and lanterns. Out in the courtyard, William and a few of the boys were trying to impress a group of girls their same age.

They decided to line up for a race to the other side of the courtyard where the girls were. The four boys counted to three.

One, two, three, go, and they were off, sprinting so fast they could barely see the others 'legs move. But young William was by far the fastest and won the race, receiving a smile from the prettiest girl in the group. In a race, the fact he had only one eye was no disadvantage at all.

It didn't hold back his legs from putting in the effort.

Richard, the son of the Duke of York, was not happy about his loss and was clearly jealous, asking, "What happened to you?"

"What do you mean?" William replied.

"The patch over your eye. What happened?" Richard enquired.

"I was born blind in this eye," said William.

"Can you show us what's underneath?" Richard asked, the girls all standing, clamoring.

"I'd rather not. I don't think it's appropriate," William replied nervously.

Richard rounded up a few of the other boys and girls and tried to convince William to remove the patch. "C'mon William, we just want to see what's underneath the patch."

William, overcome with the ongoing peer pressure, conceded and did what the future Duke of York asked. They all gazed upon the lifeless deformity in William's face, laughing and pointing without remorse. "That is disgusting. You are a freak," said Richard.

They all crinkled up their faces and made a deliberate show of disdain. "That's revolting."

"Such an ugly face I never did see," proclaimed a second.

"He should wear a bag across his whole head!" said another.

And finally, "fit for haunting a castle, and no need for a ghoulish vizard!"

The prettiest girl in the group could not look at William anymore, even showing disheartening cruelty toward him by shunning away. William wished he had his sword that night.

He felt so angry and embarrassed, a giant swell of self-pity and annoyance overcoming him. He could feel himself go deep red in the face, feeling his palms twitch too, as they did when he wanted to take a swing at someone and show them that he was not to be mocked without retaliation. He stepped forward silently and with one giant shove, pushed Richard to the floor.

Richard flailed upon the ground, shouting out, "You, you—!"

But he couldn't think of an appropriate end to his insult, so angry was he as he rose to his feet.

The onlookers appeared shocked at what they had witnessed, and Richard quickly got back on his feet and—himself stone silent just as William had been—punched William hard in the face, sending William down to the floor this time, humiliated and bleeding. In the struggle, he also dropped his eyepatch, which Richard quickly picked up and started tossing it around

Back and forth the small patch went, already muddy from the filthy ground anyway, and now it was mercilessly being thrown back and forth amongst the other children, each jumping high to catch it before tossing it to the next, then the next. They squealed with mean delight.

William raised his hand to his bloodied nose, got himself back to his feet and lurched forward, desperately trying to retrieve his indispensable eyepatch. Now, it was no fun at all, not a game anymore, not even a childish playground fight. Now, William's rage overcame him.

This time, he would get Richard well and good. He would do Richard some damage.

As soon as Richard caught the patch, he ran and tackled him hard in the midriff, sending them both flying into a bush where the prickly branches and thorns poked and shredded their faces.

Both boys were bleeding badly now, but neither wanted to put a stop to it.

They grappled and fought on the ground, both committed until a few guards rushed over and separated the two boys. Of course, the worried Duke of York quickly came to see what had happened to his son, and noticed Richard had a cut under his eye from the contact with the bush.

"William attacked me just because I am the Duke of York's son," Richard explained. "He is jealous of me, Father. I cannot seem to keep him away from me—he hounds me all the time."

"Is this true, Richard? He attacked you?" said the Duke. "This miserable wretch of a boy did set upon you, in front of all the other fellows and young ladies here?"

"Yes, Father," said Richard. "He did, Father."

Not one to be easily hoodwinked, the Duke was not going to just take his son's word for it, for he had seen first-hand how his own unruly son sometimes taunted other less fortunate children, especially those who were weak or disadvantaged by some kind of disfigurement.

"Is this so? Did anyone see the fracas involving my son? I shall give a coin to anyone who can tell me a true picture of what came to pass here, to get my son into this bloodstained mess." He reached into a small brocade pouch that hung around his waist.

All the children surged forward.

"I, sire, I saw it and can tell you," one cried out.

"And me sir, I saw it too, and here's what happened—"

"Oh sir, Duke, Duke, I did see all of it!"

The throng was now a dozen strong, some of the children never having been anywhere near the fracas but claiming to have seen everything, every little punch and blow.

"You, boy," said the Duke to a young lad he already knew as a friend to both boys. This boy would surely be impartial. His name was Alexander and he stepped forward shyly.

"Yes, sir. I am happy to tell you what I witnessed, sir. Young William did set upon your son most horribly and without just cause or want of cessation, and gave him a terrible beating, sir. I saw it all, sir." He stepped forward toward the Duke, and received a pair of small gold coins.

He delivered a slight bow to the Duke, knowing deference always helped a lie become taken as the very embodiment of the truth. "Thank you, sir," he said with humility, bowing slightly. "I watched it, sir, with my own two eyes. You can be sure it is the honest truth."

He did not seem to see all the children laughing at what he had just said. They took it as yet another slight against poor One-Eyed Willy, the boy nobody liked right at this moment.

William looked in a state of shock at what he was hearing and attempted to plead his case.

"No, that's not true. You, boy, are a liar!" he spat out to the boy who had just told all the lies.

Having his eyepatch rudely and callously stolen from him was one thing, but then having a young boy whose friendship he'd believed to be quite genuine turn against him in this way... that made it all so much worse, so much more painful and disappointing.

Then he turned to Richard and said, "And you...You filthy liar. I only hope you can live with yourself. Mark my words, this will come back to bite you someday."

He looked pleadingly at the Duke. "The truth is, sire, your own son punched me in the face for no good reason other than that he wanted to steal my eyepatch, sir, and I refused to allow him." The Duke looked at Richard again, delivering a harsh glare as if questioning the boy.

"Lies, father. He's lying; his patch fell off while we were rolling around on the ground. Honestly, I swear it. Father, you brought me up as a young gentleman. I would never set upon a disadvantaged boy in a fight because I would not feel the victor at the end of it."

"Then I want this boy arrested for assaulting the young lord," the Duke said, even though he had seen his boy do exactly what he said he would never do. The guards moved forward and quickly grabbed William. They began to hustle him toward an awaiting carriage into which they intended to bundle the insolent boy for assaulting the boy Richard, son of the good Duke.

Soon, they would see him incarcerated in a suitable lock-up, waiting to receive his just punishment. He could be jailed there for up to ninety days for such a terrible attack.

But not everyone who witnessed the spectacle of the boy being seized was happy about it.

"Unhand that boy at once!" boomed out, and everyone flinched, even the guards whose hands immediately released from William's upper arms. They let him go but still he stood there, his head down as if indeed, he was ashamed. It was an unfamiliar voice and belonged to the Earl of Essex. All eyes were upon the newcomer, and as he approached, everyone in turn bent a knee.

Teresa quickly ran ahead to check on William's condition, hugged him and then checked his face and arms for marks. "You are scratched all over, the thorns showed no mercy," she said. "What is the meaning of this?" yelled the Earl of Essex, his loud bellowing instilling the fear of God into every person there. To make a point, he whacked a vast tree with a sturdy cane until the bark fell off in strips and littered the grass. "Must I take this cane to you all to find out?" "My son says this peasant attacked him for no reason," the Duke replied.

"Come now, Duke. This is the son of one of the wealthiest men in England, whose mother was just portrayed by Rembrandt himself, and you call him *peasant?* Surely, you of all men ought to know better than that. And Richard, it's with regret I must insist as though the apple has not fallen far from the tree. This boy and his mother are my honored guests and are to be treated like royalty, am I understood?" the Earl confirmed.

"Completely, sir. Please accept our apologies," said the Duke of York.

William looked up at the Earl and bowed his head.

"Thank you, my Lord. I am indebted to you, my Lord."

"That wasn't even a race. You could have walked and beaten him," the Earl remarked. "Let's get you inside so your mother can clean you up."

Teresa pinched William on his cheek and smiled before turning to the Earl.

"Thank you, my Lord." Teresa kissed the Earl on the cheek but William noticed something strange. The Earl appeared to have just squeezed his mother's ass in front of them all.

Did I just see that? What is my mother thinking? William thought as he watched them go inside.

When James finally returned from Spain, his ship was promptly seized in the port of London.

There were no records or documents pertaining to the funds appropriated for the cargo, and James therefore found himself imprisoned by the harbormaster. News of this ploy reached the Earl of Essex along with young William at King's. Teresa Walsh used her powers of persuasion with the Earl to have James released and reinstated within the East India Company, under a different title and with less financial reciprocation. She also secured a position as a baker at the House of Lords so she could be closer to the Earl—as James had begun drinking rum all too often.

The story of William's father's treachery was but mere ammunition for Oliver and his friends, the verbal attacks continuing daily and delivered brutally, until one day, William decided to stand up for himself. He walked out into the courtyard for swordsmanship training, seeing Oliver was also there with his friends, practicing. William deliberately held back in class at the instruction of Rupert, for fear the other classmates would be injured by his superior swordsmanship.

"There he is. It's One-Eyed Willy," Oliver shouted. "Hey, One-Eyed Willy. I bet if you could handle your sword like your mother handled the Earl's, you could have got your father pardoned as well," Oliver continued, and a bunch of the classmates laughed.

"Well, at least my father didn't stab the King in his back," William retorted. "But judging by the way your father looks at other men, I'd bet he likes getting stabbed from behind!" The class erupted in hysterics.

It was a red rag to a bull, of course.

Oliver sauntered over to William and threw him to the ground.

"Pick up a sword and we shall see who stabs whom," Oliver suggested.

"Very well. You're the one who will regret you ever called me One-Eyed Willy. Don't say you weren't asking for this!"

At that moment, however, Professor Rupert came striding out to the courtyard and broke up the fight between the two lads.

A few days later, in June of 1647, Oliver Hamilton graduated from the King's School in Canterbury and the vicious feud with William had come to an abrupt end. Oliver would now be leaving school.

One year later, on the eve of William's graduation as a junior petty officer in the King's Royal Navy, James Walsh was in his study drinking rum and working on documentation for the Earl.

The room was dark, only dimly lit by two candles in fixtures on the wall, and James Walsh was seated at his desk and continuing his writing when there came a knock at the door. "Come in," said James, and William appeared in the doorway. "Goodnight, Father. I'm going to take my leave to my room." "Where is your mother?" his father replied.

"I believe she said she was baking at the House of Lords," William answered.

"That's the third time she has been baking this week," said William's father, slamming his hand down on the table and knocking over the ink that spread across the desktop in a black pool.

"But Father, I've heard her almond cake is considered by many as being *to die for.* She's only trying to make some extra coin," said William. "Surely, we all benefit from that?" His father scowled and still said nothing more.

James cleaned up the ink before it spread everywhere and William once again said. "Goodnight,

Father."

"William, wait. Before you go, my son, I have something for you. Sit down," James said, and

William sat at the table in a creaking old wooden chair. "This is for you." His father handed him a rolled-up scroll with a ribbon tied around it. William undid the ribbon and opened up the scroll.

"It's blank. I don't understand, Father. It's empty," said William.

His father laughed and handed him the feather quill after dipping it in ink. "I want you to write in the upper left-hand corner the year you were born." William wrote 1632 in neat black script in the upper left-hand corner.

"I still don't understand," William said.

"William, my son, this is a timeline of your life and all its great accomplishments. Each time you accomplish something, whether it be graduation or a promotion to Captain, anything in your life, I want you to put in a year. Now, you don't have to write down what the accomplishment was. You could even write the same year three times. It's when you go back to those years and remember those accomplishments that the meaning of this exercise will come to light for you as if a great illumination has been cast over all your lifetime's achievements. Our most important possessions are our memories, my son; they are the only true paintings we have in this world."

"Thank you, Father. I will try to fill the entire scroll," said William. "Now, I understand."

"I know you will fill out the whole scroll, son. I know you will as I have every faith in you. Oh, I have one more thing for you." James took out a silver doubloon from his pocket.

"Do you know what this is, William?"

"Yes, Father, it is a Spanish silver doubloon," William replied.

"That is correct, and it is from the year of your birth. I've been saving it," said James.

"Father, you've been saving that coin for sixteen years?" William asked, incredulous.

"I have indeed, and because of saving it for so long, you should know what it's worth," replied his father.

"Yes, Father," William answered. There must have been many times in those sixteen years in which his father could have made use of that coin. He was touched and warmed by the gesture that his good father had been holding the coin in safekeeping for him, only releasing it now, today.

"Good, it's yours. Congratulations on your graduation." William's eye sparkled.

"You can't be serious, though, Father. This could settle all of your debts. So, I mean, I appreciate the gesture and all—and I am touched by it, Father, but you need your money."

"I do need *my* money, son. But this ceased to be *my money* the very moment I knew I had a son. This coin has always had your name upon it, as true as if it had been engraved. And besides, there is no amount of money that can outstrip how proud I am of you," James replied. "And there is only one rightful place for this doubloon, my son, That is inside your pocket."

William jumped up and hugged his father, who squeezed William tighter than he ever had.

"Yes, it's for you. It's always been for you and I'm sure you'll do great things, my son." He kissed him on the forehead. "Alright, now off to bed. Goodnight, my son."

"Goodnight, Father, and again, a thousand times, thank you."

William went to bed and dreamed of filling the scroll with tremendous accomplishments. And now, he had the funds with which to do whatever he wanted in life, to help him fill the scroll.

The following morning, his father, James Walsh, hung himself from the London Bridge. His father had grave and persistent suspicions of his mother's infidelity, and feared losing his precious wife. It was too much on top of all his amassed debts.

He had picked up the bottle and begun drinking, and carried on the drinking all day long.

Rum, whiskey, ale, whatever he could get his hands on, but mostly rum. The thoughts drove him into a deep depression. William would only see it when he was home from school.

There had long since been constant and rowdy battles in the house between James and Teresa.

Finally, James's suicide was the overall conclusion to a broken home. William was devastated.

At his graduation, when the Earl himself spoke, it was hard to hold back the tears. His mother was so proud of him, and yet barely mustered up any emotion. In no uncertain terms, she callously told William, "I am crying tears of joy for you, not mourning the death of your father."

"I know, Mother," William whispered back, a solitary tear running down his face as he realized how much it would have meant to him if his father had been here to see him graduate today.

At the end of the ceremony, which took place in front of the Houses of Parliament on the River Thames, the Earl of Essex approached the junior petty officer.

He held out his hand warmly, offering his congratulations and condolences.

"If there is anything I can do, please let me know," the Earl said.

"You have a nerve, don't you? I once revered you, but now I despise you," answered William loudly, refusing to hold out his hand to meet the Earl's own. "You want the truth, Earl? Then so be it. The truth is—and I do not care whose ears this reaches—I feel disgraced to wear this uniform," William raised his voice even further, wishing for all in earshot to hear the way he was speaking to the Earl. "I should also like to ask you, how's my mother's cake, my Lord?"

"Careful, young William, I would hate to have tasted the last cake she will ever bake."

"Almond cake is sweet, my Lord, but revenge is sweeter," William replied.

Shortly after the antagonistic talk between the young William and the cake-tasting Earl, the Earl spoke with Teresa, and it was decided she would have to send William to Barbados in the Caribbean Sea. It was supposed to be a punishment for him, meted out by Theresa against his unforgivable surliness. William, however, was not at all displeased; he knew in his heart that this was the best option for him. He would never come to terms with the fact that he believed his mother and the Earl were in part responsible for his father's death.

In fact, he did not 'believe it'; he knew it absolutely. There were no more doubts in them being complicit in his father's death than he would doubt in the dawn that followed the night sky.

He could not bear to stay in London, where he would have to gaze upon their affair without thoughts of bitterness and revenge, so he left England and began his journey in the Caribbean.

He also reveled in the fact that to send him away with a clear conscience, Theresa had needed to provided more silver coinage, some of which—if not all—must have come from the Earl himself. She handed him a small sewn leather pouch, heavy with the weight of solid silver.

Gladly, he thought, the Earl would have given up the funds to get the boy out of their way, leaving them clear to carry on their shenanigans without him getting in between their lustful affair.

CHAPTER TWO

Two years later, aboard the Sea Stalker, the sky was pitch black and the seawater thrashed against the ship without mercy. The rain was pouring down as though the night was pissed, and the wind was howling like a pack of wolves in a new Amsterdam winter.

The water was breaching both sides of the ship, but even in these rough seas, the Sea Stalker was still gaining on the Spanish merchant ship less than a quarter mile away.

The captain of the Sea Stalker was John Ramos, one of the most ruthless privateers the Caribbean could muster. "Prepare to come alongside her, men. Load the bow cannons and fire a warning shot. If she doesn't allow us to come alongside her, we will send her to the depths of the sea," Ramos shouted back to his men.

The Sea Stalker was within firing range of the Spanish vessel and fired the bow cannon. The cannonball hit the portside bow of the vessel, nearly punching a hole in their hull.

The ship finally allowed the Sea Stalker to come alongside her and immediately, the men aboard the Spanish ship began firing muskets and pistols, punching small holes in the Sea Stalker, killing one of the crew. John Ramos didn't get his reputation for being kind, and ordered the starboard cannons to be loaded. Two shots were immediately fired directly at the vessel, sending shards of the Spanish ship flying into the wind, narrowly missing the ship's mast. Moments later, the guns on the top deck stopped firing.

"Walsh. Where is Walsh?" Ramos shouted, holding onto a rope to keep from falling over. Walsh appeared on the main deck from down below, sliding along the treacherous surface.

Ramos offered his hand, which Walsh grabbed, then it was followed up by a nice long length of rope for Walsh to hold on to. "I need to get every able seaman on deck. I need you to have the landsman tie us off. Can you handle that?" Ramos shouted, battling the storm.

"Yes, Captain. I can," said Walsh, and using ropes to move around the ship, he found three landsmen to tie off the other ship. Ramos appeared from below deck with twenty men able and ready to board the Spanish vessel. Armed with pistols and swords, the men threw out Jacob's ladders and began boarding the other vessel. John Ramos followed behind and jumped across, onto their top deck. Wood was scattered about from the damage of the cannon fire, and the pistols and muskets left on the deck were great additions to the Sea Stalker's ever-increasing armaments.

Ramos scanned around the deck at the dead, and held his pistol in the air.

"Where's the Captain of my new ship?" Ramos barked. With a pistol pointed at him, the Captain made his walk of shame to Ramos. John raised his pistol and put a bullet right between his eyes, dropping him immediately to the deck.

"Anyone else wants to challenge me?" Ramos shouted. No one in the crew dared to move on Ramos now. The crew of the Sea Stalker went to work on the Spanish vessel flooding the decks like ocean water in a storm. Deck by deck, the men searched for whatever goods were aboard the ship. There were spices and barrels of ale, salt, and coffee, as well as a few animal skins.

The men took it all. For some reason, Ramos was in a good mood that evening as he did not torch the ship. Normally, that was a given, and he would have no hesitation in killing everyone on board. Perhaps surviving the storm was difficult enough.

The lines were separated from the ships, and the Sea Stalker was en route back to Barbados.

A few days later, the Sea Stalker docked in Barbados on a delightful Saturday morning.

Saint Jamestown was on the western side of the island, its newly built town featuring roads to all five of the plantations, and newly built wells for water. St James's Church was right in the center of town, along with a tavern and a post office. The beaches were draped with fishermen looking to make ends meet for their families by catching and selling fish.

The farmers 'market was also set up near the church in the center of town, with baskets overflowing with fruits, vegetables, sugar, and tobacco.

The men were busy unloading the goods from the Sea Stalker, and John Ramos came down the ramp onto the dock to where William Walsh was taking, detailing, and documenting the goods received. "I was impressed with the way you handled yourself," Ramos said.

"Thank you, Captain," William replied.

"We have yet to see you use that sword. I wonder if your footwork is as good as your accounting?"

"Would you believe me if I told you it was better, Captain?" said William.

"If we are honest, then no, Walsh, I wouldn't."

"Captain, will we be shoving off tomorrow?" asked William.

"Tomorrow is Sunday, Walsh. A day of rest and prayer. I would say by Wednesday, we should be back out to sea. Are you coming into town with us, William?"

"Doubtful, Captain. I will more than likely just stay aboard the Sea Stalker," William replied.

"Walsh, you have been under my command for a few years now, and you have yet to see the plantation. I'm inviting you for supper tomorrow, after church. There is nothing you can say. It's an order. Besides, I want to introduce you to my sister. She never leaves the plantation, and you never leave the boat. Who knows, you may like each other. Two hermits made for one another." "I wouldn't know what to say. I've never courted a lady before," Walsh answered nervously.

"Look, young man, I'm not asking you to marry her, just meet her. One benefit about tomorrow is my wife and sister make enough food to feed an armada, let alone five people, and you might enjoy the time away from the ship. You know where the plantation is, correct?"

"Yes, Captain, of course. I've walked past the road that leads directly to it. Captain, are you sure I'm welcome? You're quite sure I shan't be any trouble to anyone?"

He quite hoped the Captain might change his mind; William still was quite a loner at times, preferring to stay on his bunk in the ship and think about the matters ailing the world. Besides, when men ventured ashore from the big ships was when they often ended up getting into bother of some sort. Drunken brawls and vicious arguments on land were known to be commonplace among seafarers, most of whom found the experience of being on land restrictive and irritating.

Tempers flared among some of them almost as soon as the land came into sight, let alone when they had left the vessel and gone out drinking and cavorting with local girls. But he was not to get his wish. Not today.

"Nonsense, Walsh, I wouldn't entertain such a question. Besides, what do you think you might do to cause trouble? I wouldn't have taken you aboard my ship if I had heard you were a fire-starter or a warmonger. You are neither of those, are you, lad?' "No, Captain," he said and laughed nervously.

"Excellent. Then I'll be expecting to see you at three o'clock tomorrow. And no excuses."

"See you then, Captain," William replied hesitantly. *Well, damn, now I don't get an evening of rest,* he thought. He would have to wash and press his white shirt too, the only shirt he had.

Hopefully, it would at least have dried in time.

The thought of wearing a damp shirt to supper was not appealing, especially not since he was also known to sweat copiously from the heat and his over-wrought nerves.

The church bells rang with joy at one o'clock on the Sunday afternoon, and all the patrons of Saint Jamestown who partook in the mass were hurrying out of the front doors.

With a gigantic smile on his face, John Ramos had his right arm draped around his wife Lenora and held his daughter, Isabella's right hand. John's sister Louisa was also clinging just as tightly onto Isabella's left hand as they walked down the church's steps, eventually separating and congregating again amongst the townspeople.

"John, we should begin our walk back to the plantation. We do have company arriving in a few hours," Lenora remarked. "We need to be sure we are washed and attired in good time."

"Company? Who, Walsh? I wouldn't call Walsh *company*, more like just someone to eat all the extra food," Ramos replied. "Though he is a pleasant enough young man, granted."

"That isn't very nice, John."

"You know I don't mean it. I rather like the young fellow."

"I'm going to look around the farmers 'market for a while, and I will meet you at home," Louisa suggested.

"Are you sure, love?" John said with a baffled look.

"Yes, I'm sure."

"Do you need a coin?" asked John.

"No, I have my own. You can leave me, I'll be alright."

"C'mon John, let's leave her shop around the market on her own," Lenora said, urging John forward. Isabella grabbed her father's hand and said, "Father, home."

"Yes, Isabella, we will go home now."

John, Lenora, and Isabella began their journey home leaving Louisa to her shopping.

Louisa filled her basket with a few sweet and juicy mangos, bananas, and oranges and paid across the farmer's coin, thanking him for the fruit.

All the time, she remained unaware of being watched as she put her coin back into her pouch.

She left the center of town and began to walk down the dirt road that led to the plantation, when an orange dropped out of her basket. Stopping to bend and pick it up, she noticed three men following close. She began to walk faster, stepping up her pace until she was almost running.

So did they.

She dropped the basket and began to run, but the long dress and the searing heat were not her friends. Eventually, the men caught up with her, soon surrounding her on all sides.

"What do you want?" she asked nervously.

"You know what we want, love," said one of the men, missing all his teeth and looking dirtier than a latrine. She took out the pouch of coins and threw it at the man.

"Here. Take it all. It is all I have left. Now, leave me alone."

"Apologies, love, but I would not say that is all you have," said one, leaning forward to brush her clothing with a filthy, rough hand.

"No, really. I have no coins…"

"Little lady, who told you we were after coins? We were looking for something a little softer than coins," the toothless man suggested. One of the men, one with sinful blue eyes, grabbed her from behind but she elbowed him in the stomach before another joined the struggle and wrestled her to the ground, kicking and screaming for help.

Finally, the men manage to cover her mouth with a piece of rag.

The two held her down while the smelly one spread her legs, putting his weight onto each of her knees, attempting to pull his pants down. Suddenly, something hit him on the head.

He jumped up, startled, spying a single large orange rolling away, flattened on one side.

"That—*that* is what hit me!" he cried out, very annoyed and rubbing at his head. "Well, I'll be… Who threw that bloody thing? You'll regret it when I catch a hold of you!" He looked around, spotting William Walsh holding onto a small bouquet of flowers.

"Was that you, lad? Was that you?" hollered the attacker.

William stood by nonchalantly, as though he had no idea what the matter was.

"Something hit me, here," said the man, still staring at the youth.

The other two men got up off the ground too, and the third—the one who had been struck— was still rubbing at his sore head and gazing around for the thrower.

"It was the flower boy," said the second one.

Louisa, still in shock, scrambled back to her feet and away from the would-be rapists. "Hey, one-eye, did you hit me in the head with an orange?"

"Would you have preferred a mango?" William answered. "Or a rock, perchance?"

"No, I prefer we kill you and continue with our business. Get him, lads."

Two of the men drew swords while the other picked Louisa up off the ground, holding her tightly back to his body with a knife to her throat. It seemed the boy's defense of her had only gone and made things so much worse. But he was well-equipped to do what he had to.

William drew his sword, still holding tightly onto the flowers as there was no clean ground on which to lay them down. Besides, he did not want them to get trampled in the melee.

The two men moved in on William, the first attacking from the right, trying to stab William in the abdomen. But William deflected the sword and spun 360 degrees, then kicked the man in the ass, sending him flying. The other man swung his sword in an upward, backhanded motion but was immediately stopped by William's sword and kicked in the stomach, dropping him to the floor. He gasped and groaned, flailing there on the ground, clutching at his gut.

William held his sword and drove down the handle on top of the guy's head, sending him into a deep sleep. He turned and faced the man with the knife but didn't notice the other get up from the ground, attacking William from behind, grabbing him as though he was hugging him.

The man holding Louisa threw her to the ground and went to assist his friend.

The third man with the knife lunged at William, but William slid out of the way, leaving the man's friend in direct line with the thrusting blade.

Just as William pulled away, the stabbed man managed to yank off his adversary's eyepatch. The other guy quickly tugged the knife out of his friend and attempted a backhand swing at William. William moved backward too, the knife just missing slicing him across the stomach.

"First, I'm gonna gut you, then I'll be having some fun with her," the man said.

William turned, baiting the man, who responded by swinging the knife toward William.

He stepped back out and kicked the assailant full on in the groin, instantly dropping him to his knees. William drove his own knee directly into the man's face, sending him straight onto his back where he kicked and struggled to right himself for a moment, looking like an upended tortoise.

William made a fist around the handle of the sword, stood on top of the dirty man, and punched him twice in the face for good measure, leaving him unresponsive.

Casually, as if he fended off attacking threesomes every day of his week, William sheathed his sword before turning to walk just a few hundred feet to the spilled fruits. He stooped and picked them up, putting each one gently into his basket. He walked back toward Louisa, past all three men on the road, reaching out his hand. Louisa put her hand in his, never stopping eye contact.

"You dropped your basket, milady," William said finally. He offered a warm smile.

"Thank you. And you are?" Louisa enquired.

"William, milady. William Walsh."

"Oh, well! So...you're the guest for dinner tonight! Oh no, look at me. I look horrendous."

" On the contrary, milady, as far as my eye can tell. Look, the sun is so jealous of you, it's shining with all its might, and still isn't as bright as your smile. Aphrodite herself could not compare to the beauty I see before my eye at this very moment."

She blushed and walked back to where the dirty men were scattered on the ground.

She retrieved William's eyepatch and offered it.

Now, he was mortified. Deeply ashamed and embarrassed to be seen this way in front of the

Captain's family member, he reached out to grab the eyepatch from her.

She refused his hand, gently pushing back on his wrist as he attempted to take the patch. "Please, allow me. It's the least I can do."

Louisa moved closer to William but didn't cover his missing eye. She looked deep into his other one, let her arms slide onto his shoulders—and kissed him. She quickly pulled away.

"Oh, Lord. I don't know what's gotten into me. I'm sorry," Louisa said, apologetically. "But you were just so, so brave, Mr. William Walsh, so gallant in defending me, a lady you did not even know. Anyway, my apology, William—if I may call you that."

"No apology necessary, milady, and yes, you may call me that. Oh, and these flowers are for you. I mean, they always were for you."

William handed her the bouquet of assorted carnations—yellow, pink, white, and purple. Unfortunately, they were looking a little the worse for wear now, after the fight. "Oh dear," he said eyeing the bedraggled blooms. "They were not like that when—" He was stuck for words and looked saddened.

Then he said, "Listen, let us walk together away from these unpleasant types, and when we pass the stall where I purchased them, please, milady, allow me to buy you some more." He was about to toss the damaged blooms into the gutter.

"No!" she cried out. "No. I mean, I very much would like to have them just as they are. If I may, of course. If you don't mind. I should not like to cause you any discomfort if…" She held out her hand again, tentative and yet inviting.

He slipped the broken stems into her grasp without hesitation.

She pulled them inward, toward her heart, and clasped them there. "Thank you," she said softly. "Oh…"

She seemed overcome with delight.

"Well, of course…I didn't mind," he said, "but why on earth would you prefer these tattered things to the new and beautiful ones I would have liked to buy for you?" They slowly walked as they conversed.

"Because they are the most beautiful already," said Louisa. "I never did see lovelier." "Really?" William was agog. "Why?" "Beautiful," she said again.

"I know you are. I mean, are they?" William questioned. He eyed their fractured stalks and sad, droopy and flattened petals bearing bruises all over them.

"Yes, they are," said Louisa. "These are the most beautiful and the most special because they bear witness to the amazing kindness you showed to me. I shall press the blossoms into the pages of my book until they dry out—and I shall keep them always."

William and Louisa made their way to the plantation arm in arm and heart in heart.

Louisa entered through the door to the main house on the plantation, to be greeted by the housemaid, chatty Abigail. Sometimes, the family even called her *Chatty*.

"How do you fare, Abigail? I want to introduce you to William Walsh."

"Oh dear, child. I fare well, and a good day to you but why in God's own name are you bound by dirt and mud on every inch of your body? Oh, Mr. Walsh, it is a pleasure to meet your acquaintance. I dread to think what you must make of our dear Louisa in this condition."

William acknowledged Abigail's hospitality. Slightly bending his knee, he took her hand, nodded his head and gently kissed the top of her fingers.

"I can assure you, I am most delighted to meet Miss Louisa."

And he bent his knee a second time and kissed Abigail's hand a second time for good measure. Abigail blushed for a moment and said, "Come now, boy, I'm no queen. Miss Louisa, let's get you cleaned up for supper." Louisa and chatty Abigail retired upstairs.

William, left alone in the enormous house, looked at the magnificent surroundings. A young girl came running up to him from a room behind the staircase, and tugged on William's overcoat. "Who you might be?" she enquired.

William dropped on one knee. "My name is William, and who are you, milady?"

"My name is Isabella Ramos."

"A pleasure to meet you, Princess Isabella," said William.

Isabella smiled intensely and asked boldly, "Are you a pirate?"

William laughed. "Oh, dear Lord no, I work for your father."

Lenora entered the room, wiping her hands with a towel. "Isabella, are you bothering this poor man? Run along now. I'm Lenora, John's wife. I'm delighted to make your acquaintance." "The pleasure is all mine, milady." William bowed with his arm behind his back.

"The man is both handsome and so proper. You know she didn't mean anything by it?"

"Pardon, milady?"

"She saw your eye patch and I'm afraid she assumed. She's growing up so fast," replied Lenora.

"I thought not of what she spoke; her curiosity humbles me. She has her mother's eyes and beauty."

Just as he finished his reply, John entered the room and added. "And her father's wit." "Apologies. I was going to infer that next," William said, and they all laughed aloud.

"I will take my leave," Lenora insisted. John kissed her before she left.

"William. See you again at supper," she insisted.

"Looking forward to it, milady." John pulled William to one side.

"So, Walsh, you want a tour of the place?" "I would be obliged, Captain," William answered.

"William, it's Sunday. Please address me as John."

"Yes, John."

"Good, shall we?" "After you, John."

They both walked out the front door and down the steps onto the plantation.

As he walked through the front door of the mansion, William noticed how beautiful the place was. There were tropical gardens on both sides of the brick walkway where abundant flowers blossomed, and as bees and other flying creatures enjoyed their nectar. Beyond the gardens was a stable house and then another to hold equipment. Walking down the brick walkway through the brown gates, William gazed upon miles of sugarcane fields, tasting the sweetness in the air.

"It must be such a joy for you every time you return home, is it?" William asked.

"It is a joy to see my wife and daughter. It is a joy to see my sister. But William, it is not a joy to see what has been done to the slaves on this plantation."

"I don't understand. What do you mean?"

"Well, William, my stepfather owns this plantation, and he doesn't frequent often. This plantation supplies sugar to some fifteen million Britons on the mainland.

"Its operations are run by the Crown. We merely get to live here because of our status as Cortez made my grandparents slaves, but to have to watch the treatment of these people is both frustrating and inhumane. Lenora and I give to them as much as we can without being seen as aiding them but it is not enough, William. Nowhere near enough. Sometimes, I just can't sleep at night."

"The more knowledge I am given, the less I believe in Crown and country."

"Enough of this talk, let's eat supper," John insisted, and guided William toward the house.

The table was set with red plates and serving dishes, while the battered flowers purchased for Louisa sat proudly displayed on the table in a vase, afforded pride of place.

Steam was rising off the fresh ham and candied apples, and in the kitchen was a coconut and key lime pie. Chatty Abigail was also making her famous *choffee,* a combination of coffee and cocoa mixed together. Everyone was present at the table except Louisa.

Moments later, she hurried downstairs and said, "My apologies, I'm not Mrs. Punctual." William stood up, walked around to her chair, and pulled it out.

"Your beauty is welcomed with thrilled excitement." Louisa smiled, sat down, and William pushed in her chair.

"Easy there, William. That's my sister, and I'm the only one that can tell her how amazing she looks."

William changed the direction of conversation. "Everything looks boundless with flavor."

"Don't be shy, William," said John. "Have as much as you like."

William was seated opposite Louisa and they could not stop looking at each other the rest of the evening. There was a serious conversation and laughing, but during supper or dessert, Louisa or William did not bring up the events that had led them to meet one another that day.

After dessert, John and William were admiring the moon and the stars on the porch, each one with a glass of brandy and a cigar in his hands.

"May I see Louisa again?" William asked.

John laughed. "You've taken a liking to each other, I see. As long as my sister wills it, I have no quarrels with it at all. You're a man of honor, William. I suppose, if I did not believe so, I wouldn't have brought you into my home with the company of my family."

"Then I am overwhelmed with gratitude, sir. This was a day I won't soon forget."

CHAPTER THREE

Over the next few months, William and Louisa grew inseparable. Whenever William was on leave from the Sea Stalker, he would spend his time with Louisa; there was never anything else he wanted to fo. They rode horses all over the island, spent countless days lying on the beach and swimming in the water. There were picnics out on the plantation, Sunday church, and supper.

William hadn't felt as though he was part of a family in such a long time.

The love he had for Louisa was something his heart was missing, and the love she had for him was unmatched by any other person in his entire life.

William and John were unloading goods from plunder off another one of Governor Gonzales's vessels. "There's nothing you enjoy more than destroying Gonzales's ships?" William asked. "Louisa never told you about Gonzales? She never mentioned his name?" "No, never. Is there something I should know?" William asked.

"That's something you should really discuss with her," John replied, lifting a bale of hay.

"Since we are on the subject of asking Louisa questions." William removed a ring out of his pocket. "I wanted to ask for your blessing in asking Louisa to marry me?" And he glowed when he showed John the ring.

John was blown away by what William had said, and overwhelmed with happiness. He hugged William tight, embracing him fully as if he was already a son.

"William Walsh. I would be honored to have you as part of this family."

" Gratitude, John. For all you have done for me," William replied, nodding his head.

And he meant every word of it because he could never imagine meeting a finer woman or a fairer, kinder family to take him into it.

"When are you going to do it? When will you ask her?" John asked.

"Tomorrow. We planned on watching the sunset on the beach," said William.

"That sounds wonderful. A true romantic you are, Walsh. Well, I wish you the best of luck.

The following day, around seven o'clock in the evening, the cooler air was drifting in off the ocean, the sun slowly rescinding for its slumber. William and Louisa were lying on a blanket on the beach, watching the sunset. William had his arms around Louisa, giving her warmth and protection from the breeze. "Is that a ship Louisa?" William asked, looking out to sea.

"Where?"

"There. Roughly at my one o' clock; it looks like sails to me. Take a look."

"I don't see sails, William. You must be seeing things."

She stood up and walked closer to the water to see more clearly what he had spotted.

She turned around and William was on his knee with a ring in his hand, held up in the air. She covered her mouth in awe, and tears began to fall.

"Louisa Ramos, there isn't a moment in my life where you aren't in my heart and mind. When I'm out to sea, and I'm on the top deck. When the sun is just about to set, and it dips below the horizon, and there is a pink sky that takes my breath away. I always think that sky couldn't hold a candle to Louisa, and I want to spend the rest of my life gazing upon that sky with you. Will you marry me?"

"Yes, yes, of course, I will. I love you," Louisa replied, tears of joy running down her cheeks.

William stood up and kissed her under the beautiful sky. "I love you too."

The two married in the St Jamestown Church on a Friday afternoon in the depth of summer.

The ceremony was nothing short of a fairy tale. Eleven months later, Louisa gave birth to twins— Sara and Sebastian Walsh. Sebastian was first to arrive, born on February 27th, 1651, at 11:59 p.m.

Sara emerged into the world eighty-four seconds later, at 12:01 a.m., on February 28th, 1651.

It was unusual for twins to be born on two different days.

Nonetheless, John and Lenora rejoiced at the additions to the family. The Ramos and Walsh families were one large joyful bunch by now, living their dreams on the Barbados plantation.

William was sure he had never been happier in his life, not even for a single minute of it.

There was an extra step in his walk, a wilder smile.

He truly was living his best life at this moment in time. And now, William was packing clothes in their bedroom for his voyage on the Sea Stalker the following day.

"You're leaving again?" Louisa asked. "Already? Must you?"

"Yes, my love, we set sail at dawn tomorrow. There has been something on my mind for some time now. I just haven't remembered to ask you. Do you mind if I ask it now?" "My love, ask me freely—anything," she answered.

"Why is there so much hatred within your family toward the Spanish Governor, Francisco Gonzales?"

"John never spoke of this to you?" Louisa replied.

"No, he told me to ask you about it a long time ago, but I simply forgot."

"Then please sit down, my love, and I will tell you all the reasons for our hatred for that man."

William sat down next to Louisa just as she had requested of him. He took her hand and stayed silent, just looking at her expectantly as he waited for her to speak. Clearly, whatever the story was, it was going to be a bad one and he wanted to give her all the time and space she needed.

She took in a great long breath and began. "Well, you see, William... John and I spent our childhood in a little village outside Portobello, Panama. My mother and father were farmers.

"Then, when I was ten years old, a very ambitious man named Francisco Gonzales came to see my father. He wanted to purchase working men from my father, but my father said they were not for sale. Getting hold of good men to work was always difficult, and if he let them go, then he would be struggling himself soon. Now he had his good men, he wasn't for letting any of them go.

"He told my father that he would offer him protection if he accepted the terms. My father refused, and Gonzales told him he wouldn't live to regret the mistake he had made. Two days later, early in the morning, John and I had our breakfast. My younger brother was not yet awake."

"Two brothers? You have another brother?"

"*Had* another brother," she replied, as a tear streamed from her eye.

"We were having breakfast when my father came running inside the house and told my mother to hide the children quickly. His face said it all—something terrible was afoot, something he did not want to talk about in front of us kids. My mother ran upstairs to grab my brother, Nathan, and by the time she came back down, they had tied my father's hands behind his back.

"Gonzales ordered his men to bring all of us out to the front yard. My mother wouldn't stop begging for our lives, so Gonzales hit her with the butt of his pistol and blood began running down her chin. I started crying. I couldn't stop and Gonzales walked over to me.

He wiped away my tears with a finger and tasted it, and said that all the tears I cried, no matter how sweet they were, would not put an end to the inevitability of what was to come.

The only thing that would save me would be barrels of gold and that it didn't look as if we had any. His men were laughing, but my father said that we had gold but it wasn't within the home. He asked Gonzales if he had ever heard of the vessel, the Nuestra de Atocha, and that if he let his wife and children go, he would give him the means of obtaining more gold than he could ever imagine. He had been one of the survivors on that ship.

"Gonzales said he would let the older ones go but hold onto my mother and brother for collateral. My father shouted for us both to run, and John and I ran to the top of the hill and hid underneath some bushes, but we could see everything.

"We watched them execute my mother and father. We saw my little brother, Nathan, run as fast as he could away from the captors, and I heard a gunshot and saw my brother fall in the field.

"We fled Portobello in a rowboat with no food or water. Somehow, we were found off the coast of Panama by a British merchant ship bound for London. It belonged to the cousin of the King of England, the Duke of Richmond, fifth in line for the crown. He had no wife or children.

"Despite our cultural differences, he raised us as if we were his children. My brother and I both attended Shrewsbury School and John was trained in the officers 'program, and we returned to the Caribbean with Lenora and Isabella a few years ago. This plantation belongs to my stepfather.

"The thoughts of what happened on my parents 'farm that day are inscribed in my mind, and I will never allow my hatred for Francisco Gonzales to die away."

William comforted Louisa, realizing that he himself had found a new and bona fide justifiable hatred for the man named Francisco Gonzales.

Six months later, somewhere off the coastline of Brazil, the Sea Stalker was tracking a Spanish vessel, a two-mast schooner. It didn't seem like much. Clouds painted the sky gray and the seas were slightly choppy. The Sea Stalker was preparing to come alongside the small schooner. William moved to the helm where John was.

"Why don't we blow it out of the water?" William suggested.

"William, what's gotten into you lately? Your only concern is the destruction and desecration of Spanish ships. I remember the days you used to stop me from torching them. Now, you throw the torch on yourself."

"My apologies, John," William replied, putting both hands on the wooden post in front of him.

"Not necessary. There is the occasion I can let my emotions cloud my judgment."

"No, John. My apologies are about your parents and your brother."

"Oh, she revealed the truth! Well, there's nothing we can do about it now, so let's focus on this ship, alright, First Officer Walsh?"

"Yes, Captain."

"Fire a cannon across their bow, and let them know we mean business," John instructed.

The thump of the cannon was so loud it could no doubt be heard on land. The cannonball hit off the port bow, rocking the ship. The men prepared the planks, ropes, and Jacob's ladders, and they knelt, taking cover as they came alongside.

"Captain of the ship, address yourself," William shouted.

"I am Jacob Rogers, Captain of this vessel. This vessel belongs to and is the direct property of

Governor Francisco Gonzales. There will be penalties for plundering." William looked at John, and John yelled.

"Kill them all, men." A firefight erupted and John screamed. "Load the four-pounders and fire." The air was engulfed in smoke from pistols and cannons. Wood splintered off the ship as the cannons tore it apart. William boarded the ship and its chaos, looking through the smoke.

A man appeared out of the haze to set upon him, screaming it was his ship. William quickly moved out of the way of his sword and they began to fight.

"How heroic. A captain who wants to die and go down with his ship," William said, enraging Jacob who swung his sword wildly and without proper footing. William grabbed Jacob and threw him against the side of the ship, but Jacob tried to run his sword through William's stomach. William turned and grabbed Jacob's arm with the sword, elbowing Jacob in the nose and knocking his sword out of his hand. He kicked Jacob into the side of the ship, where he fell.

Lying against the ship and bleeding profusely from his nose and mouth, Jacob reached into his pocket. "Don't kill me. You can take this." He opened up his hand, and there was an enormous bluish-gray diamond with rubies and emeralds set into a beautiful necklace made out of a reddishbronze material. William took the item but ran his sword through Jacob anyway.

"My apologies, I hate the name Jacob. I always have."

The men found a tiny bit of gold and silver, lots of sugar and tobacco.

"Why didn't you torch the ship, William?" John asked.

William showed the necklace to John and said, "*This* is the only reason why. A gift for the woman I love."

Two weeks later, on the island of Trinidad, the Governor and Commander of the entire Spanish Armada in the Caribbean, Francisco Gonzales, was having supper and was interrupted by Carlos, one of his guards, with the news. Gonzales put his utensils down and promptly picked up a cloth, wiping his mouth of the grease and grime accumulated during his nightly feast he always ate without decorum.

"Bring it here," he demanded of Carlos.

Carlos handed the Admiral a piece of paper.

"They got Jacob's schooner, sire," Carlos informed him.

"Is he alive?"

"Well, I'm afraid he was barely alive when they found him, and he passed a short time after that. To be truthful, he did not stand much chance."

Gonzales crumpled the paper and slammed his fist on the table. "I want to bring down the men responsible. Do we have any leads?"

"We do, sire."

"Well, proceed."

"Before he died, sire, Jacob proclaimed he heard some of their men speak of Barbados, and of a man with an eyepatch."

"Barbados? Eyepatch?" said Gonzales.

"Shall I send word for the fleet, sire?"

"No, Carlos, this is personal. Jacob was a friend of mine. I will take a few of the galleons, and we will find out who's been stealing from me. They are going to pay with their lives. No one steals from Francisco Gonzales and lives to tell the tale. No one."

John and William had been home for weeks when John received word that the Spanish had sent out an unprecedented number of ships to ward off pirates and privateers.

John was given orders to let the dust settle, and they would be back on the water soon enough. They were enthralled to be at home and spend time with the children, and so the whole family was seated at the table for supper. John said grace, and they began to feast.

"Ladies, once again, you have outdone yourselves—delicious," William remarked.

"Thank you, my love. Can you take Sebastian?" Louisa asked.

"Of course, let me see my son."

"My goodness, Louisa, each time I see that necklace, it's indescribable," said Lenora.

"Speaking of indescribable. William had it *inscribed* for me," Louisa replied. William was holding his son, smiling.

"Oh well, now isn't that splendid! What does it say?" Lenora asked.

Chatty Abigail interrupted. "Let me take Sara and get her cleaned up. Then I will switch with you, sir."

"That sounds just fine, Abby," William answered.

"Well, come on, tell us what it says," said Lenora.

"It says, *Your love has enabled me to see like never before; no matter what happens to me, I'll forever be yours,*" said Louisa.

"That's beautiful, William. I wish I would have thought of something like that," John said.

"William, be careful, lad, you are making me look criminally negligent." Abigail came back in and handed Sara to William, before taking Sebastian to get cleaned up.

"They are such a blessing but not easy, are they?" said John.

"No, not at all. I haven't a clue what we would do without Abigail," William answered. "She is such a Godsend, takes all the stress away."

From the other room, Abigail yelled, "That's very sweet of you, William."

"I'm being serious. My wife would agree with me ten times over."

"We are very grateful to have Abigail. We are all grateful to have each other," suggested John. "Amen to that," said William.

"William, after supper, would you like to retire to the porch for a brandy and a cigar?" asked John.

"I would be obliged, my good man."

The men retired to the porch, enjoying the spoils of life. William blew out a puff of smoke and said. "I don't know how to ever repay you. I never imagined I would have such immeasurable happiness, and find myself so blessed."

"You are repaying me right now with the happiness of my sister. I can't tell you how much it means to me. She is radiant, always smiling, always speaking of you, William."

"That's why I think of killing Gonzales every day. I can see the never relenting anguish it causes Louisa. Do you never think about killing that man?" William inquired. "Who, Gonzales?" said John.

"Yes, Gonzales."

"Oh, every moment of every day."

Back in town and just outside a grand-looking house, a man dressed in an all-white ensemble of tunic and breeches gingerly picked his way through a mud-spattered alley.

With purpose in his stride, he approached another who had taken up sleeping beside the church, wrapped up in coarse woolen blankets donated by the pastor himself.

"Pardon me, but I'm looking for someone. I was hoping you could help me find them."

"I'm sleeping, can you not see? Bugger off," said the rough sleeper, not interested in even turning to see who addressed him thus. The white-clothed man kicked the other, who in turn, got up off the ground as quick as a mouse and flashed a small knife.

It was likely to be all that he possessed, for his own clothing was little more than sackcloth and he wore no pockets in which to hold anything—if he owned a single thing, which he did not.

"Who kicked me?" the lowly man asked and he suddenly whipped around, expecting to see only the face of the man in the white attire.

But he did not; instead, he was confronted by the faces of hundreds of Spanish soldiers.

But thankfully, most sat upon the ground, taking a rest.

Now though, as if he believed he was someone quite important, the man in the white breeches crouched down, wrinkling up his nose at the sight of the mud and stinking street filth so close to his finery. He dangled a pouch of coins in the face of the other, knowing even one of the small silvers to be worth more than this lazy scoundrel could have seen in his whole lifetime.

"Stop with the nonsense," he reproached. "*I* kicked you, but 'twas not with any malice." He said it without any hesitation whatsoever. "I kicked you fully awake, sire, quite simply as I knew you would not wish to miss this opportunity."

"Oppo...oppo... what?"

"*Opportunity*. It means the same as a lucky break. That is what I am about to offer you if you can answer me truthfully."

The man leaned in, showing the wealthy visitor his yellowish, gap-toothed smile. "Indeed, sir,

I am as truthful as you will ever find."

"Then have you seen anyone on this island who sports an eye patch over one eye?" the man asked. He covered one eye as though he needed to demonstrate it. But the dusk was soon approaching and the man could barely see anyway. Nature was calling out to the night.

From crickets to snakes, the myriad of humble creatures were all making music to the tune of darkness. The windows were open in the mansion, its flickering candles also drawing in moths and flies by the dozen as they abandoned the stinking cesspits of the street to go and seek the warmth of the tiny dancing fires. The humidity was also slightly worse than normal which made for uncomfortable sleeping, and William had been tossing and turning all night.

One of the babies started to cry and William got up and went to the crib, picking up Sebastian, who was crying. Rocking him back and forth in his arms, he said, "Your grandfather used to tell me that I would not stop crying until he picked me up when I was a child.

"Seems as if it's *like father, like son.* Oh, Sebastian, I pray someday you will be a better man than I. What do you say your father sings you a song and you shall fall back to sleep?

"Pat a cake, pat a cake, baker's man, bake me a cake as fast you can. Pat it and prick it, mark it with a band, put it in the oven for baby and me.

"Pat a cake, pat a cake, baker's man, bake me a cake..."

Then, there was a piercing, ear-splitting almighty scream.

"What was that?" William said, and headed to the window to see the servants 'lodge on fire and the horses running rampant, their eyes crazed, heads thrown back and bucking wildly.

At a distance, William could see Spanish soldiers. He put Sebastian down and ran into John's room, waking John up with his hand over his mouth.

"Soldiers. Spanish soldiers. We must leave at once. I'm going to get Louisa and the children."

"I'll get Lenora, Abby and Isabella," John acknowledged. John informed Louisa of the situation, picked up a pistol from the cabinet, and they both went to Isabella's room.

Meanwhile, William grabbed Sebastian and Louisa picked up Sara. They met John, Lenora, and Abby at the top of the steps.

"There's a secret tunnel under the kitchen that comes out onto a dirt road leading to the sea," said John. Abby took Sebastian and they all made their way down the stairs slowly and quietly.

John was leading and William at the rear.

They got to the kitchen, but there was a cabinet blocking the tunnel.

"Lenora, quick help me move this," John said. William was looking out the window.

"We have to hurry. They are surrounding the house." John and Lenora removed the cabinet and opened the hatch.

"Come, Isabella," Lenora said, but Isabella wasn't there. "Where's Isabella? Where is she?" Lenora started to panic.

"Don't worry, I'll find her. Just go," John instructed. "There's no time to be hanging about." Abby grabbed Sebastian and slowly climbed down into the basement.

Louisa looked down at Abby, took off the necklace that William had given her and put it around Sara's neck, then handed her to Abby.

"Please put this on, Sebastian, I'm not leaving without Isabella."

"Abby, you go, and if we are not there in fifteen minutes, you take the boat and get the hell out of here," John instructed.

"Yes, Mr. Ramos, but please hurry, and may God be with you," Abby answered and headed for the tunnel with the twins.

"There's no time, ladies; you go, and we will find Isabella," William said.

"I'm not leaving without my daughter. We will wait here for you. But please hurry."

"This is no time to be foolish, Lenora, please take the tunnel," John bellowed. "For God's sake, don't be so stubborn and do as I say for a change."

"You can raise your voice all you like. I have told you, I am not leaving without my niece," Lenora insisted.

William kissed Louisa and went to leave, but she grabbed his arm.

Then she took off the silver cross around her neck and placed it in Williams's hand before kissing him harder than she ever had before. John kissed Lenora and said, "I love you." The two men split up to widen the search efforts and attempt to shorten the time to find Isabella. "Isabella," whispered John, as he made his way toward the living room, his pistol drawn.

"Isabella, Isabella." William was headed toward the dining area, but peeked around the corner and noticed the front door open. Gonzales was there, and he had Isabella in his arms.

The back door flew open, and Spanish soldiers flooded the house.

John entered from the living area with his pistol aimed at Governor Gonzales.

"Release my daughter, or I'll put a bullet in your skull."

Isabella started to cry, and Gonzales held her small head close to his.

William flew from the corner and grabbed a Spanish soldier by putting an arm around his neck, and aiming a pistol at his head.

"Release the girl or your man here dies," William ordered.

"Isabella, do you like candy?" Gonzales asked, and Isabella, still crying, nodded her head. "Yes," she answered.

"I love candy, pretty much anything sweet for that matter. I think it would be in both your best interests to drop your pistols and surrender immediately," said Gonzales.

"Not a chance. Now, let the girl go," William insisted.

"One move, and I'll decorate my foyer with your blood," John said, still pointing his pistol.

"I believe you men have miscalculated your odds. Guards, bring them in," Gonzales ordered, and Lenora and Louisa were brought into the room and thrown at the feet of Gonzales.

"Men, do not take your aim off these women. If one of them thinks about moving, shoot them," Gonzales instructed.

"William," yelled Louisa.

"Louisa, my love, it's going to be alright."

"Please don't hurt my daughter, please let her go," Lenora cried out.

"Tell your husbands to lower their weapons, and maybe she will live," said Gonzales.

"What guarantees do we have?" John questioned.

"Well, if you continue to test my patience, I guarantee I will just slit her throat." Gonzales pulled out a knife and gently touched the cheek of Isabella. Her tears started falling and she called for her father.

"Alright, alright. I'm lowering my weapon," John said and put his weapon on the floor. The soldiers immediately secured him.

"How about you, Mr. Eyepatch? Would you like to be the reason this girl dies?"

"William! William! Let the soldier go," John pleaded.

William contemplated and then gave up his pistol. The soldiers secured him as well.

"My, my, my, it is true what they say. History does repeat itself. John and Louisa Ramos, I couldn't have imagined in my wildest dreams that we would ever meet again. Let alone under circumstances with such similarities. The question that's weighing on my mind is how on earth you were able to procure such a beautiful piece of property.

"I've ordered my men to set fire to the crop when we leave. I'm sure your Duke of Richmond will pay a severe penalty for losing this much in sugarcane.

"A penalty your King and the duke are well deserved of, considering the amount of money you two have cost me over the last year and a half. I found it strangely odd that you would only steal the goods of ships directly owned by me, and you wouldn't bother with the others.

"We found records and talked to the townspeople. Well, we *tortured* townspeople to be exact, and they gave us the information we needed. When I heard who was living here, I said to myself, *that's preposterous. It's impossible,* yet here we are. I'm still in disbelief, what has it been, ten years? My, my, my, how time does fly." Isabella started to cry loudly. "It's alright, don't cry, little one. Everything will be fine. It's going to be ok," Gonzales continued.

"If you hurt her, I'll..." John started.

"Shh." With the knife against his lips, Gonzales continued, "I'm talking to the child. Isabella, you like candy because it's sweet, correct?" Isabella once again nodded her head. "Yes."

"Well, you see Isabella, your father and I are old friends. I even know your aunt Louisa from her tears. I bet they taste just like yours." And he wiped a tear off her face and licked his finger.

"Take the women out front and shoot them."

"Yes, sir. Sir, we found a hatch in the kitchen that leads to a tunnel," one of the guards said.

"I want the entire island searched. Do not leave one stone unturned. Do you understand me,

Corporal?"

"Yes, sir," answered the corporal.

"Go on now, get on with it."

William and John tried desperately to free themselves from their captors, but there were too many. The women were screaming and crying and called out for their husbands. The corporal and his soldiers brought the women and child down the steps and forced the three ladies onto their knees in a line facing away from the house.

There were five men and two guns pointed on each woman, and one on the child. The door was even left open so William and John could witness everything. "Ready, men. Aim," the officer instructed, and Gonzales closed the door.

Loud screams were heard, then gunshots, then there was silence.

"Did you think you were going to keep stealing from me without consequences? Both of you are going to spend the rest of your miserable existence in pain and anguish," Gonzales said. John clenched his teeth together and tears ran down his face.

"I'm going to kill you, Gonzales," John shouted. William started laughing, and John looked at him in disgust, but William continued to laugh.

"I'm going to boil your tears and drown you in them. We are going to torture your children and let *them* have children so that we can kill them. Your family bloodline will die, and your seeds will plague the earth no longer."

"You're a dead man, Gonzales. Dead," John repeated.

Gonzales laughed and said, "You two are going to be wiping someone's ass in Mexico City and working like slaves on the land. You'll be under constant watch and twenty-four-hour guard.

Remember, nobody steals from Francisco Gonzales, nobody. Have fun, my friends. "I will visit from time to time to remind you of the pain. Good luck in hell, gentlemen." "We will see you there then, Governor," replied John.

"Gonzales!" William called. He turned around, and William continued, "You will endure crushing death and grief! My hands will be soaked in your blood for the intrusion of my home and the theft of my family. Beware, I will never die before you."

The Governor walked back up the steps and pushed open the door. He took out his knife again and grabbed Willy's face, wiping the bloodied blade across it.

"This is the blood of your wife. Death is crushing, isn't it?" Gonzales said, then laughed as the Spanish soldiers carried both men away.

CHAPTER FOUR

William and John were dragged away by their captors and saw the helplessness on the faces of all the indentured servants. The pain, already so merciless, had only worsened by seeing people once considered family being ripped from their loved ones 'arms and put up into a caged carriage.

The two men were the last to be put into it. As it pulled away, they both watched what had been their life burned to the ground. The reflection of the flames within their eyes spawned the birth of a pirate named Blackheart, and the most famous of his time, One-Eyed Willy.

The sound of the officer's yelling voice had been drowned out by the scream of Louisa before she was shot dead by Gonzales's men. William thought to himself, *if only I could go back in time, I would have said or done so many things differently.* But he could not go back in time, so was left with his doleful musings, and nothing could be done about them now.

John was in sheer agony but never shed a tear or showed a shred of emotion.

There was nothing but hatred and revenge raging through his blood like a rabid mongoose, and yet all John could do was keep on rowing.

William, however, was always battling against the musings of his brain, trying to make sense of it all. And so he stopped rowing for a moment to wipe his brow, but the harsh whip against

William's back was terrifying, and he jolted forward in agony.

The chubby, filth-ridden guard with a wart on the tip of his nose shouted.

"Who told you to stop rowing?" And he whipped William again as he began to row.

They wouldn't stop rowing until they reached Villa Rica de la Vera Cruz, given its name by the brutal explorer Cortes, who had executed, ravaged and enslaved the Aztec people of this region.

They said that Fort Saint Jean de Ulua de Vera Cruz, on the eastern coast of Mexico, was built by Cortez and his men. And almost one hundred years before William or John would set foot inside her mammoth infrastructure, Francis Drake and John Hawkins had attempted to infiltrate its impervious rings of stone. Engulfed in the beauty of the emerald-green sea, the fort was the home of some of the Spanish empire's deadliest criminals.

The walls were painted with blood and smelled rancid, and all the prisoners onboard the ships were logged in by the master-at-arms before their four-day journey began to Mexico City. The journey was brutal, and not one of the prisoners had drunk a drop of water for days. Prayers for rain echoed through the long line of prisoner carriages. John Ramos was in a bad way.

"Guards, I'm dying of thirst. I need water," John pleaded.

" Which one of you said they were dying of thirst?" an officer on horseback said as he rode next to the carriage.

William looked at John and shook his head, left to right as if to say, *do not reveal yourself as the person who spoke those words.* John was beyond caring, and shouted it out anyway.

"It was me. I said it. I said I was dying of thirst. For fuck's sake, we're all in need of water," John bellowed.

The slim guard with a scarred chin and eyes that bulged out of their sockets replied, "You all want something to quench that terrible thirst, do ya? Alright, we'll give you something."

He yelled to hold the line at the front and all the carriages jolted to a halt. The officer dismounted his horse and headed to the front of the carriage where he recruited a few men. They returned to the carriage and climbed on top of the cage, waiting on the order.

"Men, these prisoners are dying of thirst, and since they aren't worthy of drinking our water, and since they have been praying every day for rain, I say we give them what they've been praying for. What do you say, lads? Do you have anything to drink *on tap* for these men?"

In unison, the five men laughed and stood, opening their pants and urinating over the prisoners within the carriage. The disturbing thing was, some of them were so thirsty they had their mouths open. The guards and the officer laughed as the men pissed over the so-called criminals, covering every one of them with their putrid waste.

William kept still with disgust as the liquid encompassed his head. John, on the other hand, reacted like a wild beast.

"You disgusting fools. If I free myself from this cage, I'll cut those off and feed them to you."

The officer responded with haste as he tied his pants. "Now, now, criminals. Be mindful of the words you speak, for they may come true. I, on the other hand, am not hungry, but you, sir, look a little starved. Men, what do you say we feed the prisoners as well?"

The men laughed as they pulled down their pants and began to defecate on the prisoners.

The commander of the battalion rode up to the carriage and shot his pistol. The officer and the guards instantly pulled up their pants.

"Is this what we are being held up for?" the commander asked, "laughs and jokes with Mr.

Gonzalez's property, Mr. Ridley?"

"My apologies, Commander, I just thought," Officer Ridley replied.

"That is the issue here; it is your thinking. You're not paid to think, you're paid to follow orders. Now, you and your men will see these prisoners are given water and properly fed," the commander bellowed.

"How do we do that though, Commander?" Ridley questioned.

"Well, I guess that would involve some thought, and you had better think quick, otherwise you will be the one eating shit."

"Yes, Commander," said Ridley.

William had a smirk on his face for the first time since the horrific events of Barbados.

When the caravan of prisoner carriages rolled into Mexico City, the prisoners were feasting on meat from a bison killed by Ridley and his men, as well as water collected from a river on route to Mexico City. Home to almost fifty-thousand people, it was New Spain's primary hub for viceroyalty and mining. The mines would become William and John's home for the better part of a decade.

CHAPTER FIVE

Five years later, in the year 1656, the hot October sun felt like hell on earth down in the depths of the mines, scorching the skin of all those who worked them, some even blistering from their burns. Pickaxes and shovels were the only weapons available against the mighty and formidable mountain and the fortunes that lay inside. In the distance, the Pyramid of the Sun could be seen, and it was said the Aztecs had made great sacrifices down those steps. Those sacrificed had had their heads cut off, and these rolled down to the bottom. The mines, ironically, were no different.

The director of this torturous business enterprise was none other than Diego Cortez Gonzales, brother to the Governor of New Spain himself.

Diego had a habit of torturing people during the day while they worked, so he would not take too well to noncompliance. He would bring those who disobeyed to the heart of the mine, so their screams would echo through every tunnel and instill fear in the soul of every man.

William was one of those who, understandably, disliked the rules. The snapping of whips was enough to make a man's teeth clench every time it was heard.

"Walsh, I'm tired of cutting you slack just because my brother has a soft spot for you and Mr. Ramos. The only time you seem to respond to my rules, Mr. Walsh, is when I threaten Mr. Ramos, and it's the same for you. So, I am faced with a dilemma," said Diego.

Walsh and Ramos were on their knees, hands bound behind their backs. The length of their beards and hair gave them a look much like cavemen. "Do I kill you both, and pretend it was an accident, or keep my brother happy?"

"That's an easy one, isn't it, William?" said John Ramos.

"I do believe it is, John; let's see if he gets the right answer," William Walsh replied. "I think I will keep my brother happy and let you two bake in the sun for a while with no water." "See, Mr. Director, sir, we knew you would be merciful," John remarked.

"Yes, gratitude and thank you for such splendid hospitality. Really couldn't have asked for more. Up until now, Lieutenant, I thought you just tickled your brother's wanker. Now, I know why your hands are always full," said William.

"Guard, remind Mr. Walsh who exactly is in charge," Diego ordered, and the guard took a step back and whipped John Ramos. This infuriated Willy and he began squirming, his hands still tightly bound behind his back. The guard smashed William in the head with the handle of the whip, and he fell to the ground, face first.

"William, get up! William! William, get up! William, dear Lord, please get up!" John called out in desperation. William finally got up, clutching the back of his head.

"What happened?" he asked, looking around.

"You opened your big mouth is what you did, getting me whipped and all." "Did it work?" asked William.

"Of course, it worked. I got the key."

"Excellent news, John, yet my head is still throbbing. Have you put it in a safe place?" William asked.

"If you mean safe as in well hidden, then yes. Tomorrow, we are going in the firebox. The thought doesn't even trouble me because we will be leaving this place behind sooner rather than later."

"We've got the key. Now all we need is a plan," said William.

"*Simple* doesn't resonate in my mind when it comes to formulating a way out of here, William," said John.

"Understandably so, yet what is that expression? I do believe it may be, *easier done than said*," William replied.

"Whatever do you mean, William? You do realize there are at least twelves guards in our way before we can make it to the canyon." John made a point.

"Then, we have to climb the canyon and pray the alarm hasn't been sounded, because then they will just try and shoot us off the canyon walls," William replied.

"We need weapons, William, and a place to hide them."

"I know, I know we do," replied William, "I've got it!"

"What have you got? What?"

"The expression. I do believe it is, *easier said than done.* That is the correct way to say it," William replied.

"Is that what your thoughts have been conjuring this whole time? Goodnight, William, I must get rest, for my energy is needed for the sun box."

"Very well. I will devise a plan to get us out of here to avenge our families. Goodnight, John."

Keys jingled and William and John's cell door opened, and the guard threw water into the eyes of the prisoners, yelling, "Get up!" Four guards escorted the inmates along the corridor of rock and out into a canyon a quarter-mile wide and almost one hundred and fifty feet below civilization.

This titan of a hole was dug into the earth by men in extreme heat, and conditions nothing short of misery. As the moonlight cast its last bit of shine before its slumber and the sun awoke to rain fire on the mine, the two men were brought to the center of the hole, where there were ten wooden boxes. Each was just large enough to contain a man.

William and John were stripped naked and forced into two separate boxes. Almost six hours later, with no water and the sun hammering the boxes with its intense feverish power, the two men had been overcome with the sweltering heat. Some of the guards spat into the holes and laughed.

The saliva would just sizzle on their skin and vanish instantaneously.

William had started to hallucinate, thinking he was aboard a ship, with Ramos asking one of the cabin boys *to fetch me water below deck!*

"Captain Ramos, would you tell your cabin boy to fetch me that water, please?" William asked. "William, we are not on a ship; we are in a mine in Mexico City. Have you lost your memory?"

When the guards had turned away from the boxes, one of the men working the mine took his canteen up to the wooden boxes and dumped water down into the drinking hole for William and Ramos. They both praised the young lad for his courage and asked his name.

"Smyth. James Smyth," the young lad replied.

John and William were kept in the sweltering boxes for three days in total, and each day, Smyth would wait until the guards 'backs were turned and give William and John water. On the fourth morning, William and John were taken out of the sun box and thrown back into their cells. Another guard appeared and threw a bucket of water over them both.

"Cool off, gentlemen. The director wants to see you two out in the canyon in twenty minutes, with the rest of the criminals," the guard announced.

Twenty minutes later, William and John were marched back out into the canyon where every prisoner within the mine stood in silence. The director walked out with two guards, carrying another who looked half beaten to death. The director of the mine, Diego Gonzales, stood in front of the prisoners.

"I'm sure you are all familiar with one of our finest guards, Mr. Suarez? Mr. Suarez does not take his job very seriously. I, on the other hand, take this occupation and all its resolutions as ancillary to the value of my life. Mr. Suarez has a responsibility to his employer, first and foremost, to never jeopardize the lives of his fellow employees or myself.

"I know you could care less about the life of Mr. Suarez—as could I. But if the person or persons who stole this man's keys does not return them to me within one minute, I will execute a

prisoner every minute thereafter until the key is returned, starting from now." The countdown continued, but no one came forward.

"Time is up. Guard, bring me a prisoner," the director ordered, and the guard brought him a prisoner and placed him on his knees in front of the director.

"You have five seconds. Five, four, three, two..." The director aimed his pistol and shot the man in the head. He continued, "I could do this all day and all night. I have plenty of slaves and prisoners coming here daily. Thirty seconds. Then the time is up again.

"Okay, no volunteers? Guard, bring me another prisoner." The guard grabbed James Smyth, the man who had given the water to both William and John.

"That's the chap who saved us," John whispered to William.

"Yes, I know it is."

"You have five seconds. Five, four, three," the director repeated.

"Wait, Wait," John yelled out.

"Well, Mr. Smyth. It appears you have escaped death with barely a second to spare." The director walked up to Ramos and said, "Do you have any information about my key?" "I stole the key. It was me," John replied.

"Very well, then where is my key?"

"The key is hidden, but I can take you to it," said John.

"No, no, no. You can take a *guard* to it right this instant."

John guided a guard to the corridor of rock where there was a loose stone in the wall, a few cells down from where his and Willy's cells were. The key lay hidden behind it. They walked back out into the canyon and presented the director with the key.

"Mr. Ramos, I do appreciate your honesty, so only five lashes for you." John seemed almost happy—five lashes for stealing keys.

"Oh, thank you, sir. I do very much appreciate your kindness."

"Mr. Smyth, back to work you go. Guard, kill Mr. Suarez," the director ordered.

A guard took out a pistol and shot Suarez point-blank in the head. "And guards. Last but not least, take Mr. Walsh to the heart of the mine. It's time we taught Mr. Ramos a valued lesson about obedience," the director continued.

Ramos, in a defiant tone replied, "No, no. Mr. Diego sir, no."

William had a shocked look on his face and started resisting the guards.

"No, not me; I'll kill you all! No!"

He was dragged away by the guards as Diego Gonzales was smiling. The only sounds John Ramos could hear for the rest of that day were the screams and cries of William J. Walsh.

CHAPTER SIX

Two years later, after Willy and Blackheart were able to escape from Mexico City, they were marooned just off the shore of the infamous island of Bones. The island had humongous rocks in front of the bay, and few ships were ever able to navigate through what they called *the Hell's Gates*. Behind the Devil's Pillars lay the bones of hundreds of thousands of indigenous people who died or were sick from cocoliztli, which the Spanish deemed *the Great Pestilence*.

The situation was so bad that at some point, the thought that they were better off in the silver mines had crossed their minds. Once they had navigated through the doorway of damnation and swum close enough to shore, they appeared to be stepping on human bones rather than sand.

They paused, and Willy looked toward the beach in front of them. It was like a boneyard. Yet surely, there had been no war great enough, or battle long enough to leave behind this much death.

Almost fifty years had passed from the last plague and there was no sign of life.

At first sight, the jungle vegetation seemed plentiful, and the palm trees were filled with coconuts, but along the tree line, the attempts of a few very poorly built places to sleep remained. It did not seem as though anyone had survived long enough to make a home out of one.

The sun was low and they were deathly tired from the swim but attempted to dig up some sand using skulls of the dead. They made a circle around the hole with more skulls, lighting a fire in the middle. It was clear that the skull and bones of humans would be vital in their survival.

Nature was making music as night fell on the tiny, deserted island. Eating a coconut by the fire,

John said, "What say you when Gonzalez is informed of our untimely departure?"

"I expect he will scour Mexico and the Caribbean for a short time, and once he has exhausted all information he may receive, he will no doubt assume we are dead and relinquish his search.

What's more concerning to me is how we get off this island of bones?"

"Isla de Huesos," John remarked.

"What does that mean?"

"The Island of Bones—as you just said yourself. We will need to sharpen some of these bones and perhaps make bowls out of the skulls."

"We couldn't! For one thing, it wouldn't be morally sound. It's justifiable to make a fire, but to eat or do anything with the bones of the dead is absurdly unsophisticated."

"Half of these bones are from my people, and I assure you they won't mind. They would be happier to provide some use to us, to give us what we need when we are in such dire straits. We should get some rest, as come morning, we will have to explore the island."

"Do you ever have thoughts? Well, I know you have thoughts of Bridgetown. Would you ever have thoughts or wishes to go back in time and save everyone?" William asked.

"I have thoughts of that night, ones that the imagination should not allow. And yes, William, that is one of them. It is as though you can see inside my mind."

There was a rustle in the bushes that startled William and John, and they both got up. The bushes were moving erratically, and William said, "Who goes there? Show yourself."

"Show yourself, you swine," John called out, holding a leg bone. Ironically, and to the men's delight, a boar appeared from the bushes and they breathed a sigh of relief.

"So, you want to travel back in time, do ya?" said a voice from behind them, sending Willy and John running in opposite directions, all a-panic. An old man with a white beard and torn, brownbreeches yelled, "Calm down, lads! Calm down, or you'll scare the dead. Take a deep breath and relax. It would be best not to venture to such a shore if you frighten so easily!"

The old man, missing a few teeth, wore no shirt, and his body was covered in a white fur resembling that of a sheepskin. Willy and John slowly made their way back to the fire and saw the old man was sitting down beside it. He gestured for the two men to take a seat there beside him.

"What is your name, old man?" John asked, still struggling to catch his breath.

"My name is of no importance; however, the knowledge I possess is of value beyond measure.

The both of you speak of traveling back in time and this I must understand. Why?" "Are you insane, old man?" William interrupted.

"I must admit that in my old age, I may have lost a tiny bit of my wits, but what I'm about to say will change your interpretation. Lost the ones you love to a terrible tyrant, did ya? Adventures of greed and voyages for revenge, clouded already cloudy minds.

"Mistakes were made and tracks not covered, yet one thing was unearthed.

"Death can change a man. Death is the harbinger of change. This island carries with it death in great lengths, and something in the both of you is of the devil's doing. What if I told you there was a way to go back in time?"

"Then I would say you are crazy, old man," replied John.

"There is a stone, but this stone is not just any stone. It is a magical stone, one that can only be accessed by one of pure heart. The light blue—almost clear—stone has striking similarities to a diamond, yet it is not one. This stone was forged into a necklace surrounded by rubies and emeralds to make it blend in. They call this the Jewel of the Spanish Main. The ancients called it the Jewel of Atlantis. It was worn by King Atlas himself, ruler of the lost City of Atlantis, ten millennia ago.

"When the city was struck by a horrendous earthquake, it sank into the sea, but the King himself attempted to put the city on his shoulders and lift it out of the water.

"Before he did, he forged a box to hold the jewel, and a sacred scroll that would activate it. He wore the box around his neck, and in this heroic display of courage trying to save his home, the box was plucked from his neck, and lost to the sea, like the King and all the city's inhabitants.

"It wasn't until 10,000 years later that the box resurfaced from the ocean on the beaches of what is now called Spain. My former Captain, Jolly Roger, had disclosed some of the wildly unfathomable stories. There are only a few who know of the power inside the jewel.

"There are those who wish to use it for evil, and those who wish to use it for the good of mankind. Yet, the power of the jewel is only accessible when the sacred scroll is open wide, like eyes, when the moon is full in the sky. Jolly lost the scroll to an armada of English ships destined for London. Outgunned and outmanned, he was forced to give up the 'the chest of the treasure buried 'which contains the sacred scroll. The jewel will lead you to the scroll, and the scroll to the jewel. One doesn't work without the other, that's the only rule."

William was in utter shock as he recalled the jewel. "John, that is the necklace that I gave

Louisa."

"What do you mean?" said the old man.

"This stone you speak of. What kind of power does it have?"

"It is said to be the last remaining piece of the lost civilization that had power far beyond the realm of imagination," the old man explained.

"I cannot vouch for such claims, but this stone you speak of, I have it."

"What do you mean, you have the stone?" the old man questioned, looking perplexed.

"I mean exactly what you heard me say. I have the stone—*I* was the one who stole it."

"You have the..." The old man began to cough and choke. "You stole the..." he continued and bent forward, coughing hard and seemed unable to stop. John was sure the old man might die right there on the spot, and he would be responsible for causing it. So he gave him coconut juice but he didn't stop coughing and sure enough, he soon fell onto his back, clutching at his heart. "You stole the stone..." he whispered, breathing ever so slowly and within a few moments, the old man breathed his last breath, taking his place amongst the myriad of other bones on the island.

For almost a year and a half, William and John spent their time on the island, building a palace out of bones and hunting and fishing with tools made of bone. The small jungle became their new plantation, except this time, they were cultivating a plot to avenge the deaths of their families.

If the old man had been telling the truth, then they could go back in time and change the events of Barbados, and that was all that was on William's mind.

One quiet night, the glow of the fire within the palace gave just enough light for William and John to continue to work on building an organ, using bone to chisel and shape others.

They were so engulfed in their work, they did not hear the commotion almost a half a mile away, a terrible cacophony headed in their direction.

One of the largest Spanish galleons within the armada fleet had laid anchor outside the walls of Isla de Huesos, and two rowboats landed on shore. A group of twenty men carried two treasure chests up onto the sand and to the edge of the plantation. The captain stopped and said, "Halt, men.

There is an old man that inhabits this jungle, so beware."

They moved on through the jungle and down a dirt path cleared out by William and John.

Half a mile into the jungle, the captain ordered, "Stop here, men! Over there on the right, that's where we shall dig the holes. On the way back from Spain, we will all be rich." One of the men yelled in excitement.

"John, did you hear that?" William asked.

"Hear what?"

"Listen, there are people," said Williamd.

Willy and John left the palace and headed in the direction of the noise.

As they got closer, the people got louder and louder and they could see the burning torches. They found a place off to the side of the dirt path and Willy observed the people.

"What are they doing?" John asked.

"There's about a dozen men digging holes. Looks like they're burying two chests. I'll give you a guess what's in them?" William suggested.

"Gold and silver?"

"I'd bet my eye on it."

The bushes rustled behind John and William, and three men were standing there, rifles pointed down at them. There was no mistaking what the gesture meant.

"Let's not go doing something you'd regret there, Cyclops," one of the men said.

The men brought William and John to the beach where the Captain and the rest of his men were gathered, forcing Willy and John to their knees facing the Captain.

"My name is Capitan Fernando De Silva, commander of His Majesty's ship, the Sea Fire. By what fortune of the devil did you gentlemen find yourselves on this godforsaken island? What are your names?"

"We were marooned here, sir. I'm John and this is William," John announced.

"Ah, yes. I know who you are. Francisco Gonzales has been looking for you for over a year. He will surely be boundless with reward when I hand you two directly to him. Although, he did say *dead or alive*. So, perhaps I will just kill one of you. The reward is the same either way."

"Perhaps, however, he would like to be advised of a ploy to steal from him. That might make for a bargain in the face of death, wouldn't you say, Captain de Silva?" said William in a confident tone, not even wavering when De Silva took out his sword and placed it under his chin.

"Well, well, well, men. It appears we have a man whose intelligence isn't in his best interest. I do believe your best interest would be living, Mr. Walsh. I'll give you the option. You can both die right here, right now, or you can fight each other to see who dies later. Either way, one of you or both of you are going to die this very night."

"I have an even better idea. We have hidden treasure worth double what you buried on this island. If you could best me with your sword, Captain, while I am barehanded, John will tell you where this treasure is. Isn't that right, John?" said William. "William, don't do this! We can both face Gonzales." "Isn't that right, John?" William repeated.

"Yes, I will comply."

"I haven't a clue as to what you morons are complying with, because I haven't agreed to any terms," the Captain insisted.

"John, during our privateering, didn't we kill a few De Silvas?" said William.

"I believe it was more than a few. They too were cowards; it must run in the family?" John replied with a hint of laughter. The captain got visibly angry, turned away and then backhanded John with the shaft of his sword.

"Men, stand Mr. Walsh up on his feet. Very well, Mr. Walsh, you shall have your chance," the Captain explained. The men lifted Willy up on his feet and pushed him to the middle of the beach. The Captain removed his overcoat and rolled up his sleeves.

"I'll have you know, Mr. William, I am one of the best swordsmen in all of the Caribbean. Are you ready to die, Mr. Walsh?"

"Aye," William answered, and immediately, De Silva threw an overhand thrust, but William moved out of the way, circling and switching sides.

De Silva again lunged forward and William kicked sand in his assailant's eyes, forcing him to drop his sword. William quickly picked up De Silva's sword and drove it straight through his torso. De Silva fell to his knees and William removed the sword.

"You first, Captain. Now release him. I said release him or face me to the death, you swine. All of you, drop your weapons. Do it, or I will gut you one by one," William shouted. The men lifted John up and let him go, then dropped their swords. "I hope you know what you're doing, William?" John asked.

"I have a plan. Just trust me, John." Willy stared at the men and said, "Now, I presume the rest of the men on the ship haven't a clue as to the debauchery you gentleman are involved in?

"Well, I say we go kill those men and take the rest of the gold and silver. I promise we will keep taking gold and silver wherever we can find it. Let me rephrase that for you.

"Either you men are with me, or you'll remain here on this godforsaken island until all you are is a pile of bones. What say you, men?"

After some deliberation, the men agreed to join William and John.

A tall, Spanish man with a bony face and wearing a typical soldier's uniform—blue overcoat and white pants—approached William.

"I am Sargento, Primero Roberto de Prima, at your service. What should I call you, sire?"

"Willy, you shall call me One-Eyed Willy."

CHAPTER SEVEN

A few weeks later, One-Eyed Willy and John Ramos were on the main deck, aboard the Sea Fire.

The skies over the Atlantic Ocean were cloudless, and the sun was beating down on them as though God's vengeance was upon them for the massacre that had occurred two weeks prior. Blood was still being scrubbed off the deck by some of the lower ranking seamen on board the ship, and the smell of gunpowder still lagged about the main deck like shit from the bow boxes, made worse by the lack of any wind. Prima came onto the deck.

"Captain Willy, sire. What of the English prisoners below deck?" Prima asked.

"There are English prisoners on this ship?" Willy asked. "Are you quite sure?"

"Yes, sire, they were privateers. We sank their ship off the coast of Port Royal, a known privateer and pirate stronghold," Prima replied.

"How many?"

"There are five, sire. Just five."

"Bring them here for judgement, Prima."

"Yes, sire," Prima replied, and quickly disappeared below deck. "What do you plan to do with them?" John asked.

"What do you plan on doing with your name?"

"What do you mean?"

"Well, John Ramos doesn't sound like a deadly pirate," Willy answered.

"Apologies, brother-in-law, I didn't know that was our new occupation. I was under the assumption that we were hiding."

"Hiding, why in the hell would we be in hiding?" William laughed.

"Then, where the hell are we going?"

"After the scroll, of course."

"I do not understand your logic, William. The last eight years of our lives nothing but misery, and you want to jeopardize our newly acquired freedom and steal the scroll," said John.

"Wouldn't the Duke like to know you are still alive? And to have the opportunity to control time. John, we could change the past."

"William, there is nothing more in this world I wish for than to change the past. But these are myths. They are stories. What about Sebastian and Sara? wouldn't you like to find them?"

"Don't talk to me about my family. What makes you think they are even alive? What makes you think they escaped from the Spanish that night?" Willy said.

"Look, Willy, they are my family too and I don't know if they *are* still alive. All I know, is that

Sara had the jewel and if that's so important to you, then that's who we should be looking for."

"Oh, yeah, you speak to me as if I don't want to find my children, as if the jewel is of more worth than my daughter. I know Sara has the jewel and I want to believe they are alive. Besides, the old man said you can't use the jewel without the scroll, or the scroll without the jewel." At that moment, Prima brought the five prisoners to Willy and John.

"Sire, here are the criminals," said Prima.

"Take a gander at this sorry bunch of scallywags. You gentlemen look as if you haven't eaten in months; how are you still alive? I'm feeling gracious today, so we are going to play an easy game. I'm going to give you each an apple, and whoever tells me who's in charge gets to eat the apple. If you try to eat the apple before I get my answer, you lose your hands. So, who's in charge of this worthless band of swine?" said Willy.

Four of the men pointed to a short, pudgy man, balding on the top of his head, with long gray hair trailing down his back. He walked forward, toward Willy.

"So you're the man in charge? What's your name?"

"My name is Devereaux, Captain, and I'm not the one in charge. You are." He then took a bite out of the apple.

Willy laughed. "Finally, an Englishman with some intelligence. You are a sharp one if ever I met one! Throw the other men overboard! Mr. Devereaux, would you like to be part of the crew of this ship?" Devereaux smiled and said, "You got fire in your eyes, Captain, so I'd be delighted.

I have just one question, Captain, if I may. What's the name of the ship?"

"Fire, you say. The name is, The Sea." Willy coughed and cleared his throat. "My apologies, Mr. Devereaux. Welcome aboard The Inferno. Now, see to the bow boxes; they need a proper swabbing. Oh, and one more thing, Mr. Devereux. If you cross me, I'll burn you alive."

Devereaux nodded in affirmation and walked away as John made his way to the helm.

"Willy, you failed to tell me our destination."

"Apologies, John. We are headed to see an old friend who can help us capture the scroll. This friend is currently in exile in the Spanish Netherlands."

"Well, I guess I should thank the Lord you're not speaking of King Charles II, because that would be a suicide mission."

Willy turned to the left with a wee smirk on his face.

John looked at Willy's expression and said, "You can't be serious? William, you are joking.

How is the exiled King of England an old friend?"

"Well, my good friend, that is a long story, and we have a long journey ahead of us. "Avast men, we've got some sailing to do," Willy instructed.

CHAPTER EIGHT

After nearly a month at sea, the newly named pirate ship, The Inferno docked in the waterfront city of Ostend on the northwest corner of the Spanish Netherlands. Disembarking, Willy could see the history embedded in the rotted, moldy smelling docks and cracks on the streets.

These streets were centuries old and proudly bore the remnants of wood from the wheels of carriages, as well as plentiful aged as well as fresh horse shit and a whole lot of gunpowder.

Willy and his men were tired, famished and in dire need of supplies.

The most important of those being a tasty beer and a good tug on the old wooden latch.

Willy had once visited this harbor in the early 1640's with his father and the King and his son. It was the one time James Walsh had taken his son with him to work and they had spent a few weeks in the bustling town of ale, drapers and blacksmiths. In fact, that was when he had met his first bagnio keeper, or brothel housekeeper. Willy had rung the bell, and a short woman, with brown hair darker than the night sky, had come to the door.

She'd answered with bosoms in clear view, and wore lipstick as red as The Inferno's bloodshed.

"My, my, my. The little boy with one eye returns, and what have you brought your old mamacita, William?"

"You, you remembered my name?" Willy stammered.

"Of course! How many boys with eyepatches do you think I know?" she replied.

"My apologies, but I have forgotten yours."

"Florence, my name is Florence."

"Ah, yes. Florence. Well, Florence, may I introduce you to my brother-in-law, John?" John grabbed the lady's hand and kissed it.

"Married are you now, Willy? And aren't you quite the gentleman, John?" Florence said.

The question Florence had asked William had sent a shocking memory of John's wife being murdered, through his head.

"Only in the presence of a lady, but believe you me, I have no issues killing a lady," John replied angrily.

"Mr. Ramos, I do believe you have a black heart that seems to go along with your black tongue," said Florence.

"I'm happy to see you two getting along so well. We come bearing jewels of course, my lady, and plenty of men with much coin to spend at your establishment. Is our mutual friend here?" asked William.

"No, he isn't, but I will have word sent to him in Breda. He can be here in a few days. Please, all of you, do come in and enjoy some of the finer things Ostend has to offer." As the men walked into the establishment, Willy leaned into John and whispered, "I think that's a good name."

"What name?"

"Blackheart, that should be your *pirate* name."

"Really, you think that's a suitable opponent for One-Eyed Willy?"

"*I* wouldn't cross him," Willy answered, and they both laughed and walked into the bagnio house to await the arrival of King Charles II.

It was late spring in 1660, a few months after John Ramos had gained a name worthy of a heartless pirate. King Charles and Willy had conjured a plan so cunning and undeniable, that when it was laid out for the men, there was no question that it was perfect.

Charles and his Scottish armies in the north were marching on route to London as they spoke. The Inferno, and a few of Charles's Spanish galleons would land on the beaches of Dover and they would all converge on London and ransack the city.

Willy and the rest of the men were waiting on the arrival of King Charles so they could begin their journey and carry out the plan.

But when Charles returned to Ostend, he brought with him some astounding news.

After a long carriage ride, Charles burst into the brothel house entrance and up the stairs and shouted, "Florence! Florence!"

He opened the door and saw William in bed with Florence, and for a second, the King froze. He certainly had not expected to see Willy—a man in whom he had a vast financial and physical interest—together in bed with Florence.

A touch of jealousy and hatred surfaced behind his usually kind eyes.

"You two." He fumbled his words. "You two are not going to fathom the news I'm about to tell you."

"What? What is it, Charles?" Willy asked, now sitting upright.

" They've reinstated the old Parliament and they are going to reinstate me as King."

"Charles, that's wonderful news."

"This is remarkable, I'm so proud of you, Charles," Florence said, and put on her robe and tied it around her waist.

"Yes, I am beyond words. This has been a dream of mine since my father's execution," Charles exclaimed.

"It's long overdue, my good friend, long overdue and without any bloodshed. When do we set sail?" asked William.

"Well, I also found out about that armada of ships who commandeered the treasure chest you spoke of. Supposedly, they never returned to England. There were four ships and three of them went down in a horrific storm. The story goes, that one ship had survived and ran aground off the coast of Guadeloupe. If I were you, I would start there," suggested Charles.

"And what of the painting of my mother in the House of Lords?"

"Ah, your mother's painting. I have a financier named Robert Perkins working for me on the Island of Tortuga. I will send the painting there. I found out some troubling information as well. Your mother changed both your name and her name to Pordobel.

"I'm told this was her maiden name. There is no record of William J. Walsh in the house of records. Your name is recorded as William B. Pordobel. I assume she didn't want the disgraced

Walsh name to plague you and her for the rest of your lives."

The King was still unsettled by the site of William and Florence in the same bed, and in a condescending tone said, "You know, William, I was deeply saddened by what happened to your father. He was a friend of my own father. Your mother on the other hand, if I may be frank, was a bit of a whore."

Willy looked the King in his eye, listening to Charles ramble on about his mother and the acts of infidelity she was involved in. He was in utter shock.

"Oh, yes. I remember when we were children at King's," Charles went on. "I would come home to London and I would hear the moans of your mother down the halls of Parliament and wonder *which member of Parliament is she fornicating with now?* I would laugh and think, *poor William.*"

Willy had always thought his mother was unfaithful and these words from the King proved him correct. Indeed, these vile words from one of his oldest friends were like sharp knives through his heart. The man clearly bore a great secret that could have changed Willy's entire life.

What if Willy had known and spoken of this to his father, and had his mother arrested for adultery? Willy was more than mad; he was disgusted that Charles would have kept this from him, but he did nothing harsh. He instead collected his thoughts, silently musing.

"My King, I am most gracious to hear the news of your restoration. My father and mother did have issues, but when it came time to choosing sides, my father risked his life for your father's.

"Indeed as I intended to do for you. I understand why you kept these words from me, yet at the same time, I do not. My men and I will take our leave for the Caribbean in the morning, and I will meet your man, Robert Perkins, on Tortuga."

William began to put his pants on and button his shirt.

"Charles, until next time, my old friend," William continued.

"Willy, I meant no harsh intentions. I thought it in your best inter-est," said Charles.

Willy stepped forward and hugged Charles tightly, he then left the room.

"So, what about you, my darling, would you like to accompany the King back to England and be his dirty little secret?" said Charles to Florence despite what he had just witnessed.

"Oh, Charlie. I'd be delighted but it would make me a bit of a whore too, wouldn't it darling?" They both laughed until they cried.

Then, the King said, "My dear, I do believe it would. But I happen to like whores quite a lot." Willy overheard the conversation and was infuriated, but it gave him the most heinous idea.

The very next morning, the sun blasted through the stained-glass win-dows of the brothel house.

There wasn't a sound; in fact, you could have heard a feather drop.

Charles woke up and stretched out both his arms, deliberately curling his right arm underneath his lover's pretty neck—and found she felt oddly cold, and his skin was suddenly soaked in a red liquid. He turned to his right, and there was Florence, unresponsive with something stuffed in her mouth. He lifted off the covers and screamed, eyes wide.

Florence's head had been cleaved from her body, and only the bloody, bony stump of her neck vertebrae were lying there, coddled by King Charles 'outstretched arm. The head, it seemed, had been stuffed into the porcelain chamber pot that sat at the side of the bed, eyes staring open.

The guards came rushing in immediately and noticed the King's arm was covered in blood.

One of the guards saw paper protruding from Florence's mouth and removed it. "What does it say?" Charles asked.

"Calmer heads prevail, Your Highness. We both know secrets are spoken with the devil's breath. We both know Florence was a gigantic whore and her moans down the hallways of Parliament may have left you headless just like your father. I meant no harsh intentions and thought it was in your best interest. Signed, One-Eyed Willy," the guard concluded.

The Inferno was departing Ostend harbor and Willy was laughing nightmarishly loud.

That laugh of his could be heard getting fainter as the ship disappeared and was finally lost into the sun. The Inferno was on its way to find the sacred scroll.

CHAPTER NINE

W hat was left of the tropical depression pounded the shores off the island of Marie-Galante.

The storm that had paid a visit to the island the night before had since raced out to sea.

There wasn't a cloud remaining in the windless sky and September 21st 1660 was without a doubt a day that would never be forgotten by any of the people of the island.

A bell rang from the newly constructed church and some of the towns-folk had gathered to say a prayer and give thanks to the Lord for saving those who had somehow survived against all odds. One of those people was Abigail La Renne, who like most of the people on the island, was of African descent—yet she spoke French as though it was her native tongue.

She had curves in the right areas, a captivatingly gorgeous smile and an explosive temper.

Abby was also one of the kindest souls you could ever be fortunate enough to make acquaintances with. And on this day, a very tall man with a bald head and a whole lot of unnecessary muscle dragged two children by the arms toward Abby.

The boy and the girl struggled to separate themselves from the man but he wouldn't let go.

"What did they do this time?" Abby asked.

"Ma, they were throwing rocks at the old church, and broke a few windows," said Quaco, Abigail's elder of two sons from her late husband. "It wasn't many windows, though, Ma, and the church has lots of them." He looked so innocent, a gentle giant, but that was deceptive.

He was also trained in the art of combat. His father had spent years privateering and had taught him the ways of both the gun and the sword.

"What did I tell you two about throwing rocks?"

"We know! *There are people in this world who get stoned to death. How would you like to get stoned to death?* is what ya told us, Mother Abigail," said Maria, the young girl with reddishbrown hair and skin as white as new sails.

"Did you take what I said for humor, Juliet?" Abigail asked. "Because it seems that you threw the rocks anyway!"

But, Mother Abigail," the younger brother added.

"Romeo, I am not yet done with Juliet. You will soon have your chance to speak."

Romeo lowered his head, and said, "Yes, Mum." "Well, Juliet?" Abigail asked a second time.

"I must admit at the time, it was rather funny, but it isn't when you think about being stoned to death. But at the time, it was. Isn't that right, Romeo?"

The children both began to laugh uncontrollably and agreed.

"Oh, so you both think it's funny? Ok, well, you know what? The crops could sure use some fertilizer. Quaco, get them a couple shovels and get them behind the livestock and we'll see how much they want to throw rocks next time."

"But, Mother Abigail!" they both blurted out.

"No buts from the both of ya. Go on now," Abigail ordered.

"I thought I was going to have a chance to speak?" Romeo then muttered under his breath.

"What was that, Romeo?" said Abby.

"Nothing, Mum. I didn't say anything," Romeo replied. "Not a word."

"And so I would think. Now, get to shoveling and I don't want to see either of you until suppertime. And leave the rocks down on the ground or there'll be big trouble."

"Yes, Ma."

There was only one plantation on the island of Maria-Galante and it was owned by Robert Perkins.

In fact, Abigail was the person who operated it for Mr. Perkins, and in return he would provide protection and supplies. He would also allow her and the other former slaves to live on the island as indentured servants. It was supposed to be some kind of great privilege.

Quaco and the children had arrived at the plantation around 08:00 AM and entered the horse stables on the easternmost side of the land. The children went from stable to stable shoveling manure into a large wooden barrel, and wheeling it to an even larger carriage.

Romeo, who considered himself a joker, decided to take a shovelful of horse shit and throw it at Juliet. The chunks of horse excrement hit her on her back and Romeo began laughing.

"Sebastian, I'm going rip that shovel out of your hand and beat you with it if you do that again."

"And I'm going to tell Abby that you're using my real name, and I promise you, she will give you far more shit than I could ever shovel at you," Romeo replied haughtily.

"Is that so, Romeo?"

Juliet picked up a piece of horse dung and threw it into the face of Romeo, resulting in them both rolling around in shit and—quite literally, as it turned out—beating the shit out of each other.

Quaco quickly ran into the barn. "What the hell is going on? Who started it?" he yelled. Both children pointed at each other and laughed.

"That's enough. I'm bringing you both back to town. You smell wretched," Quaco said.

As they walked outside, they heard what sounded like thunder over and over again, yet the skies were clear.

"What is that, Quaco?" Juliet asked. "Sounds like the gods are terribly angry with someone." "That's cannon fire. Quick, I must get you back inside and underneath the stables."

They all ran back inside and Quaco went into one of the corners on the floor. Under a pile of hay was a hatch that led underground. Quaco opened it and in a worried tone said, "You remember what we discussed.

You have everything you need. Do not, and I repeat, *do not* come out no matter

what you hear—or think you hear. Do you understand?"

Both children nodded in compliance and made their way into the hatch.

Quaco closed it and covered it with hay and horse manure, then ran outside, climbed on a horse and rode back into town.

Meanwhile, the ship named the Inferno was anchored just off the coast of Guadeloupe and members of the crew had been diving and scouring the wreckage of the English ship, the Ocean Gazer for over a month but had still not yet found the scroll. Blackheart was peering about the water for any other signs of wreckage when he spotted smoke in the far distance.

"Captain! Captain!" Blackheart yelled, running to the bottom of the steps on the main deck.

Willy looked down at Blackheart.

"You see all that black smoke?" Willy asked.

"Aye, Captain," Blackheart replied.

"What say you, Mr. Blackheart?" Willy asked.

"Could be a ship that got plundered, and in that case, I would say, let's plunder the ship that did the plundering," said Blackheart. "Plunder the plunderer."

"Agreed. Hoist the anchor, men, and get some wind in these sails. Haul wind like your lives depend on it, cause they sure as hell do. I want that booty!" screamed Willy. "And if I don't get that booty, there's going to be hell to pay!"

The Spanish had laid waste to the island of Maria-Galante.

Two galleons equipped with eight-pounder cannons had decimated the little fortifications on the beach, then begun to wreak havoc upon the town and townspeople, and the only structure left standing had been the new church.

Spanish soldiers invaded the beaches of Maria-Galante swiftly and harshly, and anyone who wasn't on their knees and surrendering was destined to face a bullet or the tip of a sword.

The man responsible for this devastation was none other than Admiral Francisco Gonzales.

The soldiers had rounded up what was left of the townspeople and brought them to the front of the church. Some were horribly injured, while others cried, scared for their lives.

Marianne Abigail La Renne showed no emotion as she stood before the most vicious tyrant in all the Caribbean, Francisco Gonzales.

"I am looking for two children, a boy and a girl. They would more than likely be the only white or Spanish here on this island. What is your name, Mother?" Gonzales asked.

"My name is Abigail."

"Well, then, you are most definitely a person of interest to me.

"I am in search of a necklace with a jewel as blue as the sky, surrounded by stones as red as a strawberry. Do you know what I speak of?"

"I do not, sire," replied Abigail. "I swear I have not seen any such things."

"Are you sure one of these children doesn't have it in their possession? I'll tell you what Abigail, and whether you choose to believe in what I say is your choice, but know this. These words I speak are valid. I will leave this island, spare the rest of you and never return if you give me what I want. If you don't, I will take half of the inhabitants as slaves.

"And the other half I will lock in the church and then burn it down. The choice is yours and you have ten seconds to decide." The Captain started to count.

"I'm telling the truth; I know of no twin boy and girl here on the island."

"They are twins? Did I say they are twins? Diego, come forth."

Diego, the nephew of Gonzales, was a young officer with a strikingly handsome appearance, the face of an angel and a heart as cruel as the devil himself. "Did I say they were twins?"

"No, sire, you did not. I believe that is very important information only a certain few would know," Diego replied.

"Indeed it is, Diego, indeed it is. Alright, enough with the games. Bring me the young man, Diego."

"Yes, sire."

Diego walked away and quickly returned with Quaco, who was a visual mess.

The young lad had obviously been badly beaten and appeared to have a cut from a sword on his left arm, just above his bicep. Diego threw Quaco to the ground.

"Diego, will you get someone to pick him up?" Gonzales ordered.

"Yes, sire." Diego looked at two soldiers and said, "Well, you heard the admiral; don't just stand there, pick the slave up."

The choice of the word *slave* did not sit well with Abigail.

"He is my son. He is *African*, and unlike you Mr. Diego, a free man. You're Spanish and an asshole," Abby shouted. "And you, sire, are the only slave around these parts. Slave to ignorance!" Diego walked over to Abigail and said, "What did you say? I couldn't quite hear you." Just as Abigail was about to repeat what she had said, he punched her in the stomach.

Abigail dropped to her knees.

"You see, we certainly don't discriminate against anyone of color or religion; we just think you *all* should be slaves," said Diego. "And we treat you all the same."

"That's enough, Diego. Kill her son and the rest of them. Take anything worth selling, along with a few slaves, and bring them aboard the ship. I want you and your men to search every inch of this island and find me those children *and* my stone. It was nice meeting you, Miss Abigail.

"I hope to see you again in the next life."

At that very second, distant rumbles were again heard overhead—the sound of far-off cannon fire. Seconds later, a cannon ball struck the church creating a loud explosion, the sudden impact forcing almost everyone to the ground and some of the townspeople started skirmishing, running for cover to hide from the Spanish soldiers.

Gonzales looked out to sea, and there was a Spanish galleon firing on one of his ships.

It was One-Eyed Willy and Blackheart, and they were boarding one of Gonzales's ships.

Gonzales's own ship was on the other side of the bay and had opened fire on the Inferno.

"Who's the captain of this vessel?" Willy asked the officer aboard Gonzales's ship.

The officer bled from a gash above his eye and sweat poured down his brow.

"You're in serious trouble. This here ship belongs to Francisco Gonzales, and once he returns from that island, you're going to be sorry," the bloodied officer said. Willy and Blackheart's eyes lit up to the point where they both heeded the words of the officer and immediately jumped overboard and began swimming ashore.

"What should we do?" asked Toothless Jackson, one of the crew.

"We came here to plunder, didn't we? That's what we should do. Come on men, let's find us some booty," Devereaux answered.

Half the crew remained on the ship to locate anything of value, and the other half boarded the smaller boats and followed Willy and Blackheart ashore.

The island was in absolute turmoil. Cannon fire and gunfire were erupting all around as Willy and his men finally got to shore. Gonzales— still in front of the church and holding Abigail hostage—said, "Woman, I am going to give you one last chance. Where are the children?"

"You can kill me and my child, but I will never tell you where those children are, because one day, those children will put an end to your tyranny," replied Abby.

Gonzales lifted his sword. "Maybe one day, but not today." Quaco threw himself in front of the sword, slicing him across his chest, and he fell into his mother's arms.

"No, Quaco," Abby cried.

Willy and Blackheart heard the scream and looked up on the hill, where they spotted Gonzales.

"Gonzales!" Blackheart screamed.

Gonzales turned and looked down the hill and saw both men. He took out his spyglass to get a closer look, and whispered to himself, "The man with the eyepatch," then yelled, "Retreat, men. Head back to the ship." He began to run down the backside of the hill.

Blackheart and Willy made their way up the front of the hill and had to fight off Spanish soldiers along the way. Two soldiers converged on Willy but he managed to kick one in the knee, then he twisted and plunged his sword into the other. As he turned back around, he shot one soldier in the head with his pistol. Blackheart, a sword in each hand and swinging wildly, cut through flesh as they made their way to the hill's summit.

Blackheart noticed the woman holding her son in her arms.

"Abigail?" he asked.

"Help! Please help me, John."

"Oh, dear Lord, Abigail," said William.

"William, this is my son. Please help me."

William and Blackheart lifted Quaco and moved him away from the fighting, and Willy instructed one of the men to fetch Prima, trained in medicine and wound repair.

"He is going to be fine. Prima will make sure of it. Abby, look at me. Do you understand? He is going to be just fine. The sword didn't penetrate deep enough. He is going to make it, trust me.

Now where are my children?" William asked.

"Never mind that; where is Gonzales?" Blackheart asked.

Abby pointed in one direction. "Gonzales sent men up there to the plantation to look for your children." She then pointed to a different area. "He fled down the hill," Abby added.

"Let's go get him, Willy." Willy looked up at the plantation, turned, and said, "Aye."

They descended the hill faster than they would have believed, the three other men who were with them trailing behind ever so slightly.

They all reached the bottom of the hill and saw Gonzales already halfway to his ship, but there was a group of Spanish soldiers left on the beach, trying to get into a boat.

Willy and his men soon overcame the soldiers and started to launch the boat back into the sea.

"Willy, Willy," Blackheart yelled, pointing as he got in the vessel. Willy looked up at the church, thoughts of Louisa overwhelming his mind. The times they had had on Barbados flowed through his head like a daydream of linear memories until they reached the birth of his children.

He looked back at Blackheart, then turned and started to run back up the hill.

Blackheart's crew began to row as hard as they could, but Gonzales's ship was hoisting its anchor, so Blackheart changed course and headed for the other Spanish galleon which had taken a beating from the bombardment from the Inferno.

Blackheart reached the helm and yelled, "Hoist the anchor, men."

Deveraux appeared from below deck, dragging a prisoner. Blackheart looked at the captive.

"Wait a minute! Do I know you?" Devereaux asked.

"No, sire," replied the prisoner.

"Well then, who the hell are you?"

"Garcia, sir, Juan Garcia," he replied.

"Well, you're either staying, or you can get the hell off my ship. I'm going after Gonzales." Devereaux and Garcia both jumped off the side of the ship into the warm water of the Caribbean as Blackheart and the few remaining men he had with him hoisted the anchor.

With only a skeleton crew, he set sail after Gonzales.

Willy had reached the top of the hill and turned to look out to the ocean, watching as the Spanish galleon sailed away. Blackheart turned and looked toward the top of the hill where Willy

was standing. It would be nine years before they would ever get to lay eyes on one another again.

CHAPTER TEN

Nearly nine years later, on a night that—like the ocean's depths—was as dark as it was chilling, moonlight reflected the Inferno's name as it entered the calmness of the harbor and hoisted its anchor.

There was a shiver in the warm Caribbean breeze, and Davey Jones lingered in the wind that swept off the water, preying on cursed souls and adding their last breath to his storm of hell on the sea.

On land, a group of men sat around a small fire drinking rum, laughing and telling stories of triumph and glory from their latest haul. The leader of this small band of dissidents was Juan Garcia, also known as Capitán de la Muerte, or as his men called him, the Captain of Death.

La Muerte was one of the most feared pirates in all the Spanish Main. He had been just a young boy when he lost his parents, and by the age of ten had committed his first murder. By the time he was sixteen, he was a full-blown pirate, and the Captain of Death was born.

La Muerte had black hair and wore black slacks with a black, half-buttoned shirt, exposing his chest, along with a black hat. He even had a black monkey, unsurprisingly named Blackie.

So, why, if la Muerte was one of the most feared pirates in all the Caribbean, was he visibly trembling with fear?

Cutthroat Cal was a widower and la Muerte's quartermaster who stood tall in his boots but had a short temper; a red bandana covered the top of his balding, blond hair.

It was said that his wife and infant child had been sacrificed by the Kalinago to their evil god, Maybouya and murdered on the island of Hispaniola. Cal had absolutely gone out of his mind after that and slaughtered the entire village, and that was how he had got the name Cutthroat Cal.

He would bend his enemies over a barrel and tie their hands behind their backs. He would then position his cutlass snug under their necks and pull his arm back, slicing through their throats.

Cal buried his feet into the cool sand and took a vicious bite out of a chicken leg. As he washed it down with a sip of rum, he wiped his mouth and looked up at la Muerte.

"What's the worry, Cap'n? We'll hide out here for a few weeks, and everything will be fine."

La Muerte walked over to Cal and gruffly said, "Do I look like someone who thinks everything is going to be just fine? He's out there and he could be on his way here right now."

"Cap'n, you really think One-Eyed Willy is going to hunt us down when the total haul was only worth 10,000 ducats? Do you honestly believe he's coming for that?" Cal asked. "I can't imagine it myself," he added.

"It's not the gold. Willy could care less about the gold; he wants the jewel. The jewel, you fool, that's all he wants. He'll come for it, you can count on that," la Muerte said confidently.

Just offshore, the men aboard the Inferno quietly disembarked and got into three boats, rowing gently toward land. Willy was on the boat in the middle, standing at the stern and smoking a pipe.

The oarsmen's strokes, synchronized to perfection, made for rapid but smooth progress, and the usually loud and riotous bunch were soundless in their endeavor.

The aspect of surprise was the aim of that night's foray.

The boats hit land, and everyone disembarked except for Willy. A few moments later, screams were heard above the sound of gunshots. Some of la Muerte's men ran toward the water and were met without mercy by One-Eyed Willy's men. Only a few were captured and they were tied up and forced onto their knees. Willy continued to smoke his pipe and jumped out of the boat into the high tide and walked up on the beach. Palm trees leaned, forced over by the direction of the wind, and a few hundred feet up on the sand, the crew of the Inferno had started a monstrous fire.

A man named Smitty, a well-known buccaneer, brought the bloodied la Muerte to Willy, who was still smoking his pipe. "Here you are, sire. We found the traitor; I knew he was hiding out here. What say you we do with the treasonous scoundrel?"

"Come now, Mr. Smitty. Is that any way to treat a former, unimportant crew member?" Some of the men laughed.

"I see Mr. Perkins can be, without a doubt, exceptional in his persuasiveness. Love the new ship, lad, but I wonder at what cost it came? Am I to understand that you and your confidants were under the assumption you could fool your old commander?" asked One-Eyed Willy.

"It wasn't for me, Señor, it was for Mr. Perkins! He kidnapped my Maria. He threatened to take her life if I did not agree to his terms," said la Muerte.

Still smoking his pipe, he rubbed la Muerte on his shoulders and patted him on the back.

"I know, I know. Love can make a man turn into a monster. I know because I am a monster, Capitán, or la Muerte, or whatever it is they call you." La Muerte squirmed around, trying to free himself but the men held him down, pressing his knees deeper in the sand.

"There's something I need you to understand," One-Eyed Willy said. "My ship is a sanctuary for those monsters and the outcasts of society. The belongings on said ship are not to be touched or removed by anyone, especially not to be taken from me. Where is the jewel?" "I do not have it, but I can get it, Captain," la Muerte replied.

"Where is it, la Muerte?" said One-Eyed Willy.

"It is safe. I put it somewhere no one would find it," said la Muerte.

"Captain, I say we take his hand and put it where no one can find it," Smitty chimed in.

"My God, have some rum! Smitty, I believe you're starting to scare some of his crew," Willy said.

"Aye, aye, Captain," Smitty replied to the question, surrounded by laughter.

"Which is his quartermaster?" Willy asked.

"I believe it is Cal," Smitty replied.

"Then bring him here," said Willy.

"Señor, Captain," la Muerte said, "I know of something much bigger. I was told something of great value."

"Is that so? Now you want to call me Captain? Perhaps, if the shoe were on the other foot, I would be running my lips pretty fast before I cut them off along with your tongue," said Willy.

"Here you are, Captain. Here is Mr. Cal," Smitty announced.

"Cutthroat Cal, I'm at a crossroad. I don't know whether to cut your throat because of the irony, or throw you into the fire. Do you know where my jewel is?" Willy asked.

"No sire, but the Governor is amassing the largest treasure the New World has ever seen," Cal explained.

"Wait, wait, wait. You didn't answer my question yet. I'll be merciful and will not make a fool of you. I extend my gratitude for the information. Love the bandana, lad, but I'll take that as you won't be needing it. Very well. Now, Mr. Smitty, throw him in the fire," Willy ordered.

"No, Captain, please!" Cal screamed with a terrified look.

The men picked him up off the ground.

"No, Captain, please. He doesn't deserve this. It wasn't him," la Muerte begged. "A bit chilly out, isn't it? Let's warm you up, lad," said Smitty.

They forced Cal into the roaring fire. His horrendous screams could be heard in the distance, but quickly faded as he was burned alive.

"He who be members of the crew of the Retribution, pledge their oath to the Inferno or be dust in the wind for Davey Jones. *Muerte, Muerte, Muerte!*

"I need you to stop crying. You've been hoisted by your own petard, and ye be the only one to blame. Now let that be a lesson to all ye intruders! Beware crushing death and grief soaked with blood from the trespassing thief. For my name is One-Eyed Willy."

CHAPTER ELEVEN

Havana

Just past noon on a magical summer afternoon in 1669, the streets of the little town of Havana were bustling with people. The sun and all its power bestowed goodwill on the people of Cuba on this day, and a breeze that funneled through the city was both welcoming and refreshing.

Fishermen were trading all types of fish and seafood, and there was an abundance of traders selling baskets of fruit and vegetables on every corner of the busy street. Local blacksmiths worked away, hammering and shaping newly molded swords, and soldiers in front of the shopkeeper's store were occupied as usual, warding out the beggars.

And, of course, there was sugar and tobacco just about everywhere you looked.

Jose, a farmer, owned one of the more prominent farm produce stalls in Havana. He handed a customer a few oranges and they exchanged coin.

"Gracias, buenas tardes, senor," Jose said to the customer.

Jose earned a living by selling apples, oranges, mangoes, corn, yucca, and carrots displayed in small baskets on three wooden shelves. The fresh flowers in between every other basket added decoration but were also an opportunity for more coin.

"Thomas, how many oranges and apples are left on the cart?" Jose asked, but Thomas didn't answer. Jose called his name again and took a few steps, and then peeked around the corner of the new cobbler stall.

He saw Thomas handing two poor boys each an orange and Jose was angered, but he went back to work and didn't mention anything.

Thomas returned to the farm stand, baby-faced and with charitable brown eyes, and tied a blue bandana around his head; it contrasted with his straw-colored hair.

"I called for you, Thomas. What were you doing?"

"I was admiring the cobbler's latest creation. My apologies, how can I assist?" "Record the amount of fruit we have left on the cart, and you are done for the day." "That's wonderful, gracias, Jose!" Thomas replied excitedly.

Then he set about counting what was left of the unsold fruit, plus the few fruits that he had given away. Then he presented the numbers to Jose.

Jose checked the numbers and said, "Gracias, Thomas, now let me pay you." Jose took out his pouch and paid Thomas three coins.

"Senor, but I'm supposed to be receiving five coins for five hours' work. I am two coins short."

"No, Thomas. You're wrong there. You gave two oranges to those beggar children, and it's coming out of your pay!" Jose responded bitterly.

"But those oranges were going bad, and you would only have fed them to the animals. So, they were just going to be wasted, just spoiled..."

"And they are my animals to feed," Jose responded. "I'm not in the *feed the public for free* business. Food costs me, Thomas, whether it goes to the animals or not—it's mine, for me to use as I will. And at least the animals help me tend to the farm.

"You know what, Thomas, don't bother coming back tomorrow."

"You're firing me?" Thomas said, surprised. "Fine, pay the balance of coins owed, and you shall never have to see me again."

"Kid, one of your beggars has a better chance of getting an orange from me than of me giving you two coins. You gave away the fruits, and that's that. End of negotiation."

"Well, I guess I'll have to purchase a whole basket of oranges then," Thomas replied and snatched the whole pouch of coins out of Jose's hand.

Thomas took off and sprinted through the town with Jose, the farmer, chasing after him, shouting, "Give me back my coins! I want my coins!"

"Sorry, no can do, *compadre*. I earned these coins fair and square!"

"If you don't give me back those coins, I'm calling for the guard, and they will lock you up for good this time! That's if they don't flog you to death first!"

"Apologies, Jose, but beggars can't be choosers. So I'll take my chance this time, compadre, if you don't mind."

"If I *don't mind?* If I don't mind! Have you taken leave of your senses? Of course I mind, and you shall see how much I mind when I catch hold of you, you—you—wretched thief!"

Thomas had just passed the guards playing dice in front of the shopkeeper when Jose yelled,

"Guards! Guards! Thief! Thief! He stole my coins; he stole my coins!" The guards looked up, saw Thomas and gave chase.

Jose stopped, bent over and out of breath, still tried to shout, "Guards, thief!" His weakened voice was carried away on the wind.

But luckily, the guards were already giving a good chase.

Thomas deliberately knocked over baskets of yucca to hinder the guards, and one of them stumbled and fell into the obstacles. But Thomas was still being hounded by a tiny, pudgy guard who looked as though he had no neck. Thomas jumped over a horse carriage then stopped at a fish stand and began to throw the wet fish at the chubby guard.

The guard ducked, trying to avoid the flying fish.

Thomas faked another throw, so the guard ducked.

Only then did Thomas launch the fish, hitting the guard fully in the face.

The not-so-slender guard fell backward into a horse carriage full of manure and rolled back onto the ground, covered head to toe in horse shit. Thomas laughed but was grabbed on the wrist by the fisherman, who had a hook for a hand. The hook clawed into his skin, almost piercing it.

"Aye, and I could slice you open from neck to navel with this here hook, young man!" cried the fisherman, clearly incensed. "So you'd best not move a muscle. Now, how do you plan on paying for the fish?"

Thomas said, "I won't have to; you will be too busy."

"Doing what, exactly?" asked the fisherman. "Guards!" he continued.

Thomas kicked over a basket of fish onto the busy street and shouted, "You'll be too busy cleaning up all the fish off the ground."

Sure enough, the fisherman unhooked himself from Thomas's wrist to clean up the fish, and held one in the air that was now attached to his hook.

"Get back here, I'm not through with you."

But Thomas had long gone, vanished into the crowded street.

He eventually slowed down in front of a brothel house and quickly walked through the door.

As soon as he was inside, the overwhelming stench of sex, rum and tobacco ravaged the establishment. Directly in front of Thomas was a set of stairs that led to a corridor with rooms on both sides and a wraparound railing so you could look back down. Candle fixtures were scattered about the walls and there was a bar in the back left corner where unfaithful men—and ladies making a none-too-virtuous living—could drink away their sorrows.

A woman, Rosie, walked up to Thomas as he was frantically looking out the window.

"Hey, Thomas, are those coins in your pocket, or are you just happy to see me?"

"Not now Rosie, the guards are after me. I'll only be a moment, I promise."

"That's what you said last time, and I spent thirty minutes holding you in my arms while you cried like a little girl, and my daddy with all the sugar went with Johanna."

"I told you my deepest darkest secrets," replied Thomas. "Don't underestimate it."

"Yeah? Well you still didn't pay me enough, so I want two coins or I'm screaming for the guards. Never mind *underestimated*."

Johanna walked over from the bar and said, "Did I overhear my name in the same sentence as *coins?*"

"Would the both of you just be quiet?"

"Thomas over here is hiding out from the guards," said Johanna.

"Ooh, this is my favorite game. I want five coins or I'm screaming for those guards right now!"

"Johanna, you wouldn't do that to me after all the coin that I've spent with you," Thomas suggested. "You wouldn't, would you?"

"Yes, I would; you spent *all that coin,* as you put it, so you could make me listen to you cry about the love you lost. Never been so bored in all my life!" cried Johanna, unfeeling.

"Exactly. We are ladies of the night and have no interest in listening to your feelings at all. We would rather let your pockets do the talking. The coins, Thomas, now!" Rosie insisted.

"OK! OK!" Thomas conceded, searching through his pockets and replying, "This is what I have for you ladies." He pulled out both hands and gently edged them forward in a clenched fist so both maids stooped to take a close look, eagerly anticipating some great gift.

Then he raised both middle fingers and shoved them into the eyes of the two brothel maids, then took off up the stairs. The ladies ran outside, half-blinded, and Rosie was yelling, "Guards, guards, he's in here. He's in here! And he owes us coins! Get him!"

Thomas reached the top of the old wooden steps, looked left then right, and continued to head left. One of the guards heard the ladies call for help, turned around, and ran quickly down the street and entered the brothel house. The ladies pointed upstairs. Thomas burst through one of the closed doors and a half-naked woman straddled an older man whose uniform was draped over a chair— it belonged to Lieutenant Claybourne, a high-ranking officer in the English Navy.

The Lieutenant, an ambassador for the King of England, was a guest of the Governor of New Spain, Francisco Gonzalez. Claybourne was commanding a secret legion of the best soldiers from the English and Spanish armies to crush the pirate rebellion in the Caribbean.

The lady screamed and covered her naked body.

"What in the name of the Lord is the meaning of this?" the Lieutenant asked.

Thomas saw an open window and shouted out as he jolted toward the open escape route, "Apologies, Lieutenant Claybourne. But I don't think the Lord would be pleased with you in your

current position, nor do I think your wife would approve either." He climbed out the window and onto a small ledge.

The guard reached the top of the steps and noticed an open door, but he was so out of breath that he stopped, leaned forward and placed his hands on his knees.

"Guard, can you explain yourself?" Claybourne asked.

"Oh, good afternoon, Mary. Lieutenant." Still wheezing, he ducked under the doorway and swiftly walked to the window where he noticed Thomas already high atop the roof. The guard turned around and said, "Thomas Copperpot is stealing again, sire. I swear I've had enough of him. He needs to be taught a good lesson."

"Well, go after him, you worthless example of an officer!" yelled Claybourne. "What is it you expect me to do about it? Have you no legs, man?"

The guard smiled as he ran out the door and shouted, "Yes, sir, right at once, sir. I'll take my leave now. My apologies, Mary, and give my best to the wife and children, Lieutenant."

"Give *my best*? I'll give my boot right up your sorry goddamned asshole," Claybourne replied.

He threw his boot but it hit Rosie in the side of the face as she walked by the door. She fell over the railing and into the arms of her sugar daddy.

"How'd you know I'm the catch of the day?" she asked.

"Hey, Johanna, you busy?" Sugar Daddy asked as he dropped her back to her feet.

Thomas Copperpot had by now jumped from roof to roof, but the third gap was wider and he thought he could make it. The guards were below, watching to see the outcome.

Thomas backed up, running as fast as he could and putting as much effort into his leap.

He fell short but caught the very edge of the top of the building with his fingertips.

He was hanging from the building for dear life, but it was slippery and he was heavy, and besides, he had not much strength in his fingers.

One of his hands lost its grip and he couldn't grab onto the building again.

The sweat from his left hand resulted in him losing his only grasp and he fell almost two stories. Luckily for Thomas, he had managed to clip every clothing line on the way down, slowing his fall, but the impact had left him unconscious even so.

"What is that smell?" Thomas asked after finally coming to.

"It's me. I fell into a shitload of manure because of you, lad," the guard answered.

"Give me those," Jose the farmer said and grabbed his coins back from Thomas.

"I think I need a doctor," said Thomas.

"There aren't any doctors where you're going, lad," the guard announced. "And believe me, it's not a doctor you need. You'll be lucky not to require the undertaker when everyone's done with you." The guards put restraints on Thomas.

One said, "Let's go, criminal. It's off to the gallows you go."

The guards each grabbed Thomas by one of his arms and took him away to be confined for the crime of feeding hungry children.

CHAPTER TWELVE

Gallows

The walk up to the Castillo de la Real Fuerza was like a glimpse into a future nightmare, the outer walls having row upon row of cannons, and their massive inclined fortifications were surrounded by a canal. Thus, unless you used the drawbridge, the fort was wholly impenetrable.

This place was home to not only the Governor of New Spain, but also to the generals and captains of his armies within the Caribbean. Once over the drawbridge and into the palace of incarceration, the fortress had soldiers covering every doorway, window and tower.

You could not help but feel that inside these walls were trapped all the virtues of the innocent and the sins of the wicked, all concealed in the same place, never to be freed.

"Which one are you? The innocent or the wicked?" the vertically challenged guard asked Thomas as they marched down the steps, across the floor to a wall with a window in it.

On the other side of this hole in the wall which they called a window was the Master of Records who recorded all the crimes in Havana.

"What's the charge?" the master asked as he turned a page in his book.

"Thievery and disrupting the peace, sire," replied the guard.

"Name of the thief?" He coughed and said, "Pardon me, I mean the accused."

"Thomas Copperpot."

"This is your third offense, Mr. Copperpot. The punishment for repeat offending is death. Sentencing is supposed to commence on the following day of the third infraction—what a shame.

Seventh cell on the right, gentlemen. Enjoy your last day with us."

"Next!" said the Master of Records and another criminal lined up for prosecution.

"This is unjust. I demand to see a lawyer," Thomas argued, but the guards laughed as they led him down the row of cells. The smell of death wreaked havoc in the air, broken fingernails lying scattered on the floor from men and women who had been dragged out with no mercy, and who had tried to claw their way back to their cells. None would have made it.

They arrived at cell seven and opened the door.

It creaked like the bones of an old salt on his last sea legs. The cell had the remnants of blood and urine from previous occupants painted in each corner.

"Look boys, whatever the Governor is paying you, I'll double it," suggested Thomas, but the guards laughed and threw him into the cell anyway, as if all the coin in the world would not sway them. He ran back out and hugged the smaller guard.

"Please, I'm begging you!" he exclaimed. "I'm afraid of my own shadow! Come on guys, I'm going to be rich, and I'll split it with you! You shall never have to work again!"

"Get in there, you swine!" the guard yelled. "Anyway, I enjoy my work. Can you not tell?" "And lad, you won't even be hanging around long enough to pay coin," the other guard said.

"Tomorrow, he will be."

"He'll be what?"

"Hanging around," the shorter guard said, laughing raucously at his bad taste joke.

They both set off laughing hysterically and slammed the door on Thomas's delusions of grandeur. They walked away.

Oh, it's a pirate's life for me! We send ships to their doom, oh, a pirate's life for me! Flames rise over the moon, it's a pirate's life for me and my booty thieving goons… Black flags on our bow cannons sing a tune… Thomas could hear singing all around him.

He peered at the cell across the way and there, could make out a faint shadow. As the darkness gave way to light, Thomas could make out a beautiful woman with light brown hair tucked under a brown tricorn hat. She had piercing and thirsty emerald-green eyes.

Based on how profoundly beautiful the woman was, her eyes must certainly have quenched many a man's pockets. "What's your name, lad? asked the woman.

"La Muerte, Capitán de la Muerte. And you, milady?" Thomas replied.

"I'm Sara. Did you say you're the Captain of Death?" Sara laughed.

"Yes madam, that's me. I fool my enemies with my appearance, but I assure you, I am deadly."

"You do know that One-Eyed Willy is hunting you and your crew?" she answered and burst into uncontrolled laughter. "I think you had better be on your guard, sir!"

"Can you teach me that song?" he asked as though she had not spoken a word to warn him.

"The real la Muerte happens to be a friend of mine and knows that song like the back of his sword. So, what's your real name, lad?"

"The name's Copperpot, Thomas Copperpot. So, Sara, are you, English?"

"That is not relevant. But I'm English and Spanish, so Cayette. Copperpot, is that English?" "Actually, milady, it's Dutch," Thomas said.

"Great, another Dutchman with dreams of fortune but a pouch full of marbles."

"I resent that statement. I happen to like my marbles! I wouldn't be so unkind, or else I won't help you escape."

"I'm not in the market for a hero, lad. My father will rescue me from this rat-infested castle soon enough. Truly, I do not need any more heroes showing up purporting to have the answer to my miserable situation. But if you do have a plan, let me hear it."

"Oh. Well, yes indeed. I can quite see your point. And I'm sure he—your good father, milady— will be here soon; however, at some point tonight, I'll be gone—according to *my plan*, as you say—and you shall be with me. Now, you had better be ready and don't be afraid," Thomas confirmed.

"I'm afraid of nothing. What is your plan, exactly?" she asked.

"Just be ready, Cayette. The plan details do not concern you. Just be sure you shall escape this wretched place with me."

"Haha, we shall see how true these lies you speak of are, Thomas," replied Sara.

Night had fallen upon Havana and the waves could be heard crashing against the beach.

The wind that came off the Caribbean could pierce the skin with their incisive gusts, although between the wind, the sounds of owls hooting and dogs barking, the infernal racket still could not begin to overpower the creepiness of the noises from inside the fort.

There sounded the horrific screams of people in agonizing pain from the brutality of the Spanish soldiers who mercilessly afflicted the art of torture upon them.

The moans of people beaten to a bloody pulp resonated in harmony with the groans from those starving, and cell doors screeched as they opened and moaned and whined as they clanged shut.

The jingle of keys against a guard's belt was but a few of the echoes heard down the hallways of the prison. The clock spun deep past midnight and announced the start of a new day.

The rooster wouldn't be crowing for at least another hour; you would surely expect this time in the morning to be silent, and it was.

Except, of course, for Thomas Copperpot, who was fiddling with the lock on his cell.

Both his hands were extended through the bars, and the clinking noise of the keys was enough to wake up Sara, who got up off the floor and slowly walked to the door of her own cell.

"What are you doing Thomas?" she whispered. "I cannot sleep. Your tinkering does keep my eyes and mind from any rest. Will it be over soon?"

"I'm just about done. There, got it." Thomas unlocked his door and it swung wide.

"How did you do that?" Sara asked. "Goodness me! Who would have imagined…"

"It was easy. I did it with these, of course."

He held up a set of keys, swinging them in his fingers.

"I got them from the guards when they were laughing at me. Who's laughing now, eh? I guess I won't be *hanging around* after all. Though I wish I could be here to witness their faces when they see that I am nowhere to be found!"

Now, Thomas used the same keys to unlock Sara's door.

"Okay, now what's your plan?" she asked.

"Did I not say you were not in need of the details?" he retorted, seemingly offended she had not admired his skills in obtaining the keys. "Anyway, one moment, milady."

He turned around. "Here you go, lads."

Thomas handed the keys to the men in the cell to his left, and turned to Sara. "Shush now and follow me. You must be very, very quiet," Thomas whispered to Sara. "No questions."

"You can't be serious?" she replied, but followed Thomas as they swiftly and stealthily walked down the hallway. Barely a footstep could be heard, Sara treading in her bare feet.

Unfortunately, it did not aid them as they were spotted by one of the guards.

"Hey, you! Stop! Prisoners are escaping! Ring the alarm! I said prisoners are escaping!"

"So much for silence," Thomas said with a loud humph, and grabbed Sara's hand, pulling her into a sprint down the hallway. The guards were converging on them both from the front and the rear. Thomas stopped, turned left into the latrine, opened up a hole.

"Okay, Sara, don't be afraid," he proclaimed.

"Ha!" she scoffed, evidently unimpressed. "Afraid? Did I look afraid? More disappointed, lad.

Aye, *sorely* disappointed. So, your big plan was to escape through the pisser? Really?" Thomas released her arm, perplexed, his brows knitting together.

Women, never grateful. Nagging wench! he thought.

"Look, I'm going back to my cell," she remonstrated now.

She turned around and made to leave but Thomas clutched her roughly again and forced her down the hole, then jumped down himself. The place stank and was fetid with urine and rats.

If the urinals had filled Sara with horror, then this place was so much worse

They landed in a cesspool that contained most of the city's human waste and garbage.

The stench was so rich, they barely smelled it anymore since the human nose would admit defeat at a certain point. Nothing could possibly match this.

The putrid sewer system was quite fascinating yet equally disgusting, and consisted of brick walls with one giant hole in the side that delivered running water.

A river of waste with occasionally bubbling froth and unrecognizable lumps—maybe feces, maybe body parts—was flanked either side by a brick walkway along what appeared to be a peculiar corridor that led to some kind of light.

Thomas and Sara both surfaced from underneath the rancid, slow-flowing sludge.

"There, Sara, that wasn't so bad, was it?"

Sara was covered in the filth and was ready to vomit, alternately retching and coughing.

Sara's eyes turned to a savage hunger for payback, and they wanted to feast on Thomas.

He climbed out of the waste and attempted to shake the shit off him. Now, he put his hand out to help Sara, but she refused, pulling herself onto the brick walkway to shake herself off.

"Thomas, I'm going to kill you," Sara commented as she wiped herself down. "We are changing your name to *El Muerto*, 'cause you're dead."

"Shush, shush. We still need to get out of here," replied Thomas. "All your whining and complaining will not make the escape any simpler."

"Copperpot, I bet all your marbles you don't get out of here alive. I can't believe I let you talk me into this. I smell wretched."

"Shush, you smelt wretched before. You may even smell better now. Anyway, follow me."

"Are you insulting me? How dare you! You haven't the slightest comprehension of my capabilities," Sara replied as she followed Thomas despite all her protestations.

"No, Sara, but I do think your unstoppable mouth is capable of getting us caught. The end of the tunnel is just up ahead. So, Cayette?"

"Ha! I'm going to remain silent and never speak to you ever again."

"Don't threaten me with a good time," Thomas replied with a hint of laughter.

They inched closer to the end of the conduit and noticed two Spanish guards securing the entrance. Lanterns swung on each side of the brick entrance, illuminating the very beginning of the pipeline. And here, the guards stood, looking deathly bored and tired as usual.

They wore blue overcoats with a white button line, blue pants, white socks and black boots.

"Which one are you taking? Are you capable of using a sword?" Thomas enquired.

"Oh, Mr. Copperpot, sir. I'm just a young lady that likes baking almond cake and making tea. Can you really save me?" Her voice squeaked plaintively.

For a second, Thomas did not know if she was lying or making fun of him, or being truthful. All he could do was play along with it. "Well, I thought so, milady," he said. "I must say, that almond cake sounds splendid. Wait here a moment."

Thomas crept to the edge of the tunnel and quickly pulled the sword out from the guard on the left and kicked him in the back. He fell to the ground and dropped his bayonet.

The other guard reached for a sword, but Thomas drove his own blade through his belly, looked him in his eyes and kicked him to the ground.

Then, Thomas turned around and was met by the other guard's pistol, directly in his face.

Thankfully, when the guard pulled back the pistol, Sara drove a long blade through his neck, pulled it out, and watched the guard fall to the ground.

"Oh, Thomas, you're my hero! I owe such gratitude for saving my life!" Sara laughed and batted her eyelids. "How can I ever repay you?" Sarah mocked, knowing it was not so.

Sara picked up the pistol and nonchalantly put it in her holster as if she killed men every day.

"You're incorrigible, Sara. You're incapable of rewarding compliments. No wonder you were in the gallows—you like to be alone. And I have no doubt that is how you shall end up as no man could tolerate you."

"Thomas, I have no need of any man—I can defend myself, as you have witnessed. You're alive because of my actions and they are much louder than the compliments of which you speak." "Sara, do you always have to be correct?" Thomas turned around and kept talking.

"You can lead a horse to water, but you can't make it drink," he said, not even sure of the relevance himself—but he certainly would not give this obnoxious so-called *lady* the final word!

"That's it, Copperpot."

She picked up a sword and lunged with an overhand slice toward Thomas.

He drew his sword with his left hand and the metals met, clanging in the air.

The swords clashed right and left, and Thomas lunged toward Sara's midsection, but she spun and kicked him to the ground, whereupon he landed face down and didn't get up.

"Come now, Copperpot. I bested you with those moves," Sara said and walked over, kicked him and pressed her sword to his back. A rooster crowed, causing her to look up. The noisy bird gave Thomas time to roll over from her sword to avoid being skewered.

And now, he was intent on taking Sara down with him.

Thomas was now on top of Sara, both of her arms pinned down.

"Those eyes have emptied many a man's pouch, but don't underestimate a Dutchman and his marbles!" Thomas said.

From the street above, they heard a commotion, a guard shouting, "There they are! Down there!

They're the prisoners! After them!"

"Delinquent vote of speech. I'll let you know if I find them," Sara continued regardless of the guards' interruption which echoed down the corridors.

"Find whom?" asked Thomas.

"Not whom… I mean your marbles," Sara replied and kneed Thomas in the testicles.

He cringed and slumped over into the fetal position, holding onto his testicles in an attempt to numb the pain. At the exact same time, four guards, along with Lieutenant Claybourne, arrived.

"Do not move, you swine, or the last thing you will taste is the blood from your filthy heart after I run my sword through it!" Claybourne ordered. But by the time he had said, "Men, arrest them," Smitty, Sebastian, Devereaux and Prima were behind the four guards.

Without hesitation, two of them sliced the guards' throats, while the other two ran their swords through the others' backs.

Claybourne turned around, dropped his sword immediately and lowered onto his knees with his hands raised.

"Hello, Juliet," Smitty said, and reached down with his hand, pulling her to her feet.

Sara went to hug Smitty, but he pushed her away, and said, "Juliet, I love ye like a daughter, but ye smell like a rotting corpse. Are ye really alive?"

The men laughed and Sebastian already had his cutlass to the throat of Claybourne.

"What say you about this varmint?" Sebastian asked Sara.

"You found them?" Thomas asked, getting to his feet.

"I'm not sure. Thomas, what say you?" Sara asked and laughed, looking in turn to Thomas.

"Claybourne," said Copperpot.

"Tell them that you know me and that I've arrested you a few times," Claybourne pleaded.

"Are you married, Lieutenant?" asked Sebastian. "Yes," Claybourne replied.

"Do you have children?"

"Yes."

"I haven't got a clue who this man is," Thomas added.

"Liar—you saw me in the brothel house this afternoon with Mary!"

"Brothel house? An adulterer? Then there is only one punishment for his kind. I know what we are going to do with him. Blindfold him, men, and bring him to the ship," Sebastian ordered.

A few of the men walked the lieutenant away as the remainder of the crew passed them, carrying heavy barrels and chests up the hill.

"Copperpot? Is that French?" Smitty asked.

"Smitty, can you direct them where to place the goods? Excuse me one moment, Thomas. Alright men—as far in as you can go! Up against the far wall in the darkness so they can't be seen and cover them with the black sail. Hurry up now—we haven't got all morning!" Sebastian ordered, turning to ask, "Who's your friend, Sara?" "We are not friends," said Sara.

"Shall I send him to the locker then?" asked Sebastian.

Thomas wore a terrified look on his face and Sara answered, "I believe we should treat this one a little differently. I think he could be useful. Maybe he could be put to good work and clean out the bow boxes? After all, he did save my life."

"Very well, my dear sister. Father will be pleased to see you, I'm sure." "And I can't wait to endure his company yet again, brother." There was a ring of sarcasm in both their voices.

"I'm indebted to you both," said Thomas.

"All finished, Sebastian. My apologies, Mr. Coppasquat, I mean Clobbertwot, or was it Coppasnot? Either way, you were saying?" Smitty continued.

"It's Copperpot, and I am a Dutchman but very fond of Shakespeare's work," Thomas replied. "Excuse me, one more moment," Smitty said. "Juliet, when were you arrested?" "Yesterday afternoon," Sara confirmed.

"Either way, with you coming out of that latrine, you just saved us a bit of time."

They headed down the hill and as they approached the docks, they walked past the bodies of soldiers who had been ruthlessly killed by the crew. Throats had been slit open ear to ear, some lying with their heads severed and placed upon their chests. Others' chests and guts had been pierced right through with a sword, while yet more appeared to have been bludgeoned.

The sun was about to rise and the group needed to depart immediately.

"You were saying something, Mr. Cobblestone?" Smitty continued.

"I said, I'm an admirer of William Shakespeare, like yourself," said Thomas.

"Shakespeare? He's captain of what ship?"

"He is a playwright who wrote Romeo and Juliet," Thomas answered.

"I'm not familiar with a playwright, and the only William I know is William J. Walsh, Captain of this here ship, also known as One-Eyed Willy," Smitty replied. "No playwright is of any consequence in a battle, unless perchance he can waft a spotted 'kerchief to indicate surrender." He laughed raucously, much amused at his own comedy.

Thomas was dumbfounded as he stood on the docks in front of the Inferno, a ship about which he'd heard so many stories as a child. She was a fine vessel indeed. "Thomas, are you any good with rope?" Sebastian asked.

"Yes sir, Sebastian, sir. I know twelve different knots."

"Excellent! Thomas, this is what I want you to do with the Lieutenant. I'll fetch you the rope."

With all the crew accounted for, plus young Thomas Copperpot, the Inferno disembarked and headed out of the bay. All that could be heard was uncontrollable laughter as the sun reflected off the docks and the ship sailed away. Sebastian looked back toward the bay and could see Lieutenant Claybourne tied securely with his back against a pole, naked and gagged, wearing nothing but his hat and boots. His hands were tied to a small barrel that covered his penis, and whenever he tried to move, it looked as though he was screwing a small barrel. On his chest was written, *Every time I go to the brothel house, it's like putting my penis in a small barrel.*

As the Inferno sailed away, a fisherman walked onto the dock and up to the lieutenant.

"Good God, lad. What happened to you? Wait a moment, there's something written on your chest." He read it out loud and said, "Ain't that the truth. Have a good day, lad," the fisherman said and waved his hook for a hand in the air and left the dock.

CHAPTER THIRTEEN

The Inferno

With the wind in its sails and the seas rolling serenely, the Inferno severed its way through to the island of Tortuga. A room aboard it was overcome with the cadence of a popular composition by Manuel Rodriguez being played on an organ. The radiance of the sun was exhibited, shooting beams of light through the glass windows at the stern of the Captain's cabin.

The sun's glow extended over the Captain's bed and down a short step, along the wooden floor onto a table in the middle of the cabin.

The newly stained wooden chairs around the table glistened like fine bone china, as did the gold and silver cups that made their home on the top of the new island of wood.

It continued through the rum bottles, lanterns, fixtures on the wall, and across a portrait of a woman with her head missing.

Finally, it stretched its brilliance to a final resting place known as darkness.

Out of the obscurity flew a lone spark from a tinderbox as One-Eyed Willy lit his pipe. Willy continued to play the organ, smoking his pipe while Devereaux and Sebastian played checkers.

Smitty put on his glasses, peered at a document on the table, picked up an apple, and took a bite.

There was a knock at the door, but no one heard.

Sara walked in but no one paid her any attention.

She slowly crept toward Willy, who was still playing the organ. She had her arm outstretched as though she was going to tap him on the shoulder and scare the hell out of him.

At that point, Smitty looked up and as Sara was just about to touch Willy's shoulder, the organ stopped and Willy grabbed her wrist, which made Devereaux and Sebastian look up toward the organ. Sara was startled.

Willy gloated, "You thought you could sneak a scare on your old Captain, did ya?" "Father, how did you know?" Sara asked.

"I cannot see as vividly as you do, my dear, but what I can see exceeds all expectations of what you thought I could. How farest thou, my darling daughter? Have you grown?" Willy put his pipe down and stood up. "Come, let me have a look at you."

Willy grabbed Sara by her hands and she did a little twirl under Willy's arm.

"Father, I'm well, very well. Most fabulous, actually. Some of the crew helped me to a bath on the crew deck."

Sebastian and Devereaux looked up in fear.

Willy had a furious look in his eye and boomed. "What filthy scalawags assisted *my* daughter in bathing? I'll have them skinned alive and bathe them in gunpowder!"

"Father, you are undoubtably the most gullible individual in the new world. It was merely a joke."

Smitty, Sebastian and Devereaux all chuckled and breathed a sigh of relief.

"Smitty, can you tell me how I produced such a beautifully astute creature?" Willy asked.

"No, Captain, I can't. Been asking myself that same question for the last few years now. You know, now that you mention it... Devereaux, remember when we had that conversation with Quaco?"

"Is ya meaning the discussion we had about the Captain's missus? And how she was not as monogamous as we thought?" Devereaux replied.

"Arrr," Sebastian said and tossed his rum in the face of Devereaux. "Eyes on the game, and thoughts off my mother, ya swine! I'll gut ya like a fish!"

"Well, I can't see now since you threw rum in my eyes, but I can smell if you're cheating," Devereaux garbled.

"No, that's not the one. You remember the one conversation?" Smitty replied.

"Are ya speaking of the one where Willy pissed off the good Lord so much that the good Lord gave him a ravishing daughter to bring his wrath upon him?" Devereaux answered.

"Aye, that's the one."

"And you remember what Quaco said?"

"No. What did Quaco say?" asked Willy.

"Aye, what did Quaco say?" Sebastian questioned.

"Quaco, tell them what you said," said Smitty.

Quaco walked in, answering, "Smite me, oh Lord, smite me. Bring your wrath upon me." Everyone laughed hysterically, except Willy and Sebastian who were reluctant to join in.

"Would you like to know what is more laughable?" As Sebastian slams his hand on the table.

"King me, Last piece! I've never been bested," Sebastian said.

"That's a farce. I've won countless times against him," suggested Sara.

"Why are you interrupting me when I'm winning? It's all your fault," Devereaux directed at Smitty, and Smitty laughed.

"So, the choice is yours. You can tend to my clothes, clean the bow boxes for a month, or rum and gunpowder, then you have to climb up to the crows' nest. Which one is it?" Sebastian asked.

"Damn you, Sebastian. Best out of three?" Devereaux asked.

"Out of my cabin, all of you, except for Sara," Willy ordered.

"Captain, the—um—*Captain of Death* requested an audience with you, sire. What say you?" Quaco asked.

"Tell *the Capitán* he can kiss me ass."

"Father, language, please; I thought cussing was a thing of the past."

"What did I say? I didn't curse, sweetheart. I am smarter than a primitive tongue."

"The certainty of such claims bears no truth, Father, so put a coin in a barrel," Sara replied, and Willy took a coin out of his pocket and threw it into a small barrel.

"That is just about full," said Quaco.

"Bring him here. I will grant Mr. Death this one request if he isn't tied up at the moment." Everyone in the cabin laughed.

"Aye, Captain, I will return," Quaco replied.

"Sebastian, stay the course and haul wind."

"Aye, Captain," Sebastian replied and flicked the back of Sara's ear. She turned and punched him in the arm.

"Sebastian, leave your sister alone," Willy ordered, and everyone except for Sara left the room.

Willy poured a cup of coffee and offered his daughter a cup but Sara refused. "What say you, daughter? Guns? Artillery? Soldiers?"

"I have it all written down, Father. I have the arrivals of ships in and out of the bay, the shifts that soldiers are on, what commanders are where and when they cap the candles at night.

"I know what time they open and drop the drawbridge to the Castillo and on what days. Who the harbormaster is and what he does and doesn't check."

"Fantastic, this is great work, my dear. Your mother would be astonished at the sea of knowledge you've soaked up with that brain of yours. I imagine your grandmother would be just as proud," Willy said as he stared at the headless portrait on the wall. "Were you able to locate the vault in the Castillo?" asked Willy while he attempted to take a sip of coffee and burned his lip.

"Jesus! That's sweltering," he continued and set the coffee down quickly.

"Father, I'm fairly certain I have a general idea where the vault is. Unfortunately, I'm not definite."

"I'm not concerned about that; your brother can sniff out coin in a church full of beggars!" "Father, did you ever believe in God?" inquired Sara.

"I can recall a time where church was routine and saying prayers was ritual in my beliefs. One thing you will learn as you grow is how the clock hands continue to advance and people become different. I'm not the same man who thanked God for my many blessings." "You're in my morning and evening prayers, Father," Sara replied.

"Sara, I beg you not to pray for me—there is no penance that can save my soul. However, since you have this unwavering belief in God, I have something for you." Willy walked to his bed and opened a drawer.

Inside was a silver coin, a scroll with a red ribbon tied around it and a tiny box. He pulled out the box and opened it. Suspended from his fingers was a silver necklace with a cross dangling at the end of it. Willy said, "This was your mother's. Perhaps you can put it to good use."

"Oh, Father, it's absolutely beautiful!"

"Turn around," Willy said and draped his arms over Sara, clasping the necklace. "It was the very last item she gave me... before... well before.... you know," Willy trailed off.

His voice wavered a bit as if he might crack and spill a tear or two. But he managed to contain his emotions.

"I know, Father. I wish that I could remember her." Sara turned around. "There is nothing in this world that could remove this cross from my neck. Thank you so much. It's a beautiful gift."

"Someday, beyond the moon and across the stars somewhere, but not too far, we will hang up our pirate hats and settle down on a piece of land larger than Tortuga. It will be overflowing with pigs, chickens, horses and enough crops to feed an army. We'll be sleeping in beds made of silk, living in a house fit for royalty," offered Willy, wishing to give the world to his daughter.

"It sounds delightful, and surely a welcoming replacement for the hammock I lay my head to rest in every night!" She smiled. "But I am more than happy with what we have, Father."

It did not ring true. She was often demanding, and not always grateful—and that caused Willy consternation. Her gentle words right now were only because of the giving of her gift.

"Sara, I can't fathom the difficulties you endure, yet please understand, everything I'm doing is to provide something more adequate and sustainable for you and your brother. But for now, like us all, you and your brother will have to call this your home."

"Father, do we have to have this conversation? Until you started to talk about that, I was just excited about my cross, and I do not want to get angry."

"Is there something on your mind that concerns you, Sara? Perhaps you're not eager to believe the words I speak. Are your living quarters not catered to your specifications?" Willy questioned. "Father, I haven't felt at home since we got here, nine years ago. You know that already. You inspire the men with your grandiose delusions, all the while neglecting the dreams of Sebastian and me. Promising a more adequate life is as believable as…"

Suddenly, there sounded a knock at the door and Quaco brought in la Muerte.

Willy was very quick to switch the conversation, saying, "Sara, I couldn't have asked for more useful reconnaissance, I am very grateful. We will discuss this further. Go and see Smitty for duties, but for now, leave us."

"Seriously, Father?" Sara replied.

"I have business with the Capitán. You may take your leave."

Sara sighed in anger and frustration and as she left, she smacked the cup of coffee off the table and stampeded out of the door.

"Kids! Quaco, you may remove his restraints, and leave us as well."

"I don't trust him, Captain. I will be right outside the door," Quaco reassured Willy. "Very well, Quaco. Very well. Juan—how can I be of service to you?" "Where is my ship?" asked la Muerte.

"Some of my crew, along with your own, sailed the Retribution to Tortuga. Robert Perkins will be expecting me to deliver gold that I no longer have in my possession because of your ambitions. Why did you not just come to me as a kinsman of the tide? If not for your actions, your quartermaster would still be alive," said Willy. "You murdered him in cold blood, Willy."

"Wrong, you were in violation of the code—an eye for an eye—and as far as I'm concerned, you paid an undervalued price for a crime worthy of a higher cost in death. Where is my jewel?"

"You're a sick man, Willy. Someday, your bones will rot on an island along with those plagued by greed. Do not concern yourself with the jewel. It is safe.

"There is something much greater at stake here."

"There is nothing on the sea with more value than the jewel. Do you even know the story behind the jewel of the Spanish Main?" Willy asked.

"I cannot say I do, Willy, yet I'm sure you will tell the tale," la Muerte replied.

"Some ten millennia ago, before Spanish sails would ever glorify the Caribbean, there was another great empire occupying these waters. Some said the land was double the size of Spain and far richer in wealth and knowledge. I will stop there.

"I would be disinclined to bore you with such tales," finished Willy.

"On the contrary! You've seized hold of my curiosity. Please elaborate?" la Muerte asked.

"I have caused you to be curious? That's wonderful. Then I will continue. Their wealth was immeasurable in gold as they used diamonds, crystals, and other precious stones for everyday life.

"The jewel is said to have washed up on Spain's shores 7000 years ago, and it's reputed that the Caribbean islands and Bermuda are what's left of the lost continent.

"The jewel is said to have the ability to travel through time. Somewhere, hidden inside this artifact, is an atlas to the lost treasures of Atlantis. Not only that, but also, when the jewel and scroll are together, the possibility of seeing the future is within reach.

"Atlas, King of Atlantis, and his empire ruled the Atlantic Ocean for thousands of years until one day, it sank into Davey Jones's locker, never to return. For thousands of years, men, women, pharaohs, kings, and very wealthy and dangerous people tried to unlock the jewel but all failed.

Now, you understand the importance of such an item.

"Tell me, what could be more important than priceless treasure?" Willy continued.

"The Spanish and English governors are compiling the greatest cache the new world has ever seen. Prince James of England and Princess Margaret of Spain are to be married, and this is their wedding gift. There is enough booty for a thousand crews to live like kings for a thousand years," la Muerte answered.

Willy, with a smile on his face, said, "This is remarkable news. How did you hear of this?"

"Perkins wants me to abduct the valuables in exchange for the life of Maria. So, you see Willy, the only way I could get you to assist me was the jewel." "Would you like some wine, Juan?" Willy asked.

"Yes, if you're offering." Willy poured la Muerte a cup of wine and continued.

"This treasure you speak of, do you know the location?"

"These details have yet to be determined, Willy. Perkins has the itinerary."

"Ah, very well, la Muerte. I recall when you were just becoming a man, barely a member of my crew. You grew to be a magnificent bosun motivated by selfishness, and in my opinion, fueled by anger and anxiety, choosing to appoint yourself Captain and cooperating with swine like Perkins. I told you, *love can turn a man to a monster.* I will help you get Maria back, but it's all mine, the gold, the jewel. Consider it payment for mutiny against your former Captain."

"That is ridiculous, Captain. Maria is the one."

"Enough! I'm exhausted hearing that woman's name. Let me divulge a bit of a secret about your Maria." Suddenly, Quaco ran into the cabin. "Sails. Aft port a few miles. They have the wind."

"Colors?" Willy inquired.

"No, sir, Sebastian requests you on the quarter deck."

"Very well, put the restraints back on the Capitán and take him below."
"Aye, Captain," Quaco replied as he restrained la Muerte.

Willy made his way to the quarter deck and spotted Sebastian at the helm with Sara.

"Here you are, Captain." Sara handed Willy the scope and he walked to the starboard side to have a look. Still no colors.

"Have the powder monkeys load the chase guns. Sara, I want every able-bodied sailor ready for a fight."

"Aye, Captain," Sara confirmed and made her way below deck.

"Devereaux, make sure all the riggers have the wind. Tighten the jib trim to the mainsail. Get this vessel up to maximum speed or you're all swabbing the deck. Understand, Mr. Devereaux?" "Aye, Captain. Let's go lads, you heard the Captain," Devereaux replied and barked his order.

Willy had a gander through the scope again. "Spanish destroyer!" Willy yelled.

"How many, Father?" Sebastian asked.

"From the looks of it, only one. Sara, ready all the cannons!" ordered Willy.

Samuel Winston was a cabin boy, a stowaway from a recent plunder. He was young, thin and light as a feather but a very skilled navigator. Samuel was up in the crow's nest and yelled down to the Captain, "They're gaining on us, Captain!"

"Yes, I realize that, boy. They have the wind. Mr. Devereaux, where is my wind?" "We are almost there, Captain," Devereaux replied.

"Mr. Devereaux, haste. Easy on the keel, Sebastian. Stay on the starboard tack."

"Aye, Captain," Devereaux said, "Almost got it!"

"There it is. Mr. Devereaux, my wind."

"Now, lads!" shouted Devereaux, and they shifted the lines and every sail filled with wind.

"That's how ya run a ship, me hearties! Now she's heeling, watch that keel, Sebastian."

"Aye, Captain," Willy yelled.

"Sara, Sara!" Willy barked. "Yes, Captain?"

"Are your guns loaded?"

"Aye," Sara replied, shaking her head and implying they were indeed ready. At that moment, the sound of thunder ricocheted off the ocean. The Spanish ship fired a cannon ball at the Inferno which nearly caught the port bow.

"Captain, do we fire?" Sara yelled.

"Wait for it! Wait for it! Now, Sara! Fire the bow chaser!"

"Aye, Captain," acknowledged Sara. One of the men lit the cannon and the explosion caused the great metal gun to jump backward two feet. The shot missed the Spanish destroyer and landed just off their stern port. "Reload the cannon," said Sara.

Willy observed through the scope. "Tortuga, dead ahead. Belay that order," he instructed.

He saw two British vessels off the Tortuga coast, no doubt en route to intercept the Spanish vessel. "Stand down, stand down," Willy yelled.

One of the British vessels fired a shot at the Spanish destroyer as a warning, forcing the Spanish to come about and turn around. Sara came back to the top deck from below and saw Thomas Copperpot swabbing the deck.

"Thomas, where were you this whole time?"

"I was on top deck, doing the duties of a swab," Thomas replied. "Can you not tell?"

Willy walked over to Sara and asked, "Who is this sad excuse for a sailor? Are you a stowaway, boy? Can't be having no stowaways aboard this ship. Come now, boy, how'd ya get on me vessel?"

"Father, this is Thomas Copperpot. He saved me in Havana. I told him he could come along, and we would find work for him," Sara answered.

"It's an honor to meet you, Mr. Willy. I heard many stories of your adventures from my father," Thomas said, looking up at Willy.

"Your father was a member of the kinsman years ago?" asked Willy.

"No, Captain. He was a cooper—the best one I ever knew," Copperpot answered.

"A cooper, you say? Well, did you pick up any of his talents?"

"Oh yes, sire. I could seal me the heck out of a barrel."

"Good, now put a lid on it and listen up! Thomas, I have two rules. One, don't let me catch you associating with my daughter, no matter the circumstances. Two, we all fight to the death. Can you handle that, lad?"

"Yes sir, I can," Thomas answered.

"Very well. Get back to work, ya slithering swine, before ya walk the plank. Welcome aboard
the Inferno."

CHAPTER FOURTEEN

Tortuga

Tortuga was one of but a few safe havens for privateers and pirates due to its natural harbor that could easily accommodate a hundred or more ships. The docks were reserved for importing and exporting goods and were controlled by a vicious financier named Robert Perkins.

Perkins had built a remarkable relationship with the French and the British, who at the time, controlled the island. Perkins owned and operated a plethora of businesses on the island, including two taverns, a blacksmith's den, five cooper mills and a plantation.

He also owned ships and paid men for their services onboard those ships.

As the Inferno slowly pulled into the old wooden dock, the view of the town with all its candles and torches looked like fallen stars. The salt from the sea left the mouth dry, and the dock wavered up and down and side to side with the motion of the water.

Some of the men disembarked from the ship and secured the Inferno with ropes around the decrepit wooden posts on the dock. Surprisingly, fifty years after being built, the docks remained in good standing, despite the challenging weather of the Caribbean.

Waiting for One-Eyed Willy at the end of the dock was none other than Robert Perkins and a few of his associates. The crew disembarked to enjoy some of the fruits of labor the island had to offer. Women, games, food and rum were at the top of the list.

As Willy and his crew came to the end of the dock, Perkins and his men stopped them.

"William James Walsh, I do believe you are indebted to me for said ship. Have you come to pay coin? Or better yet, I believe you were to procure a certain amount of gold from a plunder of which I gave the location. I would have that instead. What say you, Mr. Walsh?"

"Ahh, Mr. Perkins," Willy replied. "So kind of you to grace us with your presence on such a lovely afternoon. You know, I think I may have undervalued the Inferno when I borrowed against it. It has to be worth what I owe you."

"William, I know you have not come here to test my patience," Mr. Perkins replied.

"About that gold. Yes, I do have an idea where it was moved to. Did you receive the ship I sent as a sign of good faith?" asked Willy.

"Mr. Willy, I did receive the Captain of Death's ship, which I still own. What do you mean, where the gold was moved to?"

"La Muerte would be able to better explain where the gold is, considering he stole it from me after I stole it for you. He is currently located in the hold of my ship. I think it best you direct your questioning to him."

"William, do you take me for a fool? Coin is owed, and I will see compensation for failure to produce the gold with a new endeavor. Are you aware of a sum of gold and jewels larger than imaginable being collected here in the Caribbean?" Perkins asked.

"I have heard rumors, yet the truth in them has yet to come to fruition," replied Willy.

"Oh they are true, Mr. Willy, and this accumulation of riches will be mine and you're going to acquire them for me. Because if you don't, I will have you and all your crew hanged for crimes against the Crown, particularly for piracy. If you doubt my sincerity, I shall have you know that there are ten destroyers, including the King's Redemption, docked in Port Royal as we speak. We are both in agreement that the King himself would love nothing more than a noose around your neck, are we not? This is your chance to pay your debts and increase your wealth exponentially.

What say you to that, Mr. Willy?"

"Honestly, Mr. Perkins, the King can kiss my..." Willy replied but Sara instantly jumped in before he was able to finish.

"Father, language not appropriate."

"Right, my dear." Willy cleared his throat and continued, "My apologies, Mr. Perkins, but I've become quite humbled in my old age. Ordinarily, my response to a threat would include violence and bloodshed. Since I am a man of much wiser reasoning, I will accept your offer under the premise that you never impede such acts of cruelty against my crew and me again.

"Is this a suitable agreement, Mr. Perkins?"

"Be mindful of who you are bargaining with, Mr. Willy, and do comprehend the severity of noncompliance with this accord. We have come to terms. I will secure another ship for your endeavor as well as allow the Capitán of Death to accompany you with the Retribution. I trust three ships will suffice for such an operation?"

"That shall be fine, Robert. I will need them prepared for departure before first light. Do remember to include all the gunpowder you can muster and a formidable ship."

"Scarlets Revenge will be at your disposal and all three ships readied before the stroke of midnight. I want you and your men to enjoy an evening of pleasure at my generosity." Perkins handed Willy a pouch of gold and silver coins.

"Come tomorrow, Willy, it's business as usual. Now, if you don't mind, I will have a chat with our friend, the Capitán," said Perkins.

"Not at all, but do be gentle with the lad; he's already been through a great ordeal," replied Willy.

"Guards, go aboard and retrieve Mr. la Muerte. He will accompany us to my office." Willy walked away as Perkins's men made their way onto the Inferno to acquire la Muerte.

The stars could barely be seen from the drunken pirates firing their guns in the air.

Gunpowder, fire and meat was an interesting combination that tickled the sense of smell as people walked down the streets of Tortuga.

Black posts with candle lanterns hung every thirty feet or so, lighting up all the shops on the avenue. Willy and his crew made their way to a place called the Rusty Nail. The Nail was a hole in the wall, and entry to the establishment was gained through an old wooden door with no handle.

Willy pushed open the door and the people inside scattered.

Drunken pirates and their wenches for the evening thronged from wall to wall.

Portraits accompanied the walls, giving life to non-existent style.

Barmaids rushed around with jugs of ale and rum. Benches draped across both sides of the inn crowded with people, and leading to a fireplace in the back. Lanterns sprinkled the walls, adding light to some of the patrons sitting at tables in the middle. An open door on the left side in the rear of the inn led outside so men and women could relieve themselves.

A door was closed and guarded by a gargantuan man along the rear of the right-side wall.

As Willy and a handful of the crew made their way through the crowd, many men threw high their jugs and shouted, "Aye, Willy!" and Willy nodded his head in response to the recognition. A few of the crew recognized people and stirred up conversation.

Willy sat himself down at a long wooden table with Smitty, Sebastian, Sara, Quaco, and Thomas Copperpot. Seated at the end of the table with Smitty right next to him, Willy began discreetly speaking with Smitty.

"But Cap'n, that would take a month, maybe two," Smitty replied.

"Smitty, we have no other choice, unless you want to be hunted in these waters. I say we take our chances up the west coast," Willy responded.

While Willy and Smitty were having a conversation, Sara started a chat with Thomas.

"Not easy swabbing, is it?"

"My arms are numb, and I can barely lift my mug," Thomas replied.

"You should be thankful that it doesn't take much for you to be three sheets from the wind." "You think I can't best you in drinking?" Thomas suggested.

"You may be right, Captain. We would be the most wanted men in the new world. That's quite the journey. Can we bring women aboard?" Smitty asked.

"What's the rule, Smitty?" Willy questioned.

"No women, except Juliet. Alright, Captain, I'm with this plan, but God forbid something should go wrong," Smitty agreed.

"I've been your Captain for eight years. Has your belly ached for food?"

"No, Cap'n."

"Have you been thirsty and not had rum?" "No, Cap'n," Smitty confirmed.

"Have you wanted to wet the old pistol, but not had coin?"

"No, Cap'n."

"Then trust in the plan! I need you to leave after midnight, take Quaco as your quarter and Sam as your navigator," said Willy. "Are you on board?"

As Smitty took a sip of ale, he said, "Sam? Why the hell would I take Sam? He's no use to me, Cap'n. He's barely been on the ship a few months. I got a better idea. How about I close my eyes and just point to anyone? And they would be a better choice."

"He knows the stars, Smitty, and he knows how to sail. I need Sara and Sebastian with me."

Willy handed Smitty coins and said, "Be safe on your journey, but I need you to make haste and round up some of the crew."

"Aye, Captain," replied Smitty, then he grabbed Quaco, Samuel Winston and about fifteen of the crew. They all filed out of the Rusty Nail one by one.

A barmaid came over with two jugs of ale.

"Whoever can finish this first, wins," Sara challenged Thomas.

Willy got up, walking over to Sebastian. "Let's go pay a visit to the Queen." "Father, that woman wants to ravish me every time we see her," said Sebastian.

"I know, why do you think I bring you along every time? I'm having a laugh. Anyway, that's not true. She loves you, and she is proud of the man you've become."

"Wait, don't you want to see me crush Thomas, Father?" Sara shouted to Willy. "We won't be long, Sara. Order another two jugs, and we shall return before they arrive." "Splendid, Father," Sara thanked Willy.

"Thomas. Don't be conversing with my daughter in an inappropriate manner. The sharks feed at night." Thomas sipped his rum and swallowed very loudly, almost choking.

Willy and Sebastian made their way across the establishment. Willy noticed a fine tuzzymuzzy, tall, with brown hair and green-eyed, walk past him. Both turned around to oblige the curious-eyed lady. When Willy turned back around and took his first step, it was right into the center wooden pole of the building, knocking him to the ground and sending his hat flying off.

The people who saw this incursion laughed hysterically at this.

Sebastian was doing a terrible job trying to hold back his laughter.

"Are you okay, Father?" he asked, still trying to suppress his mirth.

"Yes, I'm okay. But that blasted wall came out of nowhere! I didn't see it."

He grabbed his hat as Sebastian helped him up. "Of course you didn't, Father, you're blind, and it wasn't a wall, it was a post. Shall I walk you to the door?"

"Sebastian, are you a jester? Because the only thing you'll be walking is the plank if ya keep laughing, savvy," Willy replied.

"Yes, Father. Come now, but be wary of your shadow, wouldn't want you to walk into that," said Sebastian with a smirk.

Willy stopped walking. "Sebastian Irving Walsh, hold your tongue or I'll cut it out and feed it to the crows."

Sebastian, instantaneously silent, replied, "Yes, Father."

When they approached the door guarded by the gargantuan man, Willy said, "We are here to see the Queen."

"One-Eyed Willy, how was your fall?" the man asked.

Willy turned his head and smirked and the man continued, "The Queen has been expecting you." He opened the door and Willy and Sebastian entered.

Surprisingly, the room was lit to a brighter capacity than the entire tavern.

A few women dressed to empty pockets scurried around with ale and rum. A table set up in the middle of the room with a few of the scourges of society playing a game of five-card poker.

The game had only been around the island for a few years and was based on the French game, Poque, which took after the Persian game, As-Nas.

However, its popularity had exploded through the population like a plague.

Sebastian and Willy sat down at the table with four other money hungry bastards looking to cash in on a few coins. Looking around the table, there was Richard 'Red Hand' Nichols, Marianne Abigail La Reine, also known as 'the Queen', London 'La Coqueta' Jade—a kinsman in training so to speak—and the young but ambitious Captain Artimus 'Young Fire' Drake, taking after his grandfather, the legendary Sir Francis. These were the 'Kinsmen of the Tide,' the brethren of pirates who each had sworn an oath to uphold piracy at every corner of the sea.

Four chairs remained empty for Francios L'Olonnais, Capitán de la Muerte, Henry Morgan and Blackheart.

The Kinsmen only met once a month, three months in a row until the following year. The

Queen said, "I'll raise ya two pieces of silver and four pieces of eight. What's say you, London?"

London had a sip of rum but folded. Queen continued, "What say you, Mr. Drake?" "I'll match your silver and pieces of eight," Artimus replied.

"What say you, Red Hand?"

"I'm in. I'll match your silver and pieces of eight," said Red Hand.

"Very well, gentleman, what do you have?"

Artimus turned over his cards with a flush—three tens and two jacks.

He smiled and then Red Hand turned over his. A flush—three kings and two tens. The Queen had a puzzled look as Red Hand reached for the pile, and she revealed her cards—four Queens.

Red Hand slammed his hand down, got up and walked to the other side of the room. The Queen laughed and with a flourish, swept the vast pile of coins closer to her. "One-Eyed Willy, we have not been graced with your presence thus far this year. To what do we owe the honor and the great pleasure?" the Queen asked.

"Deal me and Sebastian in. Here is coin."

Artimus started to deal everyone in. London said, "Another jug of rum, Senorita."

"My Queen, it has been far too long, and might I say, you look as ravishing as ever," Willy commented.

"Merci. Mais coupe la merde et continuez," she replied and smiled.

"What did she say, Father?" Sebastian asked.

"My Sebastian, you are growing into a welcoming sight for sore eyes. I told your father to cut the shit and get on with it. Sebastian, you know I have a cabin fit for a queen, and maybe you could be King tonight."

Willy smiled and chuckled.

"Tu pourrais me pilonner comme de la pate," said the Queen.

"Why does she always speak to me in French?" enquired Sebastian.

"Why Sebastian, it is common for a French woman who fancies another."

Willy whispered the translation in Sebastian's ear. *You could pound me like dough.*

Sebastian's eyes lit up and he replied, "I knew a French poet once. Jean de Conde. He was sort of a dirty poet rather like yourself, Madam Queen. May I ask you something in that context?

However, you must be completely honest, and answer without deception."

"Romeo, you may ask anything your heart desires. Speaking of Romeo, where is my little Juliet?" the Queen questioned.

"Sara is in the tavern, getting three sheets to the wind," Willy explained.

"Milady. Is there any hair in between thine legs?" asked Sebastian.

"Ooh, Sebastian, you devil! I'll have you know that there is absolutely none at all."

"Indeed. Then I was correct in my thoughts that grass doesn't grow on a well-beaten path."

The Queens's face was priceless and you could hear a pin drop. From the other side of the room, Red Hand Nichols broke out into a laugh. The Queen, who never anticipated that answer, started to laugh excessively. Willy was laughing so hard, he was coughing and fell off his chair.

London Jade spit her rum out and almost choked in hysterics.

Artimus banged his hand on the table and laughed.

Even the women carrying the rum couldn't stop laughing.

As the laughing died down, the Queen snapped apart a piece of chicken and said, "Perhaps I am used to men with larger muskets, and was willing to sacrifice pain for pleasure in the small pistol that you carry, Sebastian. But I assure you, this path is as tenacious as the first time it was walked upon. You're welcome to journey down my polished walkway."

Sebastian laughed. "Aye, well said, my Queen. You haven't got enough rum."

"Now down to business. What is it that you need from your fellow Kinsmen?" the Queen asked.

"I am here to request the assistance of the Kinsmen in the apprehension of the greatest array of riches this side of the world could ever conjure. We are speaking of an amount of gold in the realm of a billion ducats. Everyone remembers the wreck of the Nuestra Senora De La Atocha?"

The Kinsmen all shook their heads in agreement and Willy continued, "This ship was said to hold gold, silver and jewels in excess of 400 million."

"Yes, Willy, we know the story. The ship went down in 1622 in a storm 100 miles north of Havana. Supposedly, the ship was a mile from shore. That's why there were so many survivors. Still, almost fifty years later, there has been no recovery, only specks that wash up on the shores," the Queen replied.

Red Hand walked back over and sat down. "I heard it was more in the range of 750 million." "Exactly, Mr. Nichols, the estimates are outrageous. What if there is more?" Willy suggested. "Are you suggesting that we try and locate the Atocha?" Artimus asked.

"No, I'm saying that Gonzales has located it and he has been sending hundreds of men to the depths of the sea to retrieve the gold," replied Willy.

"Do these rumors hold truth? Gonzales just came back from the islands off the mainland and will be meeting with the Governor of New Britain. That is not all. Gonzales and Hamilton are amassing a comparable cache on Havana. This is to be sent back to the mainland in honor of the Prince of England's marriage to the Princess of England. The King of England has already dispatched the Armada to Havana," London Jade added.

"These rumors hold the truth beyond our wildest dreams," Willy said.

"May I suggest that we steal both the treasures and meet in Panama City?" Sebastian replied.

"And then what do we do? Where do we go? The Spanish and English Armadas will give chase," said the Queen. "And if we steal twice the treasures, they shall chase us twice as ardently."

"My grandfather used to speak of San Diego Bay, along the coastline north of Mexico. I have the coordinates on my ship. He ranted about its beauty and the friendliness of the indigenous people. Maybe we could lay our heads there for a while?" suggested Artimus.

"Whatever we do, it has to be with haste and the wind in our sails," Willy confirmed. "I agree," said the Queen.

"Now here is my plan."

Meanwhile, inside the tavern, Thomas and Sara were having fun.

"Thomas Copperpot, you are without a doubt the worst rum drinker this side of the Caribbean."

"I'm terribly sorry. I've tried to sleep up with you, but you fink too drast. I mean, you drink too fast."

"Did you just say you're trying to sleep with me?" said Sara.

"NO! NO! I said keep up with you."

Willy and Sebastian arrived back from meeting with the Kinsmen.

"Are you speaking inappropriately to my daughter?" Willy asked.

"Not at all, Captain, I would never speak openly about the quartermaster," Thomas answered before he passed out on the table.

"C'mon, Father, he was nursing that rum like his mother's titty. A drunken cabin boy, maybe, but he better learn to hold his liquor if he ever wants to make it as a pirate. The night is still young—like me." Sara lifted her cup in the air.

"Devereaux!" Willy yelled.

"Yes, sire," he said and walked up to the Captain.

"I want you, Prima and ten others to meet me on the docks at 01:00 AM."

"Aye, Captain," said Devereaux. "That we shall."

"And Devereaux? Watch my son and daughter, will you?"

"Aye, Captain," said Devereaux as he put his arm around Sebastian and said, "with my life." "Father, where are you going?" Sebastian asked Willy.

"To meet an old friend."

A knoll couch sat under a picture of King Charles II. The walls were yellow, like marigolds, with a white wood trim that culminated to a larger work of art around the fireplace. On top of the fireplace's mantle was a clock, and behind the timekeeper on the wall was a picture of the Caribbean islands. In front of the couch were new, dark oak chairs with open backs on the bottom that matched the dark oakwood desk. And behind the desk in the right-hand corner was an English flag, and on the left-hand side, a French flag. Documents were strewed about the desk, alongside a bottle of ink, feather, a magnifying glass and a miniature coin scale.

At the helm of this magnificent sculpture of wood was Robert Perkins, a pudgy, short, bald wig-wearing financial tyrant with bad breath from rotting teeth, and a long face.

He removed his spectacles and said, "You had to fulfill one occupation, and you would have had the gold and we could all be in a jubilant state. I am concerned for the safety of your loved ones with the actions you have taken as of late. Where is the jewel, Captain?"

"For me to lose a good friend to that one-eyed devil, and you threatening me with Maria, I think it's time to renegotiate," said la Muerte.

Perkins contemplated for a moment then pushed out his chair, startling even the guards. He began to walk around the office.

"Let me extend my sympathies for the loss of your friend. I'm sure his screams will haunt your nightmares for years to come, or maybe you've dreamt your last dream.

"Maybe the last thing you will ever remember in this life is the slitting of Maria's throat. It's either my way and you go with it or try to sail away in a boat with a hole. The choice is yours, Mr. la Muerte. I don't have time for games. Bring in the woman—I want my jewel."

The guards collected Maria and brought her in. She was quite stunning—long black hair cascaded over her olive skin, and she had glorious curves in all the right places.

One eye was visibly bruised, and her lip was bleeding on the lower left side.

"Sit her down next to the Capitán."

She sat next to la Muerte and they both hugged and kissed and comforted each other. "My love, my apologies. I will get us out of this situation," la Muerte promised.

"Juan, please, I cannot take this anymore. Please, my love, I just want go home."

"Juan? That's hysterical that she calls you Juan. She doesn't know about the infamous Capitán of Death? You may call him Juan, but to me, he will always be la Muerte," Mr. Perkins remarked.

"I know, my love, it will all be over soon, I promise," said Juan.

"You took the words right out of my mouth. Guards, bring in the axe man," Perkins ordered.

The man was gigantic, wore a metal mask and dressed as if it were the Middle Ages with something that resembled a chastity belt and strapped across his chest. The guards held down la Muerte while the axe man took Maria. He pushed her down on her knees and put her head through the back of one of the chairs, then tied her hands behind her back.

"Don't do this, Mr. Perkins, I will get your jewel, please don't do this," la Muerte pleaded.

"Can't you see how profound these chairs are? The sheer importance of their design? You have five seconds to tell me where the jewel is," Perkins replied.

The axe man started lifting the axe as Mr. Perkins began his count. "One, two, three, four…"

CHAPTER FIFTEEN

Back in Time

Willy made his way out of the Rusty Nail and started his journey to meet an old friend who may not even have wanted to see him. As he walked down the street past the closed shops, he heard a conversation coming from the alleyway up ahead, next to the corner of the building that was the office of Robert Perkins.

He stopped, removed his hat, and peeked his head around the corner.

There, la Muerte was getting beaten like the Queen's grassless path, by two French guards. One guard removed his pistol and smashed la Muerte in the head, causing him to fall to the ground.

"Where is the jewel? We can do this all night, Capitan. Pick him back up, Raul," one of the guards said.

"Yes, Claude," Raul replied.

Raul was holding la Muerte up—he could barely stand.

Mr. Perkins said, "If you don't tell us where the jewel is, we will have our way with Maria."

Claude and Raul started to laugh and la Muerte spat blood into Claude's face, who reached into his pocket for a cloth and wiped off the blood. He put it back into his pocket and said, "Now you are going to lose an eye." He grabbed his pistol and went to swing the handle of the weapon toward the face of la Muerte when his wrist was caught by One-Eyed Willy.

"It's not nice to take a man's eye," Willy said as he looked deep into the soul of Claude with his one eye. "I speak from experience. Take anything else from a man—just not his sight."

Claude was terrified as Raul released la Muerte to assist, but Willy kicked Raul in the chest, and he fell back, tripping over la Muerte and landing on his spine.

He grabbed his knife with his left hand, and attempted to plunge it into Willy.

Willy disarmed Claude of his pistol and narrowly escaped being cut. And with the pistol aimed at the face of Claude, he said, "An eye for an eye—it's only fair," and smacked Claude in the head with the pistol handle.

He then tied up the two Frenchmen and gagged them before he picked up la Muerte.

"Can you walk?"

"Yes, I can walk," la Muerte replied.

"I need you to listen very carefully. I am going to take Scarlett's Revenge before daybreak. I need you to accompany Sebastian and Sara on the Retribution to Isla de Juesos. Can you do that?" "What's going on, Captain?" la Muerte asked.

"Go to the ship and ask Sebastian. He will explain. He is familiar with the cause." "Aye, Captain," said la Muerte, and they both walked in opposite directions.

At the end of an old dirt road on the outskirts of town, another road was hidden away behind bushes. This other road was supposed to lead to an old, abandoned house, only the house wasn't necessarily abandoned the way that people surmised.

Willy walked with rigorous haste and could taste the sweetness in the air.

The nearby sugarcane plantations were ripe for harvest and the air was filled with molasses. The hissing of snakes, screeching of bats and other calls of nature didn't thwart Willy's ambition to see his old friend.

Kicking rocks on his walk down the dark passage, Willy was nervous, anticipating the outcome of this visit. The long road eventually came to an end and Willy, guided by the light of a full moon, easily found the other road through the bushes.

He followed a narrow dirt road for about five hundred feet and then came to an opening.

There stood the old, abandoned house, with its white paint peeling, a chicken coop to the right and a tied-up horse at the front. To the left were the remains of a structure that looked like it had burned to the ground. The entire place was a sorry sight, forlorn and tumbledown.

As Willy walked closer to the horse, it began to neigh, and Willy petted it to calm it down.

The moment Willy placed his feet upon the wooden steps leading up to the door, the steps groaned like a stomach that hadn't been fed in days. Every piece of timber was rotting.

There was a candle fixture outside the door—burning, strangely— and also a bell.

Someone had to be living here. Willy pulled the string for the bell.

The door opened and immediately, Willy reached for his pistol.

Looking around with intense curiosity, he slowly made his way inside the abandoned home. Stepping inside was like going back in time. The portraits on the wall looked as though they were from a century ago—the dust on them coated the paint, looking as if they hadn't been cleaned off for decades. The walls had cracks in them, and the paint was peeling like the outside of the house. Wax was built up on the broken-down wood from candles that illuminated the room.

An old, decrepit organ lay dormant in the corner of the room and a large dining room table had numerous maps dispersed upon it.

Willy walked around the home and toward a smaller room that contained a tiny, round table. On the table was a candle with a note against its side, propped up, as if Willy was meant to find and read it. He put the pistol down on the table and opened the letter.

Hear ye, hear ye, for all who enter my humble abode must abide by only one code. Finish this next rhyme, and you'll see. Yo ho, yo ho...

Willy turned around and standing before him was and old Indian man with a pistol.

"A pirate's life for me," Willy said.

The man put down the pistol and said, "William James Walsh, it's been some time."

"Yes, it has been, John. I see you're still playing the organ. Do you mind if I play?"

"Yes, I do mind if you play. Is this why you came, to play the organ? Well then, you shouldn't have come. Why *did* you come, William, or should I say, One-Eyed Willy?"

"John, I know I let you down on Maria-Galante," Willy said as he picked up a fixture and blew off the dust, then put it back down, coughing from ingesting the fine particles.

He continued, "I know you wanted revenge, but we both lost tremendously in Bridgetown. I have been fighting day in and day out to pay the Spanish back for their cruelty, with the same cruelty we both showed them through those tough years."

"No one knows cruelty like me, Willy, no one. You of all people know what the Governor did to my family in Portobello. What the Governor did to my wife and my daughter, your wife and my sister in Bridgetown. You know what was done. So, why, Willy? Why, when the opportune moment rose to kill this man who stole everything from us, did you choose to go after the booty?"

"Wait a moment, Mr. Blackheart. I chose to go after my children. It just so happened we were on an expedition to find the scroll. Look, I know I hurt you, and you have my sincerest apologies for that. Didn't I say so already? But we have known each other a very, very long time. Sailed and spilled blood together. We are family and, in that moment, I thought if I would have got in that boat with you and chased the Governor, we might have lost all we had built in those years, maybe our lives. For me, it was too much to lose. I had an opportunity to get my children back, and I took it."

"You forgot why you became One-Eyed Willy and why I became Blackheart. Gonzales took everything from us," said John. "Correction; *you let* Gonzales strip us of everything."

"I'm well aware of this, John. But what point in bitter thoughts, John? We can't bring them back—Isabell, Lenore or Louisa. They are gone, yet we still live. Whether it's for vengeance or not, we are still alive. You have a niece who looks just like her aunt and mother, and a nephew the same. I tell them stories, yet they are so eager to see their Uncle John—someone who was so close to their mother. We should relish what we have, not mourn what is lost."

John sat down on a chair and asked Willy, "Have I been selfish?"

"No, John, *I* was selfish. Now is the time I get to repay you for everything you have given me.

Without you, I wouldn't have my children. They're all grown up now, the young pirates." He smiled.

"So, are they any good at sailing?" John asked.

"So good they could be captains. I have to tell you that the opportune moment has arisen again, and this time, they will all pay. I have to recover the jewel first," Willy answered.

"I knew it, I knew it. You're still speaking of this jewel. Over ten years ago, marooned on Isla de Huesos with that old man who went on about tales of a power inside the jewel, you believed him. Remember you gave it to Louisa because you loved her.

"And this old man tells stories and you let that cloud your heart," said John.

"Look, John. As I said, this is getting old now. We don't have time to discuss this. But how do you think I knew where to find you otherwise? The power is real, John, that I can promise you. I just haven't figured out everything but there is still power beyond imagination.

"The Spanish are putting together a treasure so great and so vast, it's beyond the realm of thinking. We are going to steal it and kill the Governor. We will avenge your wife, my wife, your daughter, and my niece. Do you still have contacts in Portobello?" asked Willy.

"Is my horse tied up outside?" replied John.

"We need you. No, we need *Blackheart*. Perkins is going to ask for your help, so I figured I might do so before he did. I need you to play along for now and meet at the island of bones ten days from now," said Willy.

"What's in Portobello?"

"Our supplies that you will get us for our journey to Panama City." At that moment, they heard horses outside.

"That has to be Perkins and his men. I roughed up some of his soldiers," said Willy.

"What's in Panama City? And where is the Inferno?" asked Blackheart.

"Trust me, my old friend, we are going to be rich. And I promise you, we will have revenge." Willy ran out of the back door.

The sound of horses outside didn't startle Blackheart.

It merely feasted upon his curiosity to understand further what Willy had spoken of. There was a creaking of the steps and a ring of the bell. The door opened and there stood Mr. Perkins. "Yo ho, a pirate's life is mine. Mr. Blackheart! How dost thou fare?" "What is thy business here, Mr. Perkins?" asked Blackheart.

"Now, is that any way for a borrower to treat his magnanimous financier? I am here because a steep debt is owed, and if not paid, the men outside your door will not welcome this news." "Perkins, the debts are not payable at this time," Blackheart replied.

"Did you not ask me for vital information about a certain governor, who in days past, caused you utter devastation? Did I not give adequate information of where the Governor was going to be and when?"

"Yes. I agree. Half of the information was of truth, yet half of the information was borderline fraudulent, and it was even possible that he was aware of my presence."

"Absolutely not a chance! That is utterly preposterous. Now you're telling stories without merit," Perkins replied. "You speak with your ass!"

Blackheart put his sword up to Perkins's neck and said, "Are ya calling me a liar, Perkins?" Pushing the sword away with the ridge of his hand, Perkins replied, "Careful, Mr. Ramos. Wouldn't want you to die before you've made good on our agreements. Well, if you have no coin, then I do believe your navigable services are available for said payment."

"On with it, Mr. Perkins. My supper is getting cold, and I like to be left alone," said Blackheart.

"You're going to remove something of considerable worth from a ship and its captain who can't see very well," Perkins explained.

"One-Eyed Willy?" said Blackheart.

"Precisely."

"How are you positive that Willy has what you're looking for?"

"Well, he doesn't yet. However, he will. Oh trust me, he will. When he does, you will be there to steal it for me. Understood?"

"What's in it for me?" asked Blackheart.

"That's the opportune question, isn't it? You will be the captain of the Indestructible. I will prepare a crew and load the ship with all the supplies you need for this journey. You will meet with the governor of New Britain at his mansion in Port Royal in one week's time. And you will retrieve my gold the minute you have Willy in your sights," said Perkins.

"Again, Mr. Perkins, what's in it for me?" asked Blackheart.

"Something beyond your wildest dreams, and that, my new employee, is a question only the Governor can answer. I must bid you farewell. I have other business to attend to. Your ship leaves promptly at noon tomorrow."

"If I am not in agreement with the Governor's offer, I'm not taking the job," Blackheart answered, arms folded across his chest.

"But you will be Mr. Blackheart. That is an inevitable certainty," Perkins stated as he walked out the door.

Meanwhile, back at the Rusty Nail, Sebastian, Sara and Thomas were still enjoying the splendors the old tavern had to offer. Quaco and Devereaux were saying their goodbyes as they were under a restriction of time and had to be punctual in meeting Willy.

Thomas was sitting at a table and Sara and Sebastian were singing pirate songs, drinking rum and ale, swinging their mugs and feeding liquid to the air.

They were sparing no expense, every movement spilling coin on the floor.

While at the table, London Jade came to sit next to Thomas Copperpot.

London had long red fiery hair that looked as if it was made of dragon's breath. Her eyes shone a vivid green like the color of water on her favorite coastline. The fire in those eyes had burned many men alive and many a man's hearts. Her temper had a shorter fuse than a chase gun, yet her personality was wildly fearless in her attempts to have a few laughs at the expense of Thomas. "So, art thou the one of whom they all speak?" she asked Thomas.

Thomas was in another world—with his hand on his head, in desperate need of water, some food and a good night's sleep—when he realized he was being spoken to.

"My apologies milady, were you inquiring about me?"

"Obviously. I mean, that is if you truly are who they say you are, Capitán de la Muerte." "You're familiar with my adventures, are you?" Sebastian and Sara came and sat back down at the table.

"London, I see you've met?" Sebastian said.

Thomas interrupted and with his hand stretched over the table in an introductory manner, said,

"Capitán de la Muerte, at your service."

London put her hand out, and Thomas kissed the top of it.

"My, my. What a gentleman you are, Capitán."

"Yeah, Capitan, you're a real knight in shining armor," Sebastian replied in a slightly jealous spout, and sipped the ale in his jug.

"I thought it was lovely, and I think that type of chivalry is worthy of a queen," London commented.

Sebastian spat and almost choked on his rum as he laughed.

"So, what does a lady have to do to stroll upstairs with the Captain of Death?"

"I'm actually glad you asked that question because…" Thomas replied but was tapped on the shoulder. He turned and looked up. A man three times his size was standing behind his chair, his bushy goatee sporting a number of beads in it. The white shirt he wore was ripped and blood-stained and he wore a bandana tied around his bald head.

Most importantly, his arms were the size of cannons—and his name, ironically, was Goliath.

"Excuse me a moment, I'm having a bit of a chat with the lady here," Thomas said.

Goliath tapped Thomas again, but even harder this time.

Thomas turned around and said, "Look lad." He stood up quickly. "Just who do you think you are?"

"I am the giant called Goliath. Are you the Captain of Death?"

"Damn right I am, who's inquiring?"

London tried to interrupt. "Goliath, this isn't the Capitán."

"You slept with my girl Carolina in Port Royal, and she told me what you did, so now I'm going to jam my fist up your sorry ass."

"Tell the woman she's opening the wrong lips," Goliath replied.

Sebastian stood up, and stepped in.

"Wait a minute. That's unnecessary, and this isn't who you think it is."

"If you value your ass, you'll use it to sit back down in that chair," said Goliath and grabbed

Thomas's shirt. "Time to die, Copperpot."

Thomas, with a puzzled look on his face, said, "Wait a minute, did you just call me Copperpot?"

Goliath attempted to look meaner, and squeezed his fist tighter. "No, I said, Captain."

"No, you didn't, you said Copperpot."

Goliath let go of Copperpot's shirt and said, "No, I didn't. I said... wait, what did I say?" "Oh, Goliath," said London Jade as she threw her jug at him.

Half of the crowd within the Rusty Nail sighed in disappointment, throwing things at Goliath.

London Jade and Sebastian were so aggravated but Sara was overwhelmed with joy.

"What the daisies are you so charmed about?" London said.

"She's the only one that bet on Thomas not to wet himself," Sebastian said. Goliath, Sebastian and London all gave Sara two coins.

One by one, other pirates in the Nail walked over and handed two coins to Sara. The Queen also walked over with a few coins and handed them to Sara.

"Juliet, you are getting more stunning with every full moon. Your father is lucky to have such fine children. Your friend over there might be too smart for his own good; however, I see resilience in him. He may very well make it after all," the Queen said. "I have seen worse men do so."

Sara smiled and instantly caught the eye of Thomas Copperpot. The Queen walked away, and Sebastian went to take another sip of rum, but discovered his cup was empty.

"Well, I've had enough rum for one night, let's take our leave," he said.

"Why would we do that when we can just buy us more rum with these coins?" Sara asked.

"Save the coins; we have to shove off in the morning," said Sebastian.

Everyone got up from the table to say their goodbyes to London and the other pirates, then they stumbled their way to the door, swaying this way and that, and tripping over their own feet.

"Sebastian, wait," London said.

Sebastian, with a smile on his face, turned around and gave a slight bow. "Yes, milady?"

"You forgot to pay for that last jug of rum. It will be three shillings." She extended her arm and open hand, waiting.

It was possible to read the disappointment in Sebastian's facial expression.

"Yes, of course, milady. Wouldn't have it any other way," he replied as he handed her three coins. "A minor oversight," he proclaimed, bowing again as if politeness were coin itself.

She held his hand for a moment, leaned in, and kissed him on the cheek. "Good night, young Sebastian," said London.

"I bid the lady farewell and dreams of fortune."

Sebastian turned around and walked out the door again, this time with a smile on his face.

Willy came strolling down the cold sand under the light of a thousand stars. The smell of rotten old wood and fish gave him a sense of home. For a moment, Willy had thought he was back on Isla de Huenos some twelve years ago.

The men finished loading the supplies onto Scarlett's Revenge and Willy made his way onto the ship, then walked straight into the Captain's quarters. There was a small fire burning in a tiny fireplace, and Willy took out his pipe and packed it with tobacco, then grabbed ember tongs and secured a piece of coal, placing it on top of the pipe gently enough to light the tobacco.

He then returned to the main deck and up to the helm.

The men pulled up the wooden planks as Willy walked to the helm of the ship, and yelled, "Shove off, men!" and the ship began its voyage onto the dark-blue sea, guided only by a compass and the constellations.

Looking back on the island, smoking his pipe with a worried look, the Captain seemed concerned. Devereaux, a French Englishman, and one of the eldest members of the crew asked,

"What's troubling ya, Captain?"

"My children, Mr. Devereaux. I am concerned for my children," Willy answered.

"They'll be alright, Captain. I wouldn't let it worry you too much. A fine pair of pirates the two of 'em, and I'd be happy to sail with either one of 'em behind the helm."

Prima Diablo, overheard Devereaux and Willy speaking of the twins. "I agree with Mr. Devereaux—they have grown into reflections of their father, and you should be proud, Captain. I swear they shall come to no harm, taking after you as they do."

Willy took some heart from the men's statements and expressions of faith in his children. But still, something caused him consternation, even if he didn't know what or why.

"I am hopeful in the lessons I've taught Sara and Sebastian, yet I am fearful of with whom they are to sail," Willy said. "As good and capable as they are, there are rogues at sea..."

"Understandably, you worry. Capitán de la Muerte has shown a side of himself that few would like to reveal. Love can make a man do remarkable things and may also, as you say Captain, turn him into a monster. Captain, if your thoughts are teetering between faith and uncertainty, then you must put your faith in the choices of your children."

"Mr. Devereaux is correct. You must trust the decisions they make would parallel the ones you, yourself, would make," Prima replied. "They are you in all but age."

The Captain pondered the answers given by Devereaux and Prima Diablo, then he addressed the crew.

"Men, we are about to embark on a journey for the greatest treasure the world has ever seen. Every person before you plays an intricate part in the painting of this masterpiece, no matter how trivial or vital. And I assure you this is a masterpiece we are painting. From the cabin boys to myself as your Captain, we are all responsible for our piece of the painting," announced Willy.

"Captain, was I supposed to bring paint or paintbrushes?" Devereux asked.

"Whose job was it to bring the paint?" Prima said.

The crew laughed aloud.

"The next one of ya to interrupt me will be painting my cutlass red," Willy interrupted.

There was immediate silence amongst the crew.

"Now, I refuse to be dishonest about the seas we are to sail. Some of us may die or be injured. We may lose friends and crewmates. We may fall into the darkness of Davey Jones with only a speck of hope to light our way. I see that hope in the hearts of each and every one of you. I want you to hold onto that light and fight for each other, fight for me, but most importantly, fight for yourselves because there ain't enough water in the sea to douse the fire inside the crew of the

Inferno. What say you, are you with me?" The crew burst out in cheer.

They had truly been inspired, and they all yelled, "Aye!" loudly, in unison.

CHAPTER SIXTEEN

The sea played a gentle game of touch and go with the sand as Thomas Copperpot and Sebastian snored so loudly, people might have thought they were two animals having an argument, speaking in their native tongue. Sebastian put his arm around Thomas whilst dreaming of London Jade—unaware of who was lying next to him—and Thomas smiled in comfort, dreaming it was Sara.

Along with Sara, some of the men had gathered around the two dreamers on the beach. Sara kicked her brother in his back, waking him and as he opened his eyes, she said, "You lads had a bit of fun amongst yourselves last night, did you? Sure looks like it—smells like it too.

"For your information, we were supposed to shove off three hours ago. The Inferno and

Scarlett's Revenge are gone."

Sebastian, with his eyes barely open, said, "Gone? What do you mean gone?"

"Gone. Gone! *Gone*, you fools! What part of that don't you understand? Gone as in not here anymore. Departed. Left. Sailed. Moved on. We've missed them. They are gone!" she said, waving her arms wildly in the air as if about to suffer a heart attack.

Thomas, still in the fetal position, snoring, got flicked in the ear by Sebastian finally rising from his slumber. As Thomas adjusted his eyes to the sun he asked, "Doth anyone know a good axe man that may remove my head? This wretched pain is far too excruciating to live with."

"You landlubbers. Dost not know the consequences of a rum-induced evening, do you?" Sara said. "You are hopeless. I don't know why you even do this job if you can't wake up on time— and sober—ready to start a new day. You've gone and let me down, anyway. Let us all down—" She would have moaned and whined on and on but Sebastian interrupted.

"Sara, Father said there would be three ships. Three, not two. So are you sure it's too late? I mean, was the Retribution still there?" Sebastian asked.

"Of course, it was," said Sara.

"Get up Thomas. C'mon, now! That's where we are going," Sebastian insisted, pulling at Thomas' arm. A more slovenly pair you could not ever encounter, but somehow, they managed to don all their attire in the right order and—clutching their sorry heads—stood to their feet and prepared to walk. Or to stumble. Or in some cases, to crawl when the pain really overtook them. In due course, they all made their way toward the Retribution, falling and tripping as they went along. Sara still tutted and regaled them with chastising, occasionally hitting one or the other and causing them to leap forward as if in a strange and merry dance.

Robert Perkins stared angrily at his watch in front of the Indestructible as Sebastian, Sara and Thomas slowly passed him on their way to the Retribution.

"Good day, Mr. Perkins," Sebastian said as he walked down the docks. His voice had a certain singsong tone, as if nothing was amiss at all.

Under his breath, Perkins said, "Good day, peasant."

He gave a mock salute and the laughed behind their backs once they had passed by.

Claude and Raul had been found by Mr. Perkins early in the morning, tied up and gagged. They had been given a second chance to redeem themselves by keeping a watchful eye over Blackheart and Mr. Perkins' favorite ship.

Finally, Blackheart walked onto the docks toward Mr. Perkins, carrying a bag full of God only knew what—but whatever it was, it sure did not look much—and the tattered clothes on his back. "Mr. Blackheart, I do believe your knowledge of the word 'punctual' is nonexistent. Therefore, I have Claude and Raul here to accompany you on your journey. They understand the meaning and will enforce it if necessary. You have a crew of twenty-five men and supplies to last you. Any questions, Mr. Blackheart? Anything you do not understand?"

"Yes," mumbled Blackheart. "What does the Governor of New Britain want with me?" Blackheart asked, scratching his flea-bitten arms and legs.

"Thou shalt find out all in good time, Sire," said Perkins. "No point in spoiling a surprise, is there? The anticipation is riveting, and the surprise well worth the wait. Come now, Mr. Blackheart, there is no time to waste. I could let you know the consequences for noncompliance, however, the Governor will be more able to explain their severity."

"So, I'm free to board the ship and shove off?" Blackheart asked.

"Yes, you are, indeed," Perkins replied. "I would be most happy to see you shove off." He guffawed, loving his own joke.

"Avast ye!" Blackheart yelled, and the crew suddenly stopped and focused their attention to Blackheart. "What are all you scalawags staring at? Get back to work, we got sailing to do," he continued. Blackheart boarded the ship and looked down at Perkins on the dock, then screamed in Spanish, "Adiós, pedófilo cabeza de cerdo!" and they moved off within a moment's notice.

Perkins turned to one of the men working on the dock and asked, "What did he just say?" The man laughed as he replied, "Senor Blackheart said, *thank you for the ship.*" Perkins puffed himself up with grandiosity and was satisfied at the response.

Three days later, Willy and the Scarlett's Revenge were just outside the city of Port Royal, Jamaica, drifting toward the harbor through the thrashing current. The crew couldn't help but be in awe peering at Fort Charles. Even though it was an impenetrable castle built to thwart off Spanish invaders, the King invited pirates and privateers to the island specifically to ransack the Spanish fleet that would always be lurking around the city. For the pirates, this was both an alliance against, and protection from, those same Spanish invaders.

Scarlett's Revenge entered the natural harbor, passing Fort Charles and its artillery. Forty ships were anchored outside the pirate city, including five of the ten destroyers deployed by Mr. Perkins. They made an intrepid sight, as off-putting as it was possible to be.

Willy was interested in only one of those five ships—the King's Redemption. This was the most formidable ship in all the King's armada and was the King's favorite. It was one of very few man o' wars in the Caribbean, being equipped with four decks of guns armed with nearly one hundred cannons, and dwarfing its sister British ship, the Scarlett's Revenge.

The Revenge laid anchor and Willy and the crew rowed ashore, and he noticed the beaches swarming with pirates. Makeshift tents ran down the waterfront for miles as though they were preparing for battle, and great fires raged with the sizzling of meat and fish. The rum-induced gathering of heathens had to have been going on for decades.

Port Royal was known for its bustling pirate life, with warehouses, tavern keepers and goldsmiths occupying more than three quarters of the city's forty acres of land.

Willy and his crew made their way through the town, ready to indulge in the countless pleasantries Port Royal had to offer—the endless jugs of rum and the company of promiscuous women. This city was paradise for the pirates of the Caribbean and as they turned a corner onto the main strip of the city, there were women everywhere.

"Can you smell that, lads?" Willy asked.

"Prima Diablo," said the tobacco captain.

"Bullox. No, you moron. Any kind of fish your manhood could handle," said Willy.

With his nose in the air and taking in a deep breath, filthy thoughts assailing his mind,

Devereaux said, "Captain, I understand you now. Ain't nothing like a nice piece of fish." Walking down the street, many of the women were saying *good evening* and *hello* to Willy. Willy tipped his head and continued down the street until he was approached and stopped by a woman directly across the street from the Tipsy Barrel.

It just so happened that this was where he would find another one of the Kinsmen.

Charlotte wasn't that tall, but she had tobacco-brown eyes and a smoking set of bosoms. Her long brown hair laid gently on top of them added a bit of sensual elegance to their voluptuousness.

"Willy, how divine it is to gaze at thee with mine eyes. I imagined you would return to see me with haste," she said. "How much a delight it is to see you returned to me thus."

"Good evening, Charlotte. You look breathtakingly stunning, as usual, my dear. I'm actually here on business, not pleasure." Charlotte toyed a piece of her hair away from her breasts, giving the men the availability to gander at her cleavage. She stooped forward and displayed them with a little jiggle, as if a fruit vendor showing off her ripe and juicy wares.

Willy's eyes went wide and he sought to divert his gaze from her cleavage, knowing there was much work to be achieved that day. But Charlotte had yet more to offer.

In a peculiarly provocative way, she began twirling her hair around her finger, batting her big brown eyes and saying, "Oh, Willy, you're speaking my language! My business *is* pleasure, lad."

"Seriously, my dear, I am here to discuss a more, ahem, *pressing* matter, yet I assure you, my next visit will be explicitly to see you. I certainly would not like to miss out on your offerings." Without a moment's hesitation, Devereaux interrupted.

"Captain, please introduce me, if I may be so brazen…"

"Not now!" He cast Devereaux a filthy look that said, *we have work to do!* Then he added, "Charlotte, mi lady, rest assured, you are the only lady I would entertain," Willy replied.

"Liar! You spoke of the same excuses in your last visit and wound up in a room with Carolina," she retorted, spittle flying from her lips. She pulled in her bosoms and put her hair over them. Willy looked dumbfounded. "Carolina?" said Willy. "Pray, tell me what you mean." He tried to look confused but his neck and cheeks were bright red, caught in a lie. "Yes, Willy. You don't think gossip spreads like venereal disease between us women?" Willy now had a flabbergasted look on his face.

"Carolina? I do not recall spending anytime with Carolina. That gesture, it holds no evidence. Why—have you spoken with Carolina?"

She merely huffed. "If you think you are seeing me anytime soon, dearest Willy, you have another think coming!"

She moved to walk off, nose in the air, but Willy caught a hold of her arm.

"Might I ask," he inquired, "is she—Carolina—available this evening?" Willy questioned. "I mean, I will cross your hand with coin if you would ask for me…"

Some of the men were laughing and Devereaux tugged on the captain's coat, still hanging on hopes of an introduction. "See, Captain Willy, the lady hath no need for you. But I would like—" Willy ignored him.

Charlotte was giving Willy the evil eye, also ignoring what Devereaux had asked.

"As I recall, you're all balls and no… *willy*, Willy."

The laughter among the men was so loud, it was almost deafening. And she was not even done yet. She had still more to contribute and would give Willy a gift to remember.

"That being said…" Charlotte replied, "I do have a little something for you. Come closer…" She showed off her ample bosoms again and made a show of licking her lips, then pouting them. He smiled broadly and said, aside to Devereaux, "You see! The lady knows a good thing—" She leaned in as if about to kiss him—and kicked Willy sharply in his balls.

He immediately hunched over and fell to the ground.

"Oooh!" the men groaned, as if they had felt the pain that has just been bestowed upon their fearless captain. They covered their testicles with their palms, some rubbing as though they must have felt the anger with which she had booted his groin.

Charlotte bent down and said, "I was correct, and now you're no balls, and no willy, Willy!" She walked away angrily, calling back, "I am most afraid you will be out of action for a time, Sire. I shall tell dear Carolina this—that the good Captain Willy has become oddly incapacitated by way of a sad injury to his tender nether parts."

"Captain, are you alright? Did she get both of em?" Devereaux asked with a hint of concern. "Yes," the Captain muttered and nodded his head.

"She got them well and good." "In that situation, Capitan, you have to protect the family jewels," Prima said.

"You should have let me speak with her, Captain," Devereaux suggested. Willy, infuriated, made his way to his feet and dusted himself off from the filth of the street.

"Gimme my hat," he said as he snatched it out of the grip of Prima Diablo.

"Captain, you should have granted me the opportunity to swoon that swine; all she wanted was coin to feed her children," Devereaux continued.

A few hundred feet away, Charlotte was holding a baby in her arms as three tiny children clung to her legs like a dead man to his last breath.

"Devereaux, shut up, those aren't even her children. She borrows them to make morons like you spend coin thinking she has children," Willy replied and whacked Devereaux with his hat.

"Mr. Devereaux, against my better judgment, I'm placing this pouch of coin in your hands. The responsibility to ensure each one of the men gets his fair share falls upon you. If I hear otherwise... Let's just say, we'll be loading your balls into a cannon, and it won't require much gunpowder.

"We shall take the ship before dawn, so hurry and get your fill of the sins of this city, because in a few hours' time, the King's Redemption is ours. Prima, you are with me," ordered Willy.

The Captain stopped and said, "Oh, and Devereaux, do try to stay away from the Mistress

Charlotte—that tuzzy-muzzy is a fireship, and she'll have you burning for days."

"Gratitude, Captain, but not to worry, my travels aren't hindered by a little fire. Regardless, I'll just take the windward passage," replied Devereaux. "Aye, Devereaux, what a splendid idea."

The captain and a few of the men laughed.

"What is the windward passage?" Prima Diablo asked, envisaging an exotic place.

"The asshole, you asshole," Willy replied as the Captain and Prima walked toward the entrance of the Tipsy Barrel. Devereaux squared coin with the men, and one by one, they all disappeared into the chaos that was the city of Port Royal.

Upon entering the shameless Tipsy Barrel, the immediate attention of women seeking coin for company was profound. The fiddle was being played as women and womanizers danced drunkenly to a reduction of light from half of the candles that had burnt out.

The fireplace sat silent while conversations around the tavern raged on. Willy was marveled by quite a few women in the Barrel.

An enticingly voluptuous creature with sinister blue eyes and succulent red lips walked up to Willy, passing men in awe as they gazed upon her swaying, mesmerizing hips.

Prima Diablo tipped his hat to the lovely representation of the female species, but she grabbed Willy's privates and gently stroked, whispering, "Am I to hear correct that my favorite little marbles are in need of a tender nursemaid? Can I play nurse tonight, for you, Willy?" "Carolina, I am blown away by your beauty and generosity," said Willy.

"If you come upstairs with me, I'll blow you away for a few coins," she replied.

"Carolina, as much as I would love to *sit and have a conversation,* I must not entertain the idea.

I am here on business."

"Can't you spare a speck of time for your favorite lady in Port Royal?" Carolina put on a puss face. "Just a little speck. Come on, just a speck..." She stroked him again, trying her best.

"My apologies, mi lady, I want to do that, you can be sure of it, but I can't."

Ten minutes later, Willy walked downstairs, tying his pants together, a bit of sweat on his brow.

I physically couldn't, anyway, he thought. *After Charlotte's boot... Should've known better.*

"So much for business, Captain," Prima Diablo said.

"Now, ya wouldn't want to go and ruin my good fortunes, would ya?" Willy replied.

"Not at all, Captain," said Prima.

"I asked you to locate Morgan. Where does he take thy company?"
"Follow me, I will show you, Captain," said Prima.

Trudging through an array of bottom dwellers, Willy and Prima found themselves in the back of the tavern staring at a young, chivalrous man, cocksure in his arrogance.

Henry Morgan was a plum-faced brazen lad with long, fluffy, black hair and a thin mustache that assembled into a hook on both sides of his face. One of Port Royal's favorite sons, known for his prominent promiscuity, he had two large-bosomed women seated atop each one of his legs.

"One-Eyed Willy, my God. Lad, are you going to assist an old friend in milking one of these fair ladies? Trust your old friend when I say they are sweeter than a sugar plantation," Morgan said, his eyes wide with pleasure and lust.

"Your honesty comes with authenticity, I am sure; however, my presence is of the nature of business not pleasure, my friend," Willy replied. What he did not say was that having failed at pleasure already one time, that was enough.

He could not try and fail again without losing a handsome coin.

"This brings sadness to my heart and impotence to my ego. Alright ladies, off you go, I have business to attend to." The women got up from his lap and he slapped them both on the ass. They both turned around and said, "Oooh, Henry Morgan! You naughty boy!" Morgan smiled and fixed his mustache into the hooks.

"Willy, come have a seat and share in rum. Wench, two more jugs if you please." Willy and Prima Diablo took a seat at the table with Morgan.

"Henry, you remember Prima Diablo, one of my best riggers?"

"Ah yes, I do. You're the one that drank the last quarter barrel of rum and wound up passing out, pissing yourself a fair fountain there, out in the street? It was a wondrous achievement—I swear it went a full nine feet high! And you were rambling on about being caught in a rainstorm."
"I can't remember, was that before or after we pissed on him?" Willy said and they both laughed aloud as Prima stood by, looking most uncomfortable and agitated.

"Foolery, Prima, foolery. We would never do such a thing," Willy continued as the wench brought over the rum.

"Come, have some rum," Willy suggested.

"I've heard something rather hysterical involving your ship recently." "Really, Henry? And what might that be?" Willy inquired.

"Correct me if I'm wrong, but did you leave Lieutenant Claybourne tied to the docks with a barrel atop his manhood? As I say, perhaps it was but idle make-believe."

"He's a married man and should be mindful of his family," said Willy.

Morgan laughed and said, "Indeed. Well, anyway, it brought me to hysterics." He finished a cup of rum, slammed the vessel down and said, "So, Willy, what brings you to my island? I assume for booty, otherwise you would be on your back with a woman riding you like a horse."

"Indeed, Henry, a booty without measures is what brings me to your shores. A cache so incredibly large we may need two ships to transport it home."

"Two ships? Have you gone mad? Who speaks of such rumors? Two ships for a single haul?" Henry asked. "I never did hear such nonsense!"

"As ludicrous as it sounds, and crazy as I may be, the reconnaissance has proven accurate," Willy replied.

"What say the Kinsmen of the Tide?" asked Morgan.

"We are amassing a fleet off of Isla de Juesos. I have a plan in which you play a very intricate part."

"I wouldn't have it any other way. I've been longing for a haul of this magnitude. How can I be of service?" Henry responded.

"Diablo, go round up the crew and let them know I need them at the ready."

"Aye, Captain. I bid you farewell, Mr. Morgan," said Prima.

"Farewell, Mr. Diablo and be mindful of the rain," said Morgan. Prima Diablo took his leave, whispering curses in Spanish as he walked straight out of the tavern, leaving past memories of drunken stupidity at the table with Morgan and Willy.

"Now, first things first, I am in the market for another ship," said Willy.

"You expect me to believe you are here to purchase a ship?" responded Morgan.

"No, I am going to steal it," said Willy.

"Now that sounds more like the Willy I'm accustomed to. What ship?" asked Morgan as he took a sip of rum.

"The King's Redemption."

Morgan spat the rum out and replied, "I knew it, you *have* gone mad. The Redemption? Willy, you can't be serious."

"Indeed I am, my good friend. The Spanish will be expecting British ships and we are going to give them exactly what they have been anticipating. I will require your aid in acquiring the ship and a few men to assist in its operations. Any chance you are still fancied by the seamstress that works up at Fort Charles? What was the young lady's name again?"

"Patience. Her name is Patience, and contrary to her name, when in the company of yours truly, she demonstrates no restraint whatsoever," Morgan replied.

"Ah, yes, Patience, which is exactly what will be required if we are to be successful on our journey."

"Willy, I'm not quite sure what the nature of the girl's intentions toward me have to do with what we now speak of."

"Let me elaborate. The Spanish are expecting British ships. Therefore, that would require British soldiers. What do British soldiers wear?" Willy asked.

"Uniforms," Morgan answered.

"Outstanding," said Willy.

"Willy, that's brilliant! I will call on her at once and meet you and your crew in three hours' time where the beach touches the road to town."

Staring at the gate to the massive Fort Charles, Morgan appeared without fear in his stature. The gates were like black prison bars stretching all the way to the sky, disappearing in the darkness of the night. A guard marched toward him, each step of his boot crackling against the stone road like a caveman bashing rocks together to light a fire. The guard opened the gate and said, "Mr.

Morgan, the Lieutenant had been expecting you sometime later, but please follow me."

Morgan followed the guard along the stone road with towering walls on both sides, like an open tunnel. The smell of piss and shit from the occupants of the fort was unwelcoming and almost brought Morgan to vomit. Somehow keeping his composure regardless, he climbed two flights of steps, made a right turn and entered an arched doorway. Ten feet past the arch, the guard stopped.

On the left was a large, abrasive, wooden door that was open halfway.

"The Lieutenant is waiting for you. Please enter," the guard suggested to Morgan.

Wandering through the door, straight ahead was Red Hand Nichols, gazing out the window, chewing on a piece of hay and playing with marbles in his hand, as he always did.

The room felt torturously unpatriotic, although an English flag was positioned to the left at the end of the room against the wall. The pine table's size warranted the idea that military meetings were held in the room's center. However, the blood on the floor had confirmed the torturous nature, and the fresh specks of red visible on Nichol's brightly stained hands solidified any questionability. Lieutenant Claybourne was sipping a cup of tea, sitting at the head of the table.

"Mr. Morgan, how swell of you to show up during my interrogation. We had agreed on 11:00 pm, and you are usually far from punctual."

"Willy is here," said Morgan. "That is what brings me here at this hour." Nichols turned his head slowly as if not surprised to hear the news.

"We know that Willy is here. We were just interrogating one of his crew members," said Claybourne.

"Then you already know what I am about to tell you," Morgan replied.

"Not necessarily; that dirty swine wouldn't betray his beloved Captain, and so I beat him good, real good," said Red Hand. "I beat him so bad, I knocked him into the middle of next week."

"Come now, carry on Mr. Morgan. Do tell the news of Willy and his assailants," said Claybourne.

"Lieutenant, Willy is asking for my assistance in stealing the King's Redemption, three dozen

British soldiers' uniforms, and a shitload of gold from Havana."

Sipping his tea, Claybourne looked at Nichols, smiled and said, "Is that all?"

Nichols smiled and said, "Did he mention anything about a jewel? Not just any jewel—a wondrous jewel."

"Nothing of a jewel," Morgan replied. "Not a peep."

"Let him have the ship and the uniforms. We knew he would make his way here. I've been following him," Nichols said.

"I will recall the men on the Redemption and leave a skeleton crew to minimize casualties. You will simply tell Willy that most of the men retired at the Fort for the evening because of training exercises in the morning. I will have the guards fetch you a few dozen uniforms.

"We will release the prisoner and leave him at the bottom of the hill, whereupon you and your men will miraculously find him and bring him back to Willy. You will be candid in your claims that those responsible will be held accountable. We want Willy to believe, without any shroud of a doubt, that you are forthright in your voice. We want the gold and the stone. You will be paid very handsomely for your participation in its acquisition. Any questions?" Claybourne asked.

"Just to be clear, this is *my* island," Morgan insisted, puffing out his chest.

"Yes, Mr. Morgan, I do believe it is," Claybourne replied. "In that, we are agreed. Now, did you have any questions on what I just said? And on the *instructions* I clearly issued?" He carried on regardless of what Morgan had just asserted.

"Then, I understand and will inquire about the jewel inconspicuously. I will get you your gold and retrieve your precious stone."

"Very well, I do believe we have an accord. Mr. Nichols, do you have anything to add?"

"I would be facetious in saying that soaking my fair hands with your blood would bring me discomfort. Do not betray us," said Nichols.

"Then it's settled, Mr. Morgan. The men will be off the ship within the hour," Nichols said. "I'll see you on Isla de Huesos. I fare thee well, gentlemen." And Morgan made his way out of the fort.

An hour later, Willy was waiting with a few of the men at the designated location agreed with Morgan. The sea was rising faster than bread in a brick oven. The lively swarm of patrons who had scampered around the island only a few hours ago were mostly asleep, and the air was satiated with the salt from the sea water and leftover ash from the death of wood by fire.

The drowsy sound of tug of war being played between the sea and the land would be awoken by the decrepitating crackle of lighting and rumbling growl of the thunder.

There was a storm approaching.

"Is everyone accounted for?" Willy asked.

"Everyone except Mr. Connelly, Captain," Devereaux responded.

"Damn you, Connelly! Who was the last one to see Connelly? Anyone? Come on now, I'm not going to do anything rash. Where in God's name is that stupid bastard? Where has he hidden himself? Probably found a nice warm place to sleep, avoiding doing any work. Or he's passed out in an alehouse. Alright, well—we have to find him. No man left behind; you lads know the rules." "I'll go, Captain," Devereaux said.

"Ahoy, Willy!" Morgan shouted with some of his men. Two were carrying Connelly with one of his arms slung over each of their shoulders.

"What in tarnation happened to you, Mr. Connelly?"

"We found him at the bottom of the hill to the fort. Patience was the one who told me it was one of your men. He wouldn't say anything to me," Morgan replied.

"Very well," said Willy as he looked at his crew. "You and you, take Mr. Connelly back to the Revenge to see the doctor," he continued after pointing to two willing crew members.

"You left the doctor on the ship," Morgan said.

"Always do leave the doc on the ship. What good's a drunk doc or a dead doc?" Willy replied. "Well said. I may have to adopt that principle. I do, however, have a bit of good news," Morgan said.

"Aye," said Willy. "What is it?"

"It seems we have been struck with a bit of luck."

"Well, better act on that luck with haste before we are struck with lightning," Willy replied.

"The British have training exercises in the morning, and most of the men on the Redemption have retired to the fort for the evening. It is guarded by only a skeleton crew. Patience was able to retrieve a few dozen uniforms, so I do believe you can take the ship with minimal casualties if you put them to good use."

"Splendid idea, Mr. Morgan, then I believe we can handle the situation."

"I have no quarrel in my mind. As promised, I will immediately send some of my men to assist in the daily operations of the ship and rendez-vous with you on Isla de Huenos," Morgan replied.

"I shall see you later—and please be on time. As time waits for no man, as someone once said."

"Precisely! In four days' time, we will hatch the greatest heist this world has ever seen. Henry, once again, I am in your debt. I bid thee farewell, and good 'morrow," Willy responded.

"Aye, Willy, this time next month, we will be living like kings.

"And for me, it cannot come soon enough. I am tired of living this life of drudgery and hard work. It's a fool's life. So, fare thee well, old friend."

Willy sent five of his men, dressed as British soldiers and one British officer, to relieve the current soldiers on the Redemption.

The five men rowed out through what now were choppy waters with the impending storm. As they approached the ship, the officer on board yelled, "What are you men doing?" "Following orders, sir." Devereaux stood up in the boat and shouted back.

"Whose orders?"

"To replace you and your men. We were told to double shift till the morning," Devereaux replied.

"We'll gladly rest our eyes, but not at the consequence of disobeying a direct order."

"See the lieutenant. He gave us strict orders to relieve the men on the Redemption so they can be prepared for the training exercises tomorrow."

"The lieutenant has changed his mind about having us in the training?" the officer questioned.

"Are you quite sure? We were told we were not needed, and to man and guard the ship here."

"Well, not anymore. That is correct about the training, so you had all best be getting a move on if you want to compete and impress," said Devereaux. "The training needs you all alert and on your best form. And besides, I have heard that three men are most likely to lose their jobs after tomorrow—those who fail to perform their best in the training. There is not sufficient coin to go around. The price of bananas has risen, you see."

The officer's face was a pretty picture of confusion as Devereaux spun his yarn.

His demeanor seemed to say, *bananas? What has the price of bananas to do with anything?*

"Must I spell it out for you, Sire?" demanded Devereaux. "At sea, every gold coin counts and a hundred bananas to feed your gluttonous, lazy crew costs the same as three men's weekly pay."

Once the British crew all faced Devereaux's distraction on one side of the ship by having a discussion with the officer, Willy, Prima and the other men all popped up from under the gloominess of the Caribbean on the opposite side of the vessel.

Willy reached hand over hand with a knife between his teeth, cautiously climbing the other side of the King's Redemption while the remainder of the group simultaneously mirrored the movements of Willy, scaling the largest ship within the English fleet.

With little noise, they scaled the top deck and climbed over the railing, every movement hushed in its action. They crept softly and indistinctly behind the officer and his soldiers.

Meanwhile, Willy and four comrades were arming their pistols.

"Put your weapons on the deck and turn around slowly. Get down on your knees, and do not, I say again, *do not* make any sudden movements," Willy ordered. "If you do, your head shall be severed from your necks by my shot, to become a feast for the seabirds."

And as soon as they did as Willy demanded, Devereaux and the other men in the boats pointed their rifles at the officer and his men.

The officer realised they had been flanked and ordered his men to obey the demands of Willy.

"Fine choice, officer. And as a sign of good faith, I will allow you and your men to live. Now tie them up and gag them, boys; they are coming for an adventure," Willy replied as his men secured the ship. They hoisted anchor and together with Scarlett's Revenge, both began their journey to the island of bones where they had an appointment with the Kinsman of the Tide.

CHAPTER SEVENTEEN

Tranquility grasped the staggering sea in all its illustriousness, and out of the clouds, the sun shimmered its phosphorescent streaks, dazzling the deep blue and wielding intense heat upon the Retribution—a ship known for giving no mercy to any enemy it encountered.

This was as glorious a day as any that had lately dawned.

The black vessel gave new meaning to the word death. At the very tip of the bow stood an angel, crying blood with her wings clipped, and the two decks of cannon bays carried forty-two cannons, from four pounders to nine pounders that each circled the sea craft.

The black sails made for a more frightening display, drilling fear into those who were unfortunate to be boarded by her crew on the open water. As the sun bestowed its ferocity, the mighty gusts of wind were indeed without regret. Sebastian grabbed the bottom of his shirt and wiped the beads of sweat streaming down his face, then clutched a handle to the wheel of the helm.

He heard a squeaking sound coming from behind him, and turned around.

And there, as brazen as anything, he saw a little black monkey eating an apple.

"Blackie, you little thief! I was saving that for lunch," Sebastian said, smiling. "But I suppose you were more hungry than I? I must admit that I was displeased when La Muerte left and took you with him. I have missed your furry little tail scurrying about the ship. Welcome home."

Blackie continued to munch on the apple and gaily chitter to himself as he did, and Sebastian turned around to inhale a deep breath of the finest fresh air.

A disgustingly nauseating picture was suddenly painted on Sebastian's face.

"Ahoy, Sebastian. Good morning!" said Thomas Copperpot who was relieving himself of yesterday's supper in one of the bow boxes. "This air is riveting, isn't it?"

He let loose a tremendous gust of wind of his own, and promptly looked beneath him as though he was a momma bird having laid a new egg that she needed to admire.

Sebastian held his nose and said under his breath, "It *was* riveting air, yes."

Thomas finished his business and wiped himself with an oily rag, pulled up his trousers, then spent a few minutes emptying the boxes before making his way up to Sebastian at the helm. Sebastian was deep in thought, daydreaming and drifting away.

"Mi lady, would you like anything more to eat?"

Looking down at her plate, filled with three chicken legs, and not a speck of meat left on them,

London Jade replied, "No thank you, Sebastian."

The table in the Captain's quarters was filled with meat, fruits, vegetables and desserts. Candles sparkled, setting a mood of romance while the moon glamorized the night through the windows of the ship. "My Sebastian, I am so full, the buttons on my corset may break." "That doesn't sound too terrible now, does it?" Sebastian replied.

"Well, perhaps we may need more wine for that kind of talk," London replied.

"Allow me," said Sebastian as he reached over to fill her glass, but clumsily misjudged, and knocked the glass over. "Oh goodness, my apologies; did it get your dress?" "No, it did not. Here, I will clean it up," said London.

"Nonsense," said Sebastian. "I'm capable of cleaning up my own messes, mi lady, and that shouldn't be your job." She smiled as bright as the moon.

Sebastian grabbed a garment of his own from a nearby chair, leaned over Jade and began to wipe up the wine. "London, may I speak truthfully with you?" "Yes, I welcome it, please," she said.

"You have been the object of my desires for as long as I can remember. Am I being too candid?"

"No, not at all, honestly. There is something I must share with you too, dearest Sebastian. I also find myself fantasizing about you with every free moment."

He asked, "You do?"

She shook her head up and down and stood up with a great smile.

"Then would it be too forward if I..." he said as he put his hands gently on her chin and said, "kissed you at this moment?" She shook her head left to right and Sebastian took her in his arms, tilted her a tiny bit, then went for the kiss.

She was so carried away by the moment and by her passion for him, that she began to strip herself free of her bodice, so overcome with heat was the fair lady.

"Oh, Sebastian, dear! Pray, please assist me out of my constricting clothes..."

"Sebastian," said Thomas Copperpot, aiming for something akin to a response.

Well, he might have hoped, but none came.

"Sebastian," he repeated.

Still nothing but the silence, the wind in the air and the shrieks of seabirds on high.

"Sebastian!" This time, Thomas Copperpot was close enough to Sebastian and smacked him in the face. Coming out of his daydream, he saw how some of the crew were standing around in shock and awe. Sebastian looked down and oddly found he was holding Thomas Copperpot in his arms and immediately dropped him on to the ground.

"What are all you scalawags staring at? You want to kiss my cutlass? Get back to work," he ordered and the men returned back to work as Thomas got up from the deck.

"What the hell was all that about?" Thomas asked. "I swear you were fawning. Weren't dreaming up poetry again, were you? I told you; it's unbecoming to a seafarer."

"Not poetry, no," said Sebastian. "Something else."

"What then?"

"You wouldn't understand," said Sebastian.

"How do you know; you don't even know me! Who were you dreaming about?" asked Thomas.

"If you must know, I was thinking of London Jade."

"I knew it! I knew it! I *knew* you had a sweet spot for her. You're head over heels for that maiden, aren't you?" said Thomas.

Then he looked off into the distance, wistful, and eventually said, "Ahh. I was in love, once." "You were?" Sebastian said.

"Yes. Only the once, mind you. Her name was Henrietta, and her eyes were like an explosion of fireworks. I knew it the first time we met," Thomas replied.

"What happened?"

"She was killed along with my parents on our way to New Amsterdam." "Pirates?" asked Sebastian.

Sara walked up onto the quarter deck and said, "Sebastian, who is your quartermaster?"

"Sara, be quiet for a moment."

The air was still, and now, Sara dared not break the anticipation between the men.

"All I can remember is being taken aboard this ship, and the Captain saying, I was the lucky one. He always kept one person alive to tell a roaring good story. Then for the next three days, *who's jolly? He's jolly. Who's jolly, he's jolly!* was all his men kept singing," Thomas added.

"Are you talking about Jolly Rogers?" asked Sara.

"I don't know? Is that who it was?" said Thomas.

"Yes, I do remember Jolly Rogers. Father used to tell us stories of him all the time."

"Father would say anything to lay your eyes to rest," Sebastian said. "It is what fathers do."

"No, this Rogers gentleman was after a stone. Some kind of *jewel* that had magic powers inside it," Thomas chuckled. "I tell you, he was a strange one if ever I did meet one."

"I know it sounds pretty insane, but I dare say my own father can make anything sound believable," replied Sebastian.

"Anyway, they marooned me off the coast of Cuba, and here I am, three years later," said Thomas in an unusually low voice, as if he believed a wicked person may overhear.

"I'm truly sorry about your parents," Sebastian said.

"Oh dear Lord, whatever happened to them?" asked Sara.

"His parents were murdered by Rogers," said Sebastian. "So much for the *jolly* part... He sounds anything but jolly to me."

"Thomas, my apologies, I didn't know," Sara said, resting a soft warm hand on Thomas' arm.

"Forgive my intrusion. It was so amiss of me to ask so."

"It's fine, it's my loss to bear," Thomas replied. "I am past all that now." He spoke the words but a tremor in his voice said it was not so.

"I am here for comfort if you need," Sara said.

"He doesn't. Now, leave us be for a moment, Sara," said Sebastian.

"Who is your quartermaster, Sebastian?" Sara replied. "That's what I came here to ask."

"SAILS, SAILS, on the horizon," was yelled from the crow's nest. They all looked up and Sara headed to the port side to look while Sebastian made his way to the starboard.

"Sara, get the scope," Sebastian shouted and Sara ran quickly down to the cabin to get the scope, then returned to the quarter deck. She then went to the poop deck to have a look there too. "Sebastian, there are *two* ships," she said. "As plain as day, there they are. I swear it!" "Any flags?" asked Sebastian.

"They are too far out of range for the scope. But as I say—no question, two ships." "Sara, take the helm—I have to go below deck." Sara assumed command of the helm.

"What should I do?" Thomas asked.

"Stay with Sara," Sebastian said, then made haste to the middle deck where he found La Muerte still recovering from his injuries, sleeping on a hammock, accompanied by snores.

Sebastian tapped him and said, "wake up, La Muerte."

La Muerte quickly woke up and instantaneously put a knife to the cheek of Sebastian.

Sebastian calmly pushed his arm away and said, "There are ships on the horizon, La Muerte. I need you on the main deck."

"Give me a moment, and I will be on deck," La Muerte told Sebastian.

Then he returned to the helm.

"Where did you go?" Sara asked.

"To wake La Muerte. We are going to need him. For now, Thomas, I want you to wake anyone who is asleep and tell them to be at the ready. Sara, I want both decks of cannons ready. I want the stern guns especially to be prepared and in good standing to fire. Take Thomas, or anyone for that matter if you need assistance in the cannonball chamber."

La Muerte finally came to the quarter deck and passed Thomas and Sara on their way down.

"Let us have the scope, Sebastian." He climbed up on to the poop deck and had a look.

"Any flags?" said Sebastian.

"No, not yet. I would still load all the guns. Make sure you have the larger cannons to the rear." "Sara, load the nine pounders in the stern's cannons, and be ready to fire," Sebastian yelled.

"Any other thoughts, Muerte?"

"They won't be in range for an hour. C'mon men, ease off the bowline, and don't foul up the main. Everyone carry on about your way and stand at the ready," he replied. "There is to be no

panic nor hurry; hastened tasks are failed tasks. Calm about it as there is time yet." "I must give thanks and gratitude," Sebastian said.

"It's not necessary, you're doing a fine job," Muerte replied.

Meanwhile, across the sea on the ships in question, John Dampier, Henry Morgan's first mate, was at the helm of the King's Redemption, and One-Eyed Willy at the bow of Scarlett's Revenge.

The two British ships were making haste, slicing through the waves like a sharpened cutlass.

The main deck of the Redemption was buzzing, with men fluttering about on the two top decks. Diablo walked past one man who was trimming the main, just as another experienced sailor busied himself about too many tasks at once. He too was appearing calm, the same way La Muerte had hoped for on his own vessel across the heaving, windblown waves.

Diablo continued up the steps to see Willy, a hand on the rail catching himself before he

slipped. He carried on up the steps to the helm, but four feet from the top of the steps, he stopped dead. "What do you make of it, Captain?" he asked in a loud voice, against the wind.

"Well, they are ships, wouldn't you say, Prima?" said Willy as they both gazed upon the horizon and saw the faintest speck of sails. "One maybe two ships, possibly identical."

"Agreed, but what and who, Captain? Have they displayed colors?"

"Not like we could see them at this moment, Diablo, but the answer is no, they have not. They haven't come about, so that could mean one of two things. Either they are pirates and do not want to come about in case it renders them visible to us, or they are not pirates, and are committed to their course. Either way, we will know sooner than we may wonder," Willy replied.

The Captain called for Devereaux who was all the way at the bow, and he yelled back, "Aye, Captain!" He then made great haste across the deck. The sound of the fearsome wind and waves crashing into the ship as they went over swells was like history repeating itself every second.

Up, down. Up, down, resulting in some of the men, even the most experienced sailors among the crew, vomiting uncontrollably off the side of the ship from the roughest night yet.

Devereaux was at the bottom of the steps.

Right next to him, a man was heaving up his guts off the port side to great sound effects.

"First time aboard a ship?" Devereaux said and laughed, seeing how the man was leaning over with his hands gripped onto the side of the ship. His knuckles were white.

The old man lifted his head up, wiped his mouth with his sleeve and said, "Praises for all the rum, ya rapscallion."

Devereaux, already on his way up the steps, turned around and said, "Rapscallion? Well, maybe next time, *this* rapscallion won't invest coin for time spent with Carolina. How about that?" At that moment, Devereaux locked eyes with Willy—who wore a shocked and angered look. "Did you say... Carolina?" Willy inquired.

"No Captain, I said *Sara's vagina*. Who's Carolina? I didn't say Carolina, did I Jackson? I don't know any Carolina. Do you, Jackson? I said Sara's vagina, did I not, Jackson?" His mouth was running away with him, seemingly not knowing when to shut the hell up.

The old man—Toothless Jackson—shook his head left to right and replied, "Sara's vagina.

That's what I heard."

"Not *Carolina's vagina,* then? You are quite sure?" asked Willy, "Because if it was that..."

"Oh, no, Captain. Not Carolina's vagina. No, for sure. It wasn't, was it, Jackson?" stuttered

Devereaux as Captain Willy's eyes bored holes in his own. "I swear I have never been near Carolina's vagina."

"Never been near, eh?" spat Willy. "I thought you knew no Carolina! Try to explain that!"

Devereaux finally made it to the top of the steps, gasping and panting, puffing out, "I think you keep mishearing me, Captain. "I never did say anything like...whatever you thought you heard."

"Hmph!" said One-Eyed Willy. "Well, I shall give you the benefit of doubt. Though on my life, I know not why."

"How can I be of service, Captain?" Devereaux asked, desperate to change the subject and strangely fixing his private parts as though trying to remove an errant mouse from his pants.

"You didn't listen to your old Captain, did ya?" Willy said.

"No Captain, I didn't."

"Serves ya right, for Carolina. I need ya to take the helm while I take a gander out the scope." Willy raised the scope and saw the pirate flag.

"Bloody pirates. I can't read the name on the ship," he said, and snatched the helm from

Devereaux. "I need you to load the forward cannons. We will be in range in a few moments." Sara was at the helm with Sebastian by her side.

She had one hand on the handle of the wheel and the other holding the scope. Sebastian and La Muerte were down in the Captain's cabin together, looking over a map.

"The intentions are to meet off the coast of the westernmost tip of Cuba. So is there any possibility that this ship could be your father?" Sebastian asked.

Thomas Copperpot burst through the door. "Captain, Sara needs you at the helm." They both bolted out the door, up the steps and straight to Sara.

"Sebastian, it's a British ship," she said, and Sebastian snatched the scope out of her hand and had a look. He saw the flag.

"She's right," he said, then handed the scope to Thomas.

"I recommend we initiate an attack and challenge the thought in the not-so-distant future," the Captain said.

"Agreed. Ready the stern. Men, I want those cannons ready at once."

Willy's ship was catching up to the Retribution. "Steady, men. Steady. On my command, I want you to fire."

"Can you read the name of the ship?" Willy then asked Devereaux.

"Not yet, Captain, and it looks as though they are preparing their chase guns."

"Ready the bow chasers, Mr. Devereaux, and get me the name of that ship."

"They have the wind, Captain," Muerte said, implying that the British man-o-war was gaining on the Retribution. "Captain, if we don't fire now and keep them at bay, they will eventually catch up and send us to the locker."

"Sara, is the English flag still waving?" Sebastian asked.

"Aye, Captain."

"Mr. Copperpot, are the stern chasers ready?" said Sebastian.

"Aye Captain, they are," Copperpot confirmed.

"Fire!" Sebastian ordered, and the roar mirrored off the ocean like a strike of lightning, as the Retribution sent a nine-pound cannon ball soaring in the direction of the Redemption.

Willy heard the crackle of the cannon, and Diablo yelled out, "Hard to starboard, Captain, hard to starboard! Hard! Hard!" Willy turned the wheel of the helm as fast as he could, and the cannonball impacted the water with an enormous splash on the port side.

"Are the cannons ready, Mr. Devereaux?" Willy shouted.

Devereaux wiped the sweat off his forehead and looked through the scope one more time, then remarked, "It's the Retribution, Captain. It's the goddamned Retribution!"

No sooner had Devereaux confirmed the sighting, than another crackle of thunder came from the direction of the Retribution.

"Hard to port, hard to port!" Diablo yelled and the cannonball pounded into the ocean to the right of the bow, jolting the ship and everyone on board.

"Devereaux, do we have a black flag?" Willy asked. "I have not laid eyes on it myself."

Devereaux placed his hands on his pockets—first the front, then the rear, and said, "Well, bugger it; I forgot the paint, the brushes, *and* the black flag."

The Captain called for Diablo, who ran to the helm. "Yes, Captain?"

"Remove your pants."

"Apologies, Captain, I don't understand?" Diablo answered as he looked around him, bemused, if not to say more than a little worried. He had heard of some funny goings-on aboard ships, and when pants were removed, it was rarely a good outcome for the one whose ass waved in the wind. "I don't need you to *understand*. I just need your pants. Now!"

Diablo removed his pants and sent up a silent prayer for his ass.

Muerte requested a moment with Sebastian and they both left the helm and walked down the steps, speaking privately amongst themselves. "Why are they not returning fire? Something isn't right here," said Muerte. "I mean, surely they would fire. Wouldn't they?"

"Maybe they are waiting 'till we are closer," Sebastian answered. "Maybe their eyes are bad." It was not the time for jesting—and no one laughed except for Sebastian.

"No, I have outrun a man o' war before, and they just kept unloading the stern cannons." "Is there still an English flag displayed?" Sara yelled.

She removed her hand off the helm and looked through the scope, whereupon she saw a black flag. She wiped her eye and the scope, and looked through again.

Yes, definitely black but the most peculiar shape indeed.

"That's the strangest thing, Sebastian! It appears to be a black flag now, Captain," she said.

"I knew it, I knew it," Muerte said.

"Stand fast men, stand fast, and Muerte, find out who's on that ship," Sebastian ordered.

"It's Sara, Captain, she is at the helm of the ship," Devereaux confirmed.

Willy, eyes full of relief, said, "Prepare to pull alongside the Retribution and board."

"Aye, Captain."

Diablo tapped Willy on the shoulder. "Captain, may I have my pants back now?"

"Somebody get Diablo's pants down; he looks like he is getting cold," laughed Willy. "God help him if a frost sets in!"

The sun was setting on the Caribbean and the sky had colors more beautiful than the newest fashions in Europe's fashion centre of gay Paris.

Death's Retribution and the King's Redemption pulled alongside each other.

"Ahoy, Sebastian," said Willy.

"Ahoy, Father." Willy and a few of the crew crossed over to the Retribution.

"Where is my lovely Captain of a daughter?" Willy asked.

Sara greeted her father with a hug and a kiss on the cheek and said, "Ahoy, Father. To be fair,

I wasn't the Captain."

"My Sara, your beauty has the sky jealous, I'll tell you that," Willy remarked.

"I agree with you, Captain," Thomas said.

"Oh, Father, you're simply too kind. Sebastian gave me the job of sail master." "Muerte is the quartermaster. Why is the spy not in chains?" said Willy.

"Father, if it wasn't for La Muerte, we could have kept firing. He knew it was you. Don't tell me how he knew, but he knew," Sebastian said.

"Is this true, Muerte?" asked Willy.

"Captain, I won't stand here and take the credit for the impressive work done by your children. I would be proud if I were you, and *I* am proud to call them friends," Muerte replied.

"This is welcoming news from you, Muerte. We will see where your loyalty lies soon enough." Willy turned and faced the crews of the ships, yelling, "Are we ready? Are we all ready to get some booty?"

The crews on all the ships yelled, "ARRR!"

"Thomas, good of you to come along. I do like a lad that is not afraid to get his hands dirty and fight to the death," Willy said.

Thomas clenched his throat and said, "To the death?"

His voice was so plaintive, he sounded like a little boy.

"Aye, or would ya rather walk the plank?" Willy said. "Tis your choice, And pray, find your balls while you are at it. You sound—squeaky. Like the ship's rat."

A moment passed in which Thomas quivered and thought over the offer.

"No, I'll fight," replied Thomas, evidently having found his testicles in the interim.

"Good, my boy, and make sure you be staying away from mi daughter, or you'll be shark bait, you scalawag. Keep your trousers buttoned up."

"Aye, Captain," said Thomas. "Of course, Captain."

"Why don't you ask the Captain what you wanted to ask him?" Sebastian suggested.

"No, that's quite alright. It's not necessary—he has much to do."

"No, go ahead, he is very cheery on this fine day."

"Come out with it, boy. Well, go on, we haven't got till dawn," Willy ordered.

"Well, Captain… I wanted to be a part of the crew."

"Thomas, if you don't ask me a question, I'm going to toss you overboard," Willy said. "You didn't hear me. I asked…"

"My patience is running thin, boy. What's the real question? I have not yet heard one."

"I want to be part of the crew," Thomas yelled in as manly a voice as he could muster.

"Part of my crew, do ya? Is that a question, lad? Well, blow me down. In my books, it is no such thing. To be part of my crew, you have to earn the right. Ye haven't earned the right. Ye have not even earned *half* the right! After the war, if you're not dead—which you will be, but if you're not, and you show me heart—only then, when I feel you deserve it, will I make ya part of my crew. If I were you, I wouldn't be getting my hopes up. This is your chance, Tommy, my boy, so don't

part with it and get those foolish notions out of your thick skull."

"I won't fail you, Captain. I will show you, I promise," said Thomas, and as he walked away, he smiled and looked up at the stars.

He was sure the Captain had said yes to him, albeit in a round-about way.

CHAPTER EIGHTEEN

A few days earlier, somewhere outside the city of Santiago, the Governor of New Spain and Robert Perkins sat down to hold a meeting on a secluded beach. The crest of the ocean waves was like a barrel of fresh ale filled with foam. Robert Perkins and four of his mercenaries made land on a sandy beach outside the eccentric town of Santiago, Cuba, and couldn't be more grateful for the magnificence of this particular day. The sands were as white as snow and hotter than a pot of tea, basking in rays of the sun from dawn till dusk. Hermit crabs scuttled for shade as the men baked.

The hot glow gently touched the surface of the sea water, turning it to the color of emeralds.

Robert Perkins had spared no expense with his participation in the capture of the largest treasure in the Spanish Main. He not only had One-Eyed Willy, Capitan De La Muerte and Blackheart in pursuit of this literal gold mine, but he had also requested the assistance of Richard 'Red Hand' Nichols, another fierce buccaneer who was known to enjoy a bit of plundering.

He was also known to wear a brown hat with a red feather, and they called him Red Hand for all the blood he spilled with his bare hands.

He was the Captain of the Red Diamond, a rare but savage ship with a cut-throat crew.

Perkins, Mr. Nichols and two of their associates walked across this desert oasis in the Caribbean toward a white tent where waited ten soldiers in their blue uniforms on the right and left, facing each other. Perkins and company walked between the soldiers, then entered underneath the tent.

And lo and behold, there, sitting in a chair with his legs crossed and dressed in an all-white suit with a white overcoat, was Francisco Gonzales, the Governor of New Spain.

He wore a wig and had a black-grayish beard, similar to that of salt and pepper sprinkled together. Placed on the table next to Mr. Gonzales were a cigar and matches.

Also, in a basket was a selection of apples, mangoes, oranges, bananas and fresh strawberries.

Two glasses and a bottle of a new sparkling wine, called Champagne, sat in the table's middle.

"I was unsure if you were a fan of Dom Perignon's invention, so I took the opportunity of bringing a single fine bottle just in case. Have you tried this concoction before?" the Governor asked, brandishing the bottle in the air as if he might hit Perkins about the head with it.

"Actually, I have Governor, and it is most marvelous," said Perkins.

"I'll tell you something very interesting about his invention. It tastes even more amazing with certain fruits," said Governor Gonzalez. "Have you tried that too?"

His face seemed to say, *I hope you have not, as I have something to show you!*

He got the answer he desired when Perkins responded, "I have not tried that, Governor."

Gonzalez picked up a knife and cut the orange in half, then, after waving the knife around in a lethal manner again, he began speaking once more to Perkins.

"All you have to do is cut the orange and squeeze a little juice in. It's paradise in the morning," he said. "Paradise, I tell you!" And he proceeded to add the fresh orange to the two glasses.

Gonzales wiped his hands with a towel, then poured Champagne into the glasses.

"On this particular day, I choose to have it because I am an opportunist, and when great opportunity comes to fruition, it deserves of a toast. Would you not agree?"

"Indeed, Mr. Governor, and I should tell you that all the pieces are in place. The plan is going as you expected," Mr. Perkins replied. "And the drink smells…as if from the gods themselves."

"That is phenomenal news, Robert. About all the pieces being in place, I mean. Not about the smell of the Champagne, though I am sure that is quite extraordinary too. Should we have any unexpected problems, I presume we are all prepared to address them swiftly and harshly."

"What problems could you mean, Sire?" Perkins replied as he sipped his Champagne. "There are no problems with my drink, Sire. It's glorious!"

It seemed the Governor's drink was already going to his brain.

Gonzales sliced another half of an orange and started to peel it.

"By *problems*, I am not referring to the Champagne. Not by a long chalk. Robert, let me not dally and dither about the subject. My sources tell me that One-Eyed Willy stole a man o' war not too long ago and that he is amassing a fleet of ships? Does this alarm you?"

The Governor, with knife in hand, pointed to one of his soldiers who whistled and a dozen more men surrounded the tent. Perkins began to perspire, then clenched his throat. The Governor stood and walked around to Perkins, waving and pointing the knife while he spoke.

"To be more specific, I am told that ten destroyers have arrived in Port Royal from Charlestown and one of the ships that Willy stole was the King's Redemption. Do you add any validity to these claims? This probably doesn't unnerve you because you think you have it all under control. Might my assumption be correct?"

He watched Robert Perkins' Champagne glass begin to tremor in his hand.

"Robert, do not let me put you off your drink. It's awfully expensive. I should hate for you to drop it."

But Perkins' hand only jittered all the more.

Gonzales, with the knife in his right hand, put his palms on Perkin's shoulders. Perkins clenched again as the Governor leaned into his ear and continued speaking.

"Don't you understand, Robert? I've let you operate your little pirate business in my seas without consequence because of *our relationship*. A relationship built on trust."

Gonzales stood straight up and walked around the table and continued to talk.

"So, before you take another sip of my Champagne—that which you do not spill all over your fine breeches—and we toast to this glorious opportunity, I need to know if I can trust you. *Can I* trust you, Robert?"

"Yes of course, Sire."

"Then, there is something I need you to do for me. Have you heard of this pirate they call

Blackheart?"

"Yes, I have heard of him in stories. No one has seen this man in years." Robert looked at 'Red Hand' and said, "Am I correct?"

"You're absolutely correct, Mr. Perkins," Red Hand replied.

"Is that so? My sources said he arrived in Portobello as of only two days ago. Recruiting men and looking for supplies for his ship. A very *large* ship, might I add. My sources say it was an English ship that belonged to an *English*man. They say this ship is near indestructible. The manifest has your name as owner of this ship but there must be some terrible mistake, correct? Because you would not have the remotest idea of how your name came to be on that ship's papers... Indeed, it is most curious how two men could have the same name. But there we are." "Mr. Gonzalez, I c..." Perkins replied.

"Ah, ah, ah, Robert, now! I implore you to contemplate your thoughts before you respond. I'm terrified that the wrong response could forego all this opportunity, and instead of drinking the Champagne, I'll be pouring it out for the fallen warriors we have lost on the sea of opportunism.

And let me say too, I can think of a use for this rather large bottle when it is empty."

Perkins considered his words carefully and then proclaimed, clenching his ass cheeks tightly for good measure, "Sire, I have acquired the services of Blackheart to merely destroy the ambitions of One-Eyed Willy. I figured I could send you some reinforcements and I thought the ten destroyers would help secure Havana in the event one of them decides to get greedy and attempts to flee with our fortune. Basically, Governor, sir, kind sir, I was trying to protect our investment."

"Well, protect your investment this way. The Governor of New Britain will think the reinforcements are for the gift to the newlyweds of the crown and shall truly be oblivious to our plan. Willy will never make it to Portobello. I have Red Hand and Blackheart for that."

"Sire, the New World will be ours."

The Governor slammed the knife on the table, sending a shockwave through the spine of every man in that tent, including his own.

He started clapping and said, "Very well said, Mr. Perkins, I am indeed astonished. You do realize I am an extremely intelligent man? You do understand that my trust in you has grown paper thin, do you? You will need to prove to me that I can trust you. *Can* you prove it?"

"Yes, Governor."

"And do you trust me?"

Perkins played into his trap and said, "Yes, Governor, with my life."

The Governor looked up in the air, and—waving his finger—turned around and said, "Ah yes, that is it, that is exactly what I wanted to hear."

"However do you mean, Sire?" Perkins replied.

"Let me show you. Put this Champagne bottle on top of your head," Gonzales asked and grabbed a pistol from one of his soldiers.

Perkins said, "Pardon me, Sire? The…the Champagne bottle?"

"Robert, I thought we were building trust. Do you trust me to do it with you or should I rather call for one of your soldiers?"

"One of my soldiers, by all means. Edward, come sit down in Mr. Gonzales's seat." Edward left his post and walked over to sit in the seat.

"Edward, I've done this before. I would firstly put the white cloth on top of your head; we wouldn't want the glass and the Champagne bottle—which will be blown to kingdom come—to cut you up and go all over you now, would we?" the Governor said.

The Governor faked a laugh and Edward did as the Governor asked.

"Edward, I am going to take three steps, turn around and count to three. You will note I am an excellent marksman trained by the King's

Guard. Mr. Perkins, you may want to move your own chair slightly to the right."

Perkins followed the commands of the Governor, shifting his chair a little.

The Governor loaded the pistol with one bullet, took three baby steps, and turned around.

"Alright, Edward, one! Two!"

And he pulled the trigger, missing the bottle and shooting Edward in the back of the head. An explosion of blood, vile brain matter and shattered pieces of yellowy skull spattered everything that had been white in the tent, including Robert Perkins.

"If this man were anything like me, he wouldn't trust anyone. I didn't trust you, Robert, nor do I trust you now. What I did trust was for you to do exactly what you've done. Draw Blackheart out of hiding and have him feud with Willy. Conjure up a British fleet and use their ships to trap whoever stole the treasure. These are the things that I trusted you to do, and you haven't let me down. Rest assured, the second you do..."
The Governor grabbed his glass from the table and handed it to Robert; they both had blood on them. Gonzales clinked Roberts's glass and took a sip of Champagne. He picked up the bottle and poured the rest out.

"The second you do, Robert, we won't be sipping Champagne together like your friend here, missing half his brain because he trusted you. Now get out of my sight."

As Robert Perkins had his long walk down to the beach with three men instead of four, another ambitious man emerged from the other side of the dunes to speak with Mr. Gonzales.

"Mr. Governor, it's unfortunate you have such an array of disloyal people around you," said Henry Morgan.

"The words you speak are discomforting but are, in fact, real, Mr. Morgan. It would seem you can't trust anyone in the new world," replied Gonzalez.

"I disagree, sir. I believe in earning people's trust, and I'm inclined to say I will achieve yours," Morgan exclaimed.

"Is that so? How do you plan on making my trust, Captain Morgan?" Gonzales asked sternly.

"Well, for starters, I brought you your share of the raid on Spanish merchant ships minus the rum, of course. And One-Eyed Willy reached out to me just like you said he would." Morgan picked up an apple, had a bite, and continued.

"He wants me to help him steal the treasure," said Morgan.

Gonzales laughed and said, "That's precisely what you're going to do. I want to be informed every step of the way."

"Sire, I will divulge into the most intricate pieces of his plan and relay the information directly," said Morgan.

"You know what, Henry, I think you're right. It does appear I can trust you," Gonzales said.

"You can, Sire. The proof will be laid right before your eyes," Morgan replied.

"Excellent! And if you betray me, I'll string you up for the world to see what a pirate's life could be. Now get out of my sight. Cayette, *andele, andele*," said Gonzales.

"Thank you, Sire. You won't regret it," said Morgan, then he turned around and walked off the beach.

A week later, on the Cayman Islands, Blackheart arrived on a lonely island with two English warships languishing in its harbor. On land, tents had been set up along the beaches for the use of soldiers. Upon reaching the shore, he was welcomed by four English soldiers pointing muskets in his face, and one robust soldier asked, "What is your business here?"

"I am here as liaison to Robert Perkins with urgent news for the Governor," Blackheart quickly replied, and the soldier ordered the men to lower their guns and help Blackheart ashore.

The soldiers were all wearing godawful red uniforms—the white pants mixed with the red coats was why they were nicknamed *lobsters*.

The tallest of the *lobsters* said, "Well don't just stand there, you dumb pirate, get moving." Three guards gathered three torches and escorted Blackheart through the jungle.

The crickets were as loud as pistols firing and bounced off the innocence of the jungle. The path was barely wide enough for two people, and they were constantly pushing branches and stalks out of the way to proceed. The random hissing from the snakes and the high-pitched cries from bats were terrifying, but had little effect on the soldiers—they just kept on walking down this dark trail to possible death, for all Blackheart knew.

Up ahead, Blackheart noticed lights emerging through the density, which were two torches burning either side of brick stanchions and between them, a gate. The rock walls that ran along the sides of the pathway were six feet high and stretching for what appeared to be a thousand feet.

At the end of this corridor was a property unlike any other, and from it, you could see for miles. The grass was as green as pea soup with rose bushes throughout the grounds.

To the left was a stable full of horses, while straight ahead was the monstrosity of a mansion, with neatly trimmed hedges leading toward the castle.

"I quite fancy the smell of roses. How about you, gentlemen?" said Blackheart, but there was no response from the soldiers. "These are some mighty acceptable grounds and must cost a fortune to maintain," Blackheart continued. "Good God. Think of all that upkeep!" "More walking and less talking, swine," the tall guard suggested.

"We British are friendly, are we not?" Blackheart replied as they walked up the steps.

The guards stopped and doused their torches while two other soldiers who had been guarding the front door opened it up. Blackheart entered right in as Oliver Hamilton walked down a beautiful marble staircase. The paintings lining the walls were of an exceptional standard, along with the whitewood trims fitted throughout the house.

The paint on the walls themselves looked fresh, smelling brand new.

The colors were different in every room, like those of a rainbow after a thunderstorm.

"Mr. Blackheart, welcome to my home away from home, so to speak. You are just in time for the entertainment. I am sure you enjoy a bit of a fun-filled time now and then?" said Hamilton.

"Yes, Mr. Governor sir, I do like to be entertained. Unfortunately, though, Mr. Perkins sent me here on business." Oliver Hamilton was just as ruthless as a king.

Standing only five feet, seven inches tall, his ego towered over everyone in the new world— especially in his smart day attire, as he was on this day. He was generally thin but clean-shaven, wearing black shoes, all white pants, and a shirt with a blue overcoat.

The man dressed and acted as if he was royalty. One interesting fact about this evil, shameful man, was that he had a mole underneath his nose to the left side, right above his lip. He would often lick this attention-grabbing black hairy mountain when deep in thought.

"I am quite sure you are here on the business of Robert Perkins," said Hamilton.

"Sire, it is about the plan. The plan has changed, sir." "Yes, Mr. Blackheart, I am aware there is a change of plan." "Ok, Sire, so what *is* the change of plans?" asked Blackheart.

"I insist. You first, senor Blackheart," he replied.

"With all due respect, Governor, I think you should go first." Hamilton contemplated, licked his mole, and yelled for Newhardt.

Newhardt entered from a different room.

"Mr. Newhardt, this is Mr. Blackheart. Can you please escort him to the study? I had better check if Reginald has readied the tea. Tea, Mr. Blackheart?" Hamilton asked. "I'd be most obliged, Mr. Governor, sir." "Very well," said Hamilton.

Newhardt escorted Blackheart to the study where there were more books on the shelves than to be found in a library. Wooden chairs with soft cushions adorned the middle, and there were plenty of fat cigars on the table. Hamilton came back in and said, "Reginald will only be a moment and as you were saying, Mr. Blackheart?"

"I wasn't, Sire. I was awaiting your venerable response," Blackheart answered.

"You see, Newhardt. These locals and their manners never cease to amaze me. I'd given the gentleman a moment to collect his thoughts and realize maybe he was stepping out of line with his statements. Well, I guess we will have to cut off one of his ears, and I do believe he will hear me this time." Mr. Hamilton called for the guards and two rushed in.

"Mr. Hamilton, my apologies. I meant no harm; I have news for you," Blackheart quickly said.

"News for me? You hear that, Newhardt? Oh, what a delight to hear, this is wonderful. Proceed with the information?" Hamilton replied as Reginald entered.

Reginald gently set the tea down on the table and asked, "Will there be anything else, Sire?"

"We are good for now Reginald; you have my gratitude. Excuse the interruption Mr.

Blackheart, you may proceed," said Hamilton.

"Perkins plans to double-cross the Spanish Governor and steal the gold for the crown, sir."

"Why, whomever would he get that brilliant idea from? You see, Mr. Blackheart, the Spanish King and his reign here in the Caribbean will soon be coming to an abrupt end.

"The magnitude of value with this capacity of gold would cause significant disruption and damage to the port of Havana, that is without measure. Ponder it as a dagger to the heart of the Spanish economy. The destruction of ships and goods, and the removal of almost all the gold in New Spain, is certainly going to be most detrimental—if not to say, a death knell—to the collapse of Spain's trade infrastructure here in the new world. Why do you think we have ten ships on their way to Port Royal? Half of the armada is currently in pursuit of One-Eyed Willy's ship, the Inferno.

"One of my agents spotted Willy running out from the back of your house just last week. Also, what are your plans in Portobello? I understand you stopped there for not even a day, and then you made haste to see me. The Governor of New Spain's reach is not that good. And we have spies everywhere; we are that good, John. John Ramos from Portobello, Panama. Brother of the late Louisa Ramos, father and husband—now, what say you? Shall I go on?

"Need you to hear more?

"Now, fine and esteemed Mr. Blackheart, that is the plan, England will become the empire of the new world, starting right here in the Caribbean. Yes, right here! I even venture to say, right here in this very room!" Hamilton concluded with a giant waft of his arm around the room.

Blackheart, with a look of shock, said, "Bravo, I am impressed you have researched my family. It seems you have everything figured out already. If that be the case, you would presumably already know where the gold is?"

"Of course, I know where the gold is, and you're going to load it all on your ship and bring it directly to me," said Hamilton. "And then I can do with it whatever I like."

"Now why would I do that, Mr. Governor?"

"Because I have the Spanish Governor in my pocket, and Mr. Perkins, they will do whatever I command. So it works like this. You do whatever I command to avoid my wrath. And I command whatever I like for that very same reason—for you to avoid my wrath. You follow thus far?

"I admit it may be a difficult concept for one such as you to grasp, Mr. Blackheart.

"But let us be clear—Mr. Gonzales knows his strength here in the new world is diminishing, so he and Perkins want to get a nice little nest egg and retire on an island—maybe *this* island, who knows? All I *do* know is they will be rich, and you can also be a rich man, Mr. Blackheart.

"Or you can be a very sorry man. Take your pick. Now, what's it to be?"

"I am going to be a rich man, thank you, Sire. Perkins knows my price," Blackheart replied. "Ah, yes, the entertainment for the evening. Guards, bring in our guest of honor!" "I don't understand," Blackheart replied.

The Governor of New Spain walked into the room casually. He picked up a candle and lit his cigar, then placed the candle back down, drawing in on the cigar as the smoke rose high.

He burst out in a dreadful, sputum-filled coughing fit that took a full minute to cease.

Finally, he managed to gather himself again.

"Hello John, it's been quite some time?" he said and blew out the candle.

Blackheart's heart started racing; he was very anxious and had shortness of breath, then the memories hit him, and it turned into anger, rage, and excitement.

Hamilton asked Blackheart, "Is this not the man who callously did destroy your life? The very orchestrator of the hideous murder of your entire family? Your wife and daughter's parents, whom you love, fell victim to the hands of this coward. I will give you an option of how you want to kill this man. Slowly and harshly, or quickly and mercifully? You will choose how he dies."

"Neither slowly nor quickly, Mr. Governor," Blackheart replied, pleased to come up with another option in his own mind. A better option by far.

"Why is that, senor?" replied Hamilton.

"Because I want it to be long *and* painful!" said Blackheart.

Gonzales laughed, took a puff of his cigar, and with a smile said to Blackheart, "Ah, but did you know that your family is still alive?"

"Ooooh, and the plot thickens; I love a good love story," said Hamilton.

"Don't you lie to me," Blackheart said as he attempted to grab hold of Gonzales, but the guards grabbed him and held him back.

"No, I'm joking—or am I not joking? Of course, I'm not joking about something so serious. I am telling the absolute truth to you. They are still working on a plantation.

"They always laugh and cry without you. They have beautiful dresses and are very well taken care of. They don't need you anymore. It's been so many years. I am a monster, I will admit, but I did not kill your wife and daughter. I tell you what, you make sure we get our gold and you will get your girls in return," said Gonzales.

"Tell me where they are, right now!" Blackheart shouted.

"Barbados, where they have always been, just on a different plantation."

"And my sister?" inquired Blackheart. "She is there too?"

"They are all there, I can assure you. This is a favor for which Francisco has been in debt to me for years, now. They will return to you safely when my gold returns to me in the very same manner," said Hamilton. "A fair trade, wouldn't you say?"

"I see how you hold all the cards, don't you?" Blackheart replied.

"I cannot deny it. I've been dealt a really good hand in life, unlike our mutual enemy Cyclops and his band of miscreants," Hamilton said.

"And what of Willy?" Blackheart asked.

"He deserves to die painfully," said Hamilton.

"And Gonzales?" Blackheart said.

"Oh yes, don't we all wish our dreams would come true in a fell swoop? Unfortunately, that cannot be as I need him for this whole *take over the Caribbean* thing, so you won't be touching him. Unless, of course, you bring me my gold. There is no need for any more conversation. Just get me my gold," said Hamilton. "Chit chat never won a war yet."

"One more thing, Mr. Governor. Where will the exchange be?" Blackheart questioned.

"Exchange?"

"Yes, exchange. I want my family, and you want your gold. Where is this taking place? Clearly, I would wish to set eye upon my family before I give the gold."

"Ah, indeed. How rude of me. Well, how about two weeks from to-morrow? What more poetic a setting than your hometown of Portobello, Panama? Now off your go. Fetch me all my gold or your family dies a second time," Hamilton said and licked at his repugnant hairy mole.

Blackheart departed the Governor's mansion and was escorted back to the beach by the guards, then members of his crew rowed back to the ship where Claude and Raul were eagerly waiting.

"What did he say?" asked Raul.

"He has a message for Mr. Perkins and wants you to come ashore," Blackheart said.

"This is a lie. No, I don't believe you. It doesn't smell true. It stinks of a rat."

"Look, have it your way. We can't waste any time. If you want to be like that, I will go back ashore and tell the Governor of New Britain you refused to come ashore," said Blackheart, "And

that's that. I haven't all day to stand chin-wagging like two old maids."

"No, wait, we will go," said Claude.

"Claude, he is lying," Raul insisted. "Please, let's not go. It smells most foul to me."

"And what if he is not lying? I'm not willing to take the risk. Go, we must."

"Can the two of you hurry up and go, in that case? I want us to be on our way. We have pirates to kill," said Blackheart. "Some of us have work to do."

Claude and Raul got into the rowboat and began rowing toward land. Once they reached more than halfway, Blackheart yelled for the men to *hoist anchor.*

Once the brothers noticed the anchor being hoisted, and attempted to turn the boat around but it was too late. They were yelling for them to stop, but Blackheart was laughing as they sailed away into the moonlight.

Back at Hamilton's mansion, both Governors were in deep conversation.

"You are going to let them take the gold, Francisco, or you will never see Louisa again," said

Hamilton. "Think about it. Be sensible."

"I am beginning to think this is a dictatorship, not a partnership. I know the extent of my position and what is warranted of me. Do you know yours?" asked Gonzales.

"Are you questioning my ability to execute a plan?" demanded Hamilton. "Perhaps One-Eyed Willy would like to know that his wife is alive and well. You came to me, remember, Mr. Gonzales, not the other way around. It's you who has lost control. Regardless, we must make sure that some of the gold makes its way back to the mainland for the wedding to avoid suspicion.

"On that topic, what news from the old wreckage of the Atocha?" Hamilton asked.

"My men were able to salvage almost twenty barrels of gold, silver, and stones.

"Twenty big barrels, too, not half-barrels, Sire! And it weighs so much, I swear the bottom did almost fall out of our ship when we picked it up! The ship, she heaved and she groaned...

"It took four-hundred men to retrieve that amount—*four hundred*, I say!—and still, there is more but a storm was approaching," explained Gonzales. "We were almost at risk of becoming a wreck ourselves, I say. But luckily, good fortune smiled upon us and we made it back."

"This is splendid news, Francisco. I knew this partnership would be filled with fortune. As I was saying, One-Eyed Willy will be kept under discretion. The only family that will be waiting in the bay of Portobello is Blackheart's. To ensure your cooperation, Louisa will be brought along just as a precautionary measure. I'm sure you understand?" said Hamilton.

"I do indeed comprehend the nature of your delicate negotiations and find similarities in my processes. Governor, I knew you'd act familiarly, and so did I. Yet, unlike you, it is for the mutual benefit of us both," Gonzales said. "I knew that two fine men as we are, could reach an agreement in which we *both* reap a pretty reward."

"Is that so? I beg your pardon, senor, but if you may enlighten me as to what you mean?" Hamilton asked. "I am aware the Spanish galleon with most of my gold and a small percentage of yours, is on its way to Lima, Peru. Why on earth would you let hundreds of millions of gold coins and bullion just sail around the world—and you not even be with it?

"As I said before, sir, are you out of control? This is disappointing news, Francisco, and yet again, you have underestimated my ability to procure information. I knew you would pull a foolhardy stunt like this, so to ensure my gold's safety, I have enlisted the services of the most feared pirate in the history of the Caribbean. He will make sure your Louisa is safe," said Hamilton. "Who could you possibly have hired that I don't already have in my pocket?" said Gonzales.

"Well, Francisco, you see… This pirate will not accept money. This pirate will travel to the ends of the earth to find that which he desires the most," Hamilton replied.

Gonzales had a sip of wine and sarcastically said, "Who are you speaking of, Jolly Rogers?" "Precisely," said Hamilton.

Gonzales spat out his wine with laughter.

"Now, who's gone mad? We've all heard the stories, but who has seen the man or his ship? Who has ever set his two eyes—or even his one eye—upon this Jolly Rogers fellow? He is a ghost, the original pirate, a myth! An old wives' tale, a bedtime story that they tell children to make them sleep—a total make-believe!"

"So, you remember what they said about his ship, the Incinerator? It could breathe fire like a dragon. Anyone who wasn't crew and who tried to touch the ship would be incinerated with flames," said Hamilton. "You remember that too, do you, Governor? Go on, laugh—laugh if you must! And we shall see who is still laughing in due course!"

Gonzales laughed again wildly, slapping at his knees in mirth. Fat tears of laughter ran down his wobbling cheeks. He took another great glug of wine.

"Oh my goodness, oh…" He clutched at his gut. His sides were splitting from all the laughing. "I swear you must have been drinking in a tavern all day to come out with such nonsense! But it pleases my ear as I have not laughed so much in many a year! What a hoot. What a jolly jape!"

"But they are stories, only stories, Oliver! Jolly Rogers, my ass! Look…"

He leaned in closer and made as if to whisper, as though he was saving Hamilton's skin.

"My good man, Hamilton… I have a few extra men on my payroll if you are in such dire need of need the assistance," Gonzales suggested as he continued to laugh and slap at his own legs in merriment. "Jolly Rogers…oooh, haa! I will do you a discount for my men. Oooh, haa!" Hamilton, with an angered look on his face, called for his guard.

And in through the doors to the study walked the most horrific sight ever gazed upon.

The man's beard was thick, grayish-black with insects buzzing around it, and he had teeth that rivaled that of a skeleton. Only now and then, a gleaming gold tooth did shine forth—misshapen and ugly all the same, but gold nonetheless and forced into the gap where his own had fallen out.

Rogers wore a black hat with skull and crossbones on the front, and an old dirty gray overcoat with a black shirt and black pants that stopped at his knees.

The red socks were the same color of the blood spattered on the satchel across his chest.

His cutlass was secured through his belt on the right side, and it reeked of stagnant death.

It was as though you were looking at a real ghost. The pirate approached the left side of Gonzales, had a gander at the Governor and said. "So, you been telling pirate stories? See, there's a history between us that you couldn't possibly imagine, Mr. Gonzales. See, we do know each other through mutual acquaintances. My son, Jacob Rogers, was your first officer when you were a captain scouring the Caribbean and burning villages."

"Jacob Rogers was your son?" Gonzales said with the most daunting look. His jaw hung open.

"Yes, he was my son, and later became a captain on one of your ships. This particular ship got raided and torched. The stories in the papers were that the cargo caught fire and the ship burned and sank. The Captain and his men sank to the depths with Davey Jones.

"How come I find out just a short time ago that the Captain lived to tell the tale—and we as pirates know dead men tell no tales..."

Rogers grabbed a cigar and a match, lit it off Gonzales' leg, and smiled when Gonzales ran out of the room, intimidated and terrified. A cold breeze followed him out, so fast had he shifted, as if he had seen a ghost with his very own eyes. His bones almost clattered, he was so afraid.

"Keep an eye on that one for me, Mr. Jolly, and please make sure he does what he is told," Hamilton said with a wry smile that seemed to stretch out from ear to ear.

"That will not be an issue. Now, Willy and Blackheart will be at the designated place at the designated time, am I correct? I look forward to incinerating both of them with the utmost pleasure. An eye for an eye." Rogers guffawed, a long and deep laugh that shook the room.

"I will ensure they are, Mr. Rogers, and if that is the case, you will be a wealthy man. You know William and I have a history, and I actually gave him that name, 'One-Eyed Willy' back at

Kings', some twenty plus years ago," said Hamilton. "Did you know that?"

"I don't want yer spoils, Mr. Governor, nor do I want your stories. These are the only three things I want in this world. I want blood. I want my revenge. And most of all, I want my jewel back. They killed my son, and they will pay dearly for that. They will never see their families; they will die long before they're with them. But let them believe what they wish…" "And Gonzales, you will kill him and Louisa as well?" Hamilton said.

"If you wish me to do so, it will be done. Louisa has something that belongs to me. My son was going to give to his fiancée what my wife gave to him before she passed.

"They stole it, and I want it back," Rogers answered.

"Aha, the jewel of the Spanish Main? How do you know she has it?"

"Just call it a feeling of pirates' intuition. Just make sure everyone plays their part, Mr. Governor, and I will play mine. If you dare try to use me as you used these pawns, checkmate will come quicker than previously conceived. Lovely home. I do hope it stays that way. Goodnight, Mr. Governor. Keep the missus warm for me," Rogers said and laughed on the way out.

Hamilton choked on his drink, coughed, and said *goodnight*.

A troublesome look crossed his demeanor as he contemplated with a cold shudder the alliance it appeared he had made with the most feared pirate, Jolly Rogers.

CHAPTER NINETEEN

William looked at himself in the mirror in the Captain's quarters of the Retribution, and while he trimmed his wiry beard, he recollected all the things in his past that had led up to these moments.

He was about to embark on the greatest adventure he had ever endured.

The decisions he would have to make were too difficult to bear.

Some of the choices would send men to their deaths, even put their children at risk. This was all calculated by one of the most intelligent minds on the planet.

Willy was a graduate of King's School, and was the first officer in the British Navy. Willy had received plenty of knowledge from one of the wealthiest businessmen in England, his father. And everything in Willy's life thus far had led him to become the genius he was and put him in a position to steal the largest treasure ever known in the new world.

As he reminisced, there came a knock at the door.

"Who goes there?" asked Willy.

"It is I, Sebastian, Father. May I come in?"

"Yes, you may, Sebastian," answered Willy.

"Father, Captains are arriving from the Kinsman," Sebastian stated.

"How many thus far, Sebastian?"

Sebastian walked over to the little table with the checkerboard and moved a piece, then replied,

"Three, Father. I've counted three thus far."

"Have the preparations been made on the island for their arrival?" Willy asked, staring back at Sebastian through the mirror.

Sebastian sat down at the table and didn't respond to his father's question. It seemed he was away in his own world sometimes, lost in thoughts.

"Is everything in order?" Willy asked for a second time.

"Yes," Sebastian sternly replied and continued, "well, except for one thing, Father." He stared at the back of his father's head, a look that seared into Willy.

Willy stopped looking at Sebastian through the mirror, turned around, and asked, "What is it?" "Some of the men are wary about the island, Father. They are saying all kinds of strange things. They... they believe evil spirits curse the land there," answered Sebastian as he stood up and went over to where there was a jug of wine, pouring himself a glass.

"Any news of Connelly? Has he awoken from his wounds?"

"No, not yet Father, the doctor is tending to him, yet he is still unconscious," Sebastian said.

"Very well, any sign of Blackheart?"

Taking a sip of wine, Sebastian said, "Not yet, Father. Can you be sure which side he's on, as

I've heard some of the men speak of him as a traitor?"

Willy put down the blade and wiped his face. "The thought would never enter my mind as to the loyalty of your Uncle John," Willy replied. "I beg you not to say such things."

Sebastian looking shocked asked, "Father, are you implying that I am related to this man?"

Willy laughed, "Sebastian, my boy, there is much you do not know, but one thing is certain, Blackheart is John Ramos, your mother Louisa Ramos's brother, so to put it plainly, yes. He is your uncle."

"Are you serious? Why have you never told us?"

"Timing, my son; the north star wasn't in the correct position."

"Father, the north star never moves."

"Ha, I have taught ya speck about sailing, ain't I."

Sebastian laughed and asked, "The message I should deliver to the Captain, sir?"

"Send word that we shall meet an hour after sundown on the island. Your sister is baking my favorite. Almond cake. We shall meet *after* almond cake. Nothing is more important than that." "Father, don't you find that strange, a ruthless pirate that bakes? And a woman, to boot?"

"You know where she gets it from, don't ya?" asked Willy.

"No, Captain, I don't."

"Her father! Now, send the message before I send you a message. Oh, and Sebastian, don't worry about the men. I have everything under control," said Willy.

"Aye, Captain."

Sebastian left the cabin but shortly after, there was another knock at the door. Willy, with a razor in his hand, turned away from the mirror and said, "Oh bugger, what is it now?"

Prima entered the quarters. "My apologies, Captain. Some of the men were wondering if they could remain on the ship?"

"Scared of a few bones, are they?" Willy replied, still staring in the mirror, a pair of scissors in hand as he attempted to keep in order his facial hair.

Prima removed his hat and with a voice that mimicked that of a young adult going through puberty, replied, "Indeed, that would be the case, Captain."

The Captain turned to Prima with the pair of scissors in his hand, and walked over to him.

"Would ya rather me cut your heart out with these here scissors and feed it to the sharks? Or would you like to accompany me to the island?"

"The island, Captain. I'll go with ya to the island."

The captain stabbed an apple with the scissors and took a bite.

"It was only food for thought. Deliver that message to the men and have them ready the boats.

Tell Sebastian and Sara we will be departing for the island shortly."

"Aye Captain, and what about the others that still refuse?"

Willy, with the scissors in his hand, grabbed a carrot off of the table and sliced it in half, then replied, "I would hate for their time here on the Redemption to be cut so short.

"So, do be courteous and make them aware that refusal to abide by a direct order from their Captain is mutiny, and the punishment for said crime is death. Nay—not just death. A *painful* and drawn-out death."

"Aye, Captain. I will inform the men of that," said Prima.

"You know what, Prima? I will inform the men myself and put an end to this very quickly." Willy followed Prima out of the quarters and up to the quarter deck to address the men.

With one hand on the helm of the ship and the other holding the handle of his cutlass, Willy began his speech. "Are you not the same men who threw Cutthroat Cal into a blazing fire?

"Are you not the same men who've plundered over a hundred great ships in these seas, and left no one to tell the stories? Are you not the most fearsome crew that sails these waters? Gentlemen and lady, I have never encountered a more devout bunch of deviants in all my days as a pirate.

"Now, I regret to say there have been rumors of fear, and I am here to simply say as your Captain, that I would give my life for each and every one of you.

"Fear is nonexistent as long as you know that your Captain is fearless in his endeavors and will protect this crew with every ounce of my soul. For those of you who have families you haven't seen in months, or women you enjoy spending your booty on, this could very well be the last time you ever have to pillage and plunder. What awaits us as a crew is destiny, and as we all know, death *loves* destiny. If I am destined for the locker on this journey, then so be it, and Davey Jones will regret that day. And I don't know about you, but I'm going to make damn sure that my children and my crew will be rich and indulge in pleasantries beyond the realm of expectation.

"So, men and lady, I ask you—and I want to hear your voices echo across the sea like a cannon singing tunes in battle—*are you with me?*"

In one heartfelt voice, the men on the Redemption, as well as Sara, all yelled "Aye!"

The yell was so loud that it rattled some of the bones on the island. Willy's speech had renewed the confidence in the men, and they were ready to go to the island and coordinate the capture of the treasure with the other crews of the Kinsman of the Tide.

The spoils that would soon be theirs were impossible to ignore or resist.

And not a single one had resisted.

Their mouths were watering already at the thought of all the booty soon to come their way.

As they approached the bloodcurdling Isla de Juegos, rocks poked out of the water like the heads of a dozen alligators waiting for the right moment to attack their prey.

Each one of these stones was massive, stretching out deep under the sea.

Two of the stones were lit up with fires on each side of them, and this was the entrance known as the Gates of Hell. Upon passing through these gates, a pretty little bay sat filled with rowboats, and the island swarmed with pirates.

Massive fires burned a hundred feet from the water, and the many skulls of those who had perished were lined across the tree line. Some had candles in them, and others did not.

Palm trees stood bending, clearly having been moved at the speed of the wind which was inexplicably absent at this time, yet at some distance, there were ominous shadows of dark clouds traveling silently in this direction.

The crews had all assembled on the beach while the captains met at the palace of the damned.

At some point, those men and women who had been forced here against their goodwill because they were thought to be uninfected, had begun building themselves a large house.

It was about half a mile into the jungle, these people keeping their distance as long as they could from those who were sick but had still contracted the disease.

Unfortunately, they had died before its completion.

Amid their tenure on Isla de Huesos, Willy and Blackheart were able to complete a portion of the structure, and over the years, some of the crew of the Inferno finished the job, sprinkling a bit of fear using the skulls and bones of the very souls who no longer occupied the island.

A sound of a bell was heard on the beach and everyone made their way along the walkway through the jungle, following a path of skulls and torches lighting the way to the palace.

The creatures of the island this very night were particularly loud, for they had not had company in quite some time. Upon reaching the steps to the palace, the desire to stare upon the railings made of bone and the stool post made with skulls was overwhelming.

Handprints of blood on the top of those skulls on the stool post signaled a meeting of the utmost importance for the Kinsman. The prints in deep red were a language all of their own.

They entered through the doorway and the sight was remarkable, nearly everything inside this house having been made with bone. The steps that led upstairs were constructed of pelvis bones with wood infills, and the railings were made from the long bones of legs and arms.

To the left was a room with a rib cage made into a bar set-up, and here, rum and wine were being served to the Kinsman and its top advisors.

Across the way was a monolithic table with chairs made of bone, and one chair at the head of the table with an indescribable design. All the Kinsman crew were present for this meeting.

Gathered around this monstrosity of wood standing on eight leg bones were John Ramos, aka Blackheart, with a knife in one hand, his other hand placed palm down on the table, stabbing the spaces in between his fingers, faster and faster.

Francois L'Olonnais, the cruelest out of all of the pirates was seated at the table with the look of death in his eyes as he scanned the other Kinsman crew.

Richard 'Red Hand' Nichols, with a usual piece of hay clutched between his teeth as if being used as a toothpick, had his leg draped over another, patiently waiting for the Queen.

Artimus Drake was the favorite of all the Tide, being that his grandfather had been one of the first pirates of the Caribbean, and a legend in the minds of the others.

Henry Morgan quietly sat in his chair, belching the remainder of the jug of rum staring at him on the table. Sebastian was there too, the only son of One-Eyed Willy and the heir to the Inferno.

La Muerte, also known as the Capitan of Death, sat close to him, twisting his mustache with both hands, and directly across from him sat One-Eyed Willy himself, attentively observing the actions of all the Kinsmen. The Queen, sitting at the head of the table with her rosy, red cheeks, white wig, and dazzling green eyes finally said, "Hear ye, hear ye! This is the seventh meeting of the Kinsman of the Tide on Isla de Huesos, and I want to welcome you all.

"We have been called here by a fellow Kinsman for a terrible and unforgivable violation of our code. It has also come to my attention that a ploy has been plotted and its perpetrator may very well be amongst us. Richard 'Red Hand' Nichols, you are hereby accused of plotting against the Tide and of coercing with the financier Robert Perkins to steal the jewel of the Spanish Main and the greatest treasure that ever existed in the new world."

Red hand removed the piece of hay out of his mouth, and stood up.

"This is preposterous, you have no proof," he said. Spittle landed atop the table.

"Bring in the witness," the Queen ordered, and two guards brought in Mr. Connelly who had been beaten pretty badly by Red Hand and Claybourne.

"Are you indeed a member of the crew of the Inferno, Mr. Connelly?" she asked.

"Aye, yes I am," said Mr. Connelly.

"Can you take us through the events that caused you to appear in the condition in which you find yourself presently, as you stand before us?"

Connelly, who had bandages around his head and covering his eye, looked up as best he could with nothing more than a bloody slit for one eye, and the other obscured.

"Mr. Nichols and Mr. Claybourne wanted information about the jewel and the treasure, and I gave them nothing."

"Aye," said some of the captains, shaking their heads in support of the crew member's statement. Red Hand pushed his chair back and stood up.

"This is utterly outrageous. I am a well-respected member of the Kinsman. You will take the word of a cabin boy over a Kinsman of the Tide?"

"I say we vote on it," said Henry Morgan, who raised his mug of rum in the air.

"What the hell are we voting on, Morgan?" the Queen asked.

"Well, who we believe."

"Kill ;em both and be done with it," L'Olonnais said.

"What says the scroll?" said Willy.

"Aye," said Sebastian, "What says the scroll?"

"Aye, what says the scroll?" Morgan and Artimus also agreed and added.

The Queen then nodded her head. "Aye, what says the scroll? Red Hand, if you are the accused, then you must be the one to unlock the treasure of the buried."

"I say we vote." La Muerte stood and kicked Willy in the shin to draw his attention.

Red Hand walked around to the Queen.

"My apologies, Capitan of Death. We have voted, and we all agree with, *what says the scroll*." The Queen removed the key from around her neck and placed it in Nichol's hand.

Red Hand left the room to fetch the chest and bring it before the council.

"But my Queen," said La Muerte.

"Sit down, Capitan," she replied.

The Capitan sat down, leaned into Willy and said, "Do you remember that safe place I said I had put the stone?" Willy's eyes lit up and he stood from his chair. "The place for safekeeping?" "Connelly, how can you be sure it was Mr. Nichols?" Willy asked.

"Because Claybourne called him by that name, and he's been follow-ing us this whole time. He is planning on stealing both the jewel and the treasure just as quick as you get them."

"Captains, we all know this is the booty to end all plundering, and Red Hand knows as well," La Muerte said.

"Where is Red Hand?" asked Willy.

Willy rushed out to try and find Red Hand in the other room, but he was no longer there.

The window toward the back of the room was open and there was no sign of him.

Willy looked down at the floor and noticed the treasure chest of the buried booty was opened and the sacred scroll and the stone were missing.

"He's taken the scroll! Traitor, he has taken the scroll!" Willy yelled to the rest of the group.

"I want every able crewman after that scroll, and bring me Red Hand alive," the Queen ordered.

The message was delivered to the hundreds of men outside the palace and they immediately scattered back to the beach to find Red Hand, who would obviously be heading to his ship.

The Queen acknowledged the traitor and vowed to capture and personally incinerate him.

"I can't have you incinerating nobody without me ripping out his heart first. Willy, will you need my ship for this delightful treasure hunt of yours?" L'Olonnais said.

"Indeed, we will," Willy replied.

"Then, you shall have it—and my men, as many men as you can use. Just make sure I never have to rip out a man's heart," said L'Olonnais.

"Aye. Sebastian, ready the men," said Willy.

"L'Olonnais, you're coming aboard my ship?" the Queen said.

"Aye," answered L'Olonnais.

"After that traitor, men," the Queen ordered, a look of thunder on her face.

All the captains ran out the door after the treasonous Red Hand, and as they did, the crackle of two cannons one after another was heard. The cannonballs unleashed havoc through the trees, sending shards of wood in every direction, then exploding as they hit the Palace of the Damned.

Willy and the other captains turned and watch the palace crumble as it was engulfed in flames. The Queen yelled, "Quick men, to the beach." Devereaux, Prima and Sara were amongst the first wave to hit the tree line before the beach. Once they and the others came from out of the jungle, Claybourne and 150 soldiers were gathered on the beach, awaiting information.

"Fire," the lieutenant shouted.

"Get down," Sara yelled as she hit the ground.

Prima and Devereaux instantly obeyed and did the same.

The gunfire from the soldier's rifles ricocheted through the trees, hitting and taking down crew members as they took their first steps onto the beach.

"Return fire," Sara yelled as the second wave of men came to the edge of the tree line just as the British were reloading and opening fire on the soldiers. The cannons were still raining fire down on the captains and the rest of the men making their way toward the beach.

"Charge," Sara yelled, as did Claybourne, and the opposing groups of men came to the middle of the beach and clashed with swords clanking, and pistols popping.

Sara, who was an excellent swordsperson, was in the heat of the battle, taking her sword and pummeling it into the flesh of British soldiers. Indeed, she appeared to be rather enjoying herself.

The other captains and the rest of the respective crews finally arrived at the beach and immediately charged into the action against the tyrannical Lieutenant Claybourne.

Willy, his pistol aimed, shot a red coat with a shot right to the heart—just as if he was bringing down a deer in the forest—while L'Olonnais stabbed one through the heart with his cutlass.

The Queen came up from behind one of the soldiers, sliced his throat, picked up his bayonet, and immediately shot another. Artimus Drake and a few of his men silently swam out to the British ship that was still blasting the cannon fire toward the island.

They climbed aboard the ship stealthily.

A few of the men took to the lower deck where the cannons were being fired.

The other men initiated a battle with the British soldiers on the main deck and not long after, the cannons stopped firing. Claybourne turned and looked out to sea, knowing something was wrong. He yelled to his men, "Retreat! Retreat men, back to the ship."

But the pirates had them flanked on both sides. The lieutenant looked around him, saw there was no way out and ordered, "Lay down your swords, men."

Shortly after, Sebastian came up to the lieutenant who was kneeling on the sand.

"Isn't it hysterical how we keep meeting this way? The last time we saw you, you had your manhood caught between a pole and a small barrel."

Sebastian placed the edge of his sword under Claybourne's chin and lifted his head to see the angered expression in the eyes of the lieutenant.

"Where has red hand taken the scroll?" Willy yelled as he made his way through the men.

"Why, I haven't a clue. Whatever you do mean?"

"Pick him up," Willy ordered, and the men quickly picked up Claybourne.

Willy then punched Claybourne in the stomach with one almighty blow and he fell back to the sand, coughing in displeasure, spitting up his guts.

"Now, this could go one of two ways. You die right here right now and never see your beloved family again, or you live with the slightest chance you may. The choice is yours, Lieutenant—and my patience has just ran its course," Willy said. "Now, make a choice and say it loud."

"Come now, Lieutenant, where?" said Sebastian as he placed his sword deep into the throat of Claybourne.

"Alright, alright. I will tell you but under one condition."

"I'm afraid you're not in the position for any requests," Willy replied as Claybourne raised his chin up high.

"Very well! Kill me, and the information will rot with my corpse. Then 'tis lost. So be it."

"I'd be beyond happy to kill you, Claybourne. Do not think that I won't. Sebastian, send him to the locker," Willy said.

"Belay that order, Mr. Claybourne. You will tell us where that scroll is, or I will personally hunt down your family and hang them for all to see. After all, it's a pirate's life for me. I'm sure Mary will be quick to give information about your family for a little bit of coin.

"Or maybe I ought to have my crew have their way with her. What say you, Mr. Claybourne?" the Queen yelled.

The lieutenant, disgusted and concerned, revealed the location of the scroll to Willy and the Queen. He could bear this onslaught of insults and threats no longer.

"My Queen, I will retrieve the scroll and return it to the Kinsman," Willy said.

"Nonsense, I will go," Artimus suggested.

The Queen, deep in thought, replied, "No, Willy. You and Artimus will stay the course and go after the vault. Olly and I will seek out Red Hand and get back the jewel and sacred scroll." "Where is La Muerte?" asked Willy.

La Muerte was aboard the Retribution with two of his crew members, preparing to ready the ship for departure. The two men were concentrating on the anchor while La Muerte was at the helm, and La Muerte heard fussing around at the bow of the ship.

He ran downstairs and said, "What is taking you fools so long? Ricardo, are you there? We haven't got the time to mess around. Felipe? Where are you, two bumbling idiots?"

The Capitan of Death looked over the side of the bow and saw two bodies floating in the water, then he turned around to find Blackheart was standing staring at him.

"Trying to make a quick getaway, lad? Have you not forgotten something? Where is the stone?" Blackheart asked.

"Red Hand has the stone. I'm just trying to go back to Tortuga to save my Maria," La Muerte replied. "That is all I am doing. I was not trying to flee... I really was not."

"La Muerte, the few years that I have known you, I always had this feeling that we have met before. I feel as though you were once in the employment of one Francisco Gonzales?" "The only job I have for Mr. Gonzales is killing him," La Muerte said.

"Is that so? So you don't recall killing a mother, a father and a child with him thirty years ago in Portobello?" Blackheart questioned La Muerte. "Are you sure of your memory? Have you taken a knock to the head, perchance?"

"Why do you even ask these questions?" replied La Muerte.

"Because I believe you were there, and you killed my parents."

"I was there but I was only five years old. I was just a child. Is that you John?" replied La Muerte.

"Nathan, this can't be real, am I dreaming?" Blackheart said, his mouth wide.

He dropped his sword and they both hugged.

John, with two hands on Nathans' face, said, "Oh the Lord has blessed me this day, my baby brother is alive. How did we not know this for so many years?"

"Well, you left the Inferno just as I came aboard. The only time we saw each other was at a Kinsman meeting once in a harvest moon. You never trusted me," replied La Muerte. "No, I didn't. Not until this very moment. What of this woman you love?" "Robert Perkins has her captive on Tortuga," said La Muerte.

"Then go to her brother. I will deal with One-Eyed Willy."

The two newly reunited brothers hugged and Blackheart helped La Muerte hoist anchor, took a rowboat from the ship and headed toward land. The Retribution headed into the dim light that would eventually turn into the sunrise.

Back on land, the respective crews of the Kinsman were tying the last few soldiers' hands together.

"What say you with the lieutenant?" Artimus asked.

"He is our ticket into the bay of Havana," said Willy.

"And what are we going to do with these soldiers?" asked Artimus.

"We will take them aboard the Retribution," Willy insisted and at the same time, Black Heart walked up to them.

"You can't, the Retribution has gone. You missed it." "La Muerte, you swine," Willy replied.

"Walk with me, Willy," Blackheart said and they both began a stroll down to the beach.

"How much do you know of La Muerte's past?" Blackheart asked. "Much?"

"Not much, he bounced around from crew to crew to survive. That is all," Willy replied.

"Willy, his parents were killed in Panama thirty years ago, and his name is Nathan," said Blackheart.

"Like your little brother, Nathan?" "Willy, he *is* Nathan," Blackheart replied.

"But that's impossible."

"*Is* it impossible? I saw his eyes; that is my brother," said Blackheart.

"This is shocking news. I am utterly speechless," said Willy.

"Willy, I have other news. They are alive."

"*Who* is alive?" asked Willy. His brows knitted together and he was very confused by the way this conversation was heading.

"Lenora, Louisa and Isabella," said Blackheart

With both hands, Willy grabbed Blackheart by the shirt. "Don't be telling tales about the dead." Blackheart ripped Willy's hands away.

"Get off me. It's true, you moron, Gonzales never shot them. He wants the treasure and the stone in exchange."

Willy sat down in the sand.

In exchange? He wants to barter for them as though they are fresh-plucked fruits?

"First Nathan and now Louisa, how do I tell my children? How could we not have known?" said Willy.

Blackheart sat next to Willy, digging his hands into the sand.

"How could we have known? Gonzales did whatever he had to do to keep this from us. He kept us chained in captivity for seven years. He kept us worse than household swine."

The Queen walked down the beach toward Willy and Blackheart, and sat next to them.

"Why the glum faces, gentlemen? We will get the scroll and the jewel back. Concentrate on your job and that's the treasure," she said.

"They are alive, Abby," Willy replied. "I can barely grasp it myself. They live…"

"Who is alive?"

"Lenora, Louisa and Isabella," Blackheart said.

The Queen stretched out her two hands and put them around Blackheart's neck.

"Don't be talking about the dead like that."

"It's true! How many times do I have to say it? It's true." The Queen took off her hat and started to fan herself.

"It's too hot. This is too much to take in. Are you sure, Blackheart?"

"Yes, I'm sure."

"What do we do?" said the Queen.

"We get the gold and get them back, is what we are going to do, Abby. Red Hand has the stone and the scroll. Be careful, he is trying to play both sides. He is wily as a fox."

"Aye Willy, he won't fool this Queen."

"Blackheart, let's round up the captains and the crews and go to Havana, and burn that Castillo

to the ground."

CHAPTER TWENTY

Some distance away at Windsor Castle on the outskirts of London, England, King Charles II was having breakfast with Queen Catherine, sitting demurely at a lavish breakfast table that was as long and wide as one of the docks on the River Thames.

The assortment of fruit, cakes, birds, beasts and cheese was without bounds—there wasn't a delight you could dream about that couldn't be found on the royal breakfast table.

The King was stuffing his face with every one of these finer delicacies when Catherine asked,

"Oh Charles, do you have to eat like that?"

Indeed, his mouth was often open, chewed food dropping back onto his plate. Various horrifically sloppy masticating sounds aggrieved her ears.

Charles stopped eating, grabbed a napkin, wiped his face, and with food still in his mouth, inquired, "Like what, Cathy? What am I eating like? Please do me the courtesy?"

"Like a peasant that hasn't eaten in days, that's how you are eating. Like a hungered pig. Like a gathering of crows feasting on the sorry carcass of a dead animal. Like a—" He interrupted, aware the nagging could go on until nightfall.

"Well, come to think of it my love, I haven't eaten since supper last night. So, yes, I am feeling rather starved. But do you have to bother me every time I'm famished? The sooner you allow me

to be done with it, the sooner you can stop seeing me eat."

"On the contrary, my darling King. I do not think it is you who is bothered, I think you fancy the way you eat, and you do it on purpose just to agitate me," replied Queen Cathy.

At that moment, Prince James walked in to have his fill of morning treats to start his day.

The King and Queen were delighted to greet him this morning and he was scheduled to be married in a month's time to the Princess of Spain.

The prince walked alongside the table where his stepmother, Queen Cathy was seated, and gave her a kiss. Then he went around the edge and put his hands on his father's shoulders, wishing him a fair morning before grabbing a plate and began serving himself.

"And what of the Princess of Spain, are you enthused and eager to meet? I heard she is quite the spectacle," the Queen asked.

"I have heard the same, Mother. I'm indeed thrilled to meet my new bride, yet more excited for the riches that shall come from the wedding."

"James, that's terrible that you would think of your wedding as a chance to gain wealth," the Queen replied.

"Humor, my Queen, only humor," said James.

"Don't believe him, my love. He speaks truth in his words. I only know this because it is costing me a fortune. If the prince only knew what he was getting into, he would mind his tongue and not speak with so many flies on the wall."

"Father, my apologies. I don't expect any wealth, only good blessings from both our families."

A guard rushed in and said, "My King, apologies for the intrusion, but there is an urgent message for you, all the way from the West Indies."

"Ah, it is good news about the gift for the wedding, I suppose. See, my son, you say good blessings and here we have one. What is the message?"

"That the Redemption has been stolen, Sire."

"Stolen? *Stolen?* Are you sure? Who would be able to steal my greatest ship?"

"One-Eyed Willy, Sire; he has stolen the Redemption and there are rumors he is going to attempt to steal the wedding gift," the guard answered.

This news infuriated the King who began waving his arms like a madman, clearing food off the table as plates and glasses smashed against the floor.

The Queen immediately took her leave as the King grabbed his chair and smashed it against the table, breaking it. He was breathing heavily, like a great pair of fire bellows, huffing and puffing with a huge amount of fuss and noise.

Then he fixed his wig, put both hands on the table in front of him, and said, "Guard, I want One-Eyed Willy's head. You get word to Hamilton and Perkins that if they don't produce our friend Willy's head along with my wedding gift, then he can be sure that King Charles of Spain and myself will personally remove *their* heads. And I would take great pleasure in it, too." "Yes, Sire. Who do you want me to send?" asked the guard.

"I want the whole damned armada there yesterday, do you understand?" said the King.

Choppy waters clashed with the hull of the Inferno as it battered its sorry way through the waves, spilling vast amounts of water over the top of the bow.

The Atlantic Ocean was a mighty beast to reckon with, especially during mid-summer, and early in the afternoon just off the coast of the small seafaring town of Rio De Janeiro, gray clouds blanketed the skies as far as the eye could see.

Samuel Winston and Quaco were up on the main deck in the sun and the fair breeze, playing a game of liar's dice. Smitty came down the steps from the top deck.

"Who thinks they can best ole Smitty?"

"Ain't nobody wanting to play you. It's terrible that we have to even be on this journey," said Quaco.

"Did you not spend coin with one of the village girls the night before last?" said Smitty.

"That's as may be but I'm not comprehending how we got picked for this duty. Sail all the way around the south of America and rendezvous with the Captain in Panama City. That's ludicrous if you ask me. My apologies, but the odds of the Captain actually being there are better than you ever besting me in a game of dice," Quaco said, and Samuel Winston laughed.

"Is that so, Quaco? And what are you laughing at, swab? So you're questioning your Captain's ability to put a plan together or execute it? I'll have you know the Captain saved my life and then came back and rescued me from Mexico City," Smitty said.

"We know the story Smitty, I've heard you tell it a thousand times. Every time you tell it, we are playing dice and there is coin involved," Quaco replied.

"I haven't heard the story. I want to hear it," Samuel Winston said.

Quaco got aggravated and threw the cup of dice down.

"I can't hear this story another time or lose any more coin."

Smitty sat down after Quaco got up, and said, "You big goon, now go get us some more rum, and clean the bow boxes, ya scalawag. After all is done, I'm going to need you to relieve
Cannonball Joe at the helm."

"Aye Captain, relieve Cannonball Joe. Got it." Samuel Winston was filled with excitement.

"So, tell me Captain Smitty, how did One-Eyed Willy rescue you?"

"I'll tell you but it's going to cost you a few coins. Now take a bit of Smitty's good ole advice and shut ya hole—and roll the dice."

Meanwhile, two-thousand miles to the north, the skies roared and rocked the Redemption like a baby being rocked to sleep. The only lights displayed in the sky were the lightning forks, and the absence of the moon and the stars meant trouble for a captain and his ship.

Rain pounded off the wooden deck so hard and fast that it almost looked as though it was also raining from the deck itself, upward toward the skies.

Thomas Copperpot was learning firsthand about the daily routine of a pirate, holding onto a rope for dear life when the wind swooped in with such force that it damn near picked him up off the deck. Yet, Copperpot was still hanging on after the ocean threw, time and time again, a deluge of salty water at his body. Willy was smoking a pipe from inside the captain's quarters while he watched Copperpot hanging on for dear life.

He turned around and said, "Sara have you paid much attention to Mr. Copperpot?" Sara was lying on her father's bed throwing a pillow in the air, and catching it.

"I can't say I have, Father. Why do you ask?"

"The boy has heart. He works hard. He has something to prove. Do you know his story?"

"He told Sebastian and I that Jolly Rogers killed his parents and marooned him on Cuba. He's been on his own for three years and truthfully, I think he misses his family," said Sara.

"It's a terribly cruel way to lose your family. I am far too familiar with that kind of pain, as you know, but I cannot say I know *his* pain," Willy replied. "But do you know the most painful thing he lost that day, Father?" "No, my dear, what did he lose?" asked Willy.

"Love, Father. He lost love. He lost his fiancée whom he adored like no other before."

"Then I believe I do know his pain all too well, my darling daughter. When I lost your mother, it was as if I lost all sense of emotion. The mines were nothing compared to the loss of your mother.

I stayed there for as long as I could to divert the pain rendered.

"Thomas is putting all his emotion into this opportunity, and that pain is what drives him." "Father, why did you marry my mother?" asked Sara.

"Your mother was unlike any other woman I have ever met. She saw me for who I really was," replied Willy.

"Father, I find that hard to believe considering who you are. I mean, how did she get past all the brutality and selfishness?" Sara continued.

"Selfish? You think I'm selfish? Everything I did, and I am doing, is for you and your brother." Sara got up off the bed.

"Lies, Father. Everything you are doing is for you and your crew."

"Yes, Sara. And you are part of this crew."

"Father, I just want to be a girl, a woman who wears dresses and lives in a house."

"You, wear dresses? Come now, you haven't worn a dress since you stepped aboard a ship," Willy laughed.

"See, I knew you wouldn't understand; I bet Mother would," she replied as she stormed out of the Captain's quarters and walked right past Sebastian.

He entered the door and looked back. "Father, what was that about?"

"Your sister wants to wear dresses."

"She hasn't worn a dress in years!" Sebastian said with a laugh. "Father, the storm has passed, but more importantly, Morgan's ship has entered the Bay of Havana."

"Very well, then it has begun. What of the other five ships?" Willy asked.

"L'Olonnais's ship, the Marquis de Louis, the Revenge and Claybourne's ship will remain out at sea. Artimus and his crew are awaiting your orders there. I will board the Indestructible with Blackheart and we will hoist anchor just offshore, half a mile from the bay in Almendras Cove.

We will be in place and ready for the signal."

"Very well, my son," Willy said and walked over to Sebastian, looked him in the eye and said,

"So, lad, tell me. Are you ready to make history?"

"Aye Captain," Sebastian replied. "I have never been more ready, Father."

"Then let's go steal us some treasure. But there is something I need you to do before you depart for the Indestructible, I want you to bring your sister and Thomas Copperpot with you."

"Why, Father? They will just slow us down? This is not a task for ladies." "No, my boy, they will stay aboard the ship when you are on the mission," said Willy.

"Fine, then I will take them with me," replied Sebastian.

"Very good. And also, have someone bring Lieutenant Claybourne up to the main deck and have all the men at the ready."

"Aye, Captain," said Sebastian.

"Oh, and Sebastian," said Willy.

"Yes, Father," he replied, wondering if his father's list of wants would end anytime soon.

"Be mindful, that if we are successful, this will be the last time we ever have to plunder. So do be careful, my son. This goes to plan, and we shall bring home rich spoils."

"Yes Father, I intend to. See you when we are rich."

Willy smiled and Sebastian departed his quarters. Willy looked in the mirror, put on his hat over his red bandana, pulled out his cutlass then thrust it back into the sword scabbard.

He checked his knife was slipped inside his boot as usual and made sure both of his pistols were loaded, then headed out to the main deck where Lieutenant Claybourne, with his hands in chains, was standing next to Prima.

"Ah, Lieutenant Claybourne, so nice of you to join us. How do I fair in this godforsaken awful uniform?" The lieutenant spat on the ground.

"Careful, Lieutenant, the locker is just over the side of the ship and well, we wouldn't want to make your wife a widower or even worse, for something to happen to those charming little children of yours. We would not wish for that now, would we?"

"No, we wouldn't, Mr. Willy," the lieutenant replied in disgust.

"Very well, then. Mr. Diablo, would you be so kind as to remove the chains from Mr. Claybourne?" Prima eagerly removed the shackles from Claybourne, and feeling his wrists no longer bound, said to Willy, "You know, Willy... May I call you Willy? My cousin Oliver Hamilton told me stories of you when you were children, and he will make sure you will never get away with this."

"On the contrary, Lieutenant. I would, however, if I were a man in your position, focus my thoughts on whether or not I would see my children again, and not on the ambitions of a pirate or the tales of your family members."

"Captain, I can play his part. What say we just feed him to the sharks?" Devereaux said as he came to the main deck.

"Devereaux, that is no way to treat a lieutenant in the King's Navy. The man at least deserves an officer's death," said Willy. "A finer death than becoming live fish food."

"Then, let me dispose of this swine in a manner which he deserves."

"Come now, Mr. Devereaux, I need you to ensure all the men are dressed and at their ready.

We are approaching the island and will reach the blockade within the hour."

"Aye Captain. I still say we send him to the locker," Devereaux insisted as he walked past Claybourne with blood in his eyes and rage running through his veins.

"You'll have to excuse Mr. Devereaux. He was not well brought up, thus does not have the characteristics of a gentleman. He sees an officer, and without thought, just wants death.

"It is understandable. Perhaps the memories of his childhood could account for those feelings. Either way, Mr. Claybourne, you play by the terms we agreed or I assure Mr. Devereaux will pay a visit to your home. And as much as I try to teach him the rudiments of etiquette in polite society,

I am afraid he remains, at best, a savage wishing to tear you limb from limb. Are we understood?" "I will do as you command as long as my family is unharmed," the lieutenant replied.

"Then I do believe we have an accord. Men, raise the English colors and prepare for what inevitably will be the greatest plunder in the history of these here seas," Willy yelled to the crew.

The Spanish had set up a blockade in the bay of Havana. The Governor had two ships at the entrance on the Caribbean side and three on the bay side at the entrance to the bay. Henry Morgan and his crew tied off the Rum Runner as the harbor master greeted him with a smile.

"Mr. Morgan, another delivery and at this hour? I do not have you on the manifest at all, Mr.

Morgan. What is the meaning of your visit today?"

"Out of my way, you impudent swine. I have an urgent message for the Governor that cannot wait!" said Morgan. "Now move! Shift your ass!"

"Yes, Sire. I shall have you escorted to the Castillo," replied the harbor master.

"Nonsense, I'm perfectly capable of delivering the message, or shall I tell the Governor I was delayed because of your incompetence? Which do you opt for?"

"Not necessary. Very well, Mr. Morgan, do enjoy your stay and be sure to tell the Governor I was able see you off with haste to deliver the message," the harbor master replied. "And do add how much I relished seeing your friendly face on this fair day."

"I certainly will. Now out of my way," Morgan ordered. "Get gone!"

Henry Morgan and a few of his men made their way from the docks up to the Castillo. It was 04:40 am by now and the element of surprise was in their favor.

The Indestructible sailed within a few miles of the bay of Havana under the scraps of darkness left of the night, and the ship dropped its anchor in a cove at the beginning of the Rio Almendras, just off the coastline.

There, with nothing more than light from the moon and stars, Blackheart, Sebastian, Thomas and thirty men got into rowboats and silently rowed ashore.

They pulled the boats up onto the land and Sebastian noticed Sara helping pull one of the boats on shore. "Sara," he yelled, stamping his feet hard into the sand.

He walked hastily toward his sister.

"Did Father not specifically tell you to stay aboard the ship? Did he not give you an order?"

"Sebastian, I want to help and you're making me look unfit in front of the crew. I am as capable as you are, and well you know it."

"My, my, my. You two are your mothers' children," Blackheart said as he walked over.

"What do you mean by that?" Sara asked.

"If you stay here and guard these boats for your dear old uncle, he will tell you all there is to know about your mother when we return with the gold."

"That is quite the offer, and I can honestly say I am excited."

"Excellent idea, Uncle. Now where is Thomas? Thomas, Thomas?" Sebastian called out.

"I'm here, Sire," Thomas answered as he zipped up his pants and speed-walked up to Sebastian.

"I need you to guard these here boats with my sister. Most importantly," Sebastian leaned into him and whispered, "I need you to watch my sister to make sure she does nothing stupid. Do you think you could handle that, lad?"

"Without a doubt in my mind, Sire," Thomas replied.

"Good, and if you let me down, I'll maroon you with Lieutenant Claybourne on Isla de Juesos."

"Oh, you needn't worry, she will be fine, Sire. I won't let her out of my sight. If she as much as sneezes, I shall know about it."

"You both know I'm standing right here. Uncle John, I look forward to a swift return." "Aye, mi lady, as well as I," Blackheart replied.

The men gathered their weapons and essentials and headed off on their short journey back to the tunnel near the docks where Sara and Thomas had once escaped.

The sun had yet to show itself as Willy and Artimus Drake slowly progressed to the mouth of the bay of Havana. The Spanish had two ships anchored on the east and west sides of the entrance. The Castillo de la Punta and the Castillo el Morro and all their gun power overlooked the Spanish stronghold with a mighty gaze. Willy was hidden in the Captain's quarters with a dozen of the crew on the main deck dressed in the most fashionable British Naval uniforms.

Lieutenant Claybourne, attired most sumptuously in his dashing dress blues, was for all intents and purposes, the commander of the King's Redemption, or so it would seem.

Just a few hundred feet in front of the Spanish blockade, a long chain was draped across the entrance to the canal that led to the bay connecting both the Castillo de la Punta and Castillo el Morro. In recent days, with the threat of One-Eyed Willy, the chain had been kept raised at all times. Any ship attempting to gain entry was to be tied off to the most feared of all Spanish ships, the Nuestra Senora de la Conception, equipped with one hundred guns, and subsequently searched.

The Redemption pulled alongside the Conception and a few of the men aboard the Redemption threw their ropes over to the Spanish vessel to be tied off.

A short man with a ponytail and wearing a black hat, who looked to be in command, tapped his finger on a book with palpable impatience.

He waited as his men laid a board across the two ships. Once in place, this ponytailed, short fellow and a few soldiers made their way onto the Redemption.

"Hola, and welcome to Cuba," he said. The lieutenant, who faced the opposite direction with his hands behind his back and glaring over the ocean, turned.

"Senor Capitan Juares, very good to see you."

"Senor Lieutenant Claybourne. It is not Tuesday. To what do we owe the honor of your most esteemed visit at such an hour? And might I say in such splendid fashion. What a remarkable ship."

"I was informed by Senor Perkins to lead the first five of ten destroyers to assist in the security of the tremendous gift for the newlyweds and the ultimate apprehension of One-Eyed Willy." "We were not expecting any of the destroyers until midday," said Juares.

"Precisely why I am here. I am rarely ahead of schedule and fancied a change. You are indeed surprised to see me here this early are you not?"

"Why, yes senor, I am. It is not like you," Mr. Juares replied.

"Exactly my point Mr. Juares. I find myself just as surprised as you are. One-Eyed Willy himself would be shocked, do you not agree?"

"Oh yes, Senor Claybourne, I do believe he would be. That's why your arrival unannounced at

05:00 a.m. has me concerned. You are not being held against your will, are you?" Senor Juares and a few of the men laughed.

"We won't search the ship and find One-Eyed Willy hiding in the Captain's quarters, will we?" Claybourne, with a smirk on his face, laughed extra hard and then stopped immediately.

"I have it in my right mind to slay you right where you stand and tell Francisco Gonzales how my honor was in question and I had to defend it in a most unfortunate way." He made a throat-slashing motion with his outstretched hand.

"But Mr. Claybourne, I was... I was merely... It was a..."

"My cousin is the Governor of New Britain, I should have you reminded! Has that matter slipped your notice? Well, maybe we should take our fine ships elsewhere, and you can fend for yourselves against Willy's armada with what little defense you have!

"Maybe the Monarchy from both of our respective countries would like to know that it was Senor Juares who failed to protect their property because he thought it was a joke. Yes, a joke! A jest and a jape! But the problem with that, Mr. Juares, is that this isn't a joking matter. I find no humor in spilling blood, but if the cause warrants bloodshed, I'm *happy* to oblige for the cause." Senor Juares cleared his throat and coughed.

"My apologies, Lieutenant. Truly, I apologize for my most grievous offense. I should have thought before I launched into mirth but it is a nervous habit, Sir."

"You were nervous?"

"I was, good Sire. I am always nervous in front of one so... so..."

"Very well," Mr. Claybourne conceded. "It must be hard to encounter one as fearsome as I am." He puffed out his chest and popped a button.

"Indeed," said Juares, happy to have wriggled off the hook. "Erm, are you carrying any cargo?" "Just the usual gifts from Perkins for your men."

"Yes, he is a most gracious financier one who is a favorite of the Governor of both New Spain and New Britain. What of the other ship's lieutenant?" Juares replied.

"We are five in total, three will remain out at sea. I will allow my colleague to take lead into the bay, if that's alright with you?"

"Well, I would ordinarily have to check the ship, but out of mutual respect for both our countries I will allow it this time, and my apologies, I meant no dishonor."

"No pun intended, but I'm sure you were just having a laugh. Oh, I forgot to remind you that Mr. Perkins will be bringing new women to the city this afternoon with the arrival of the other five ships. I'm sure this is welcoming news? I believe Carolina is one of the women aboard, and correct me if I'm wrong, you fancy her?"

"Alright Mr. Claybourne, off you and your ships go. Men, let's get back to the Conception and untie the ropes. Enjoy your stay here on the island of Cuba."

"Gracias senor, I'm certain we will."

The chain was lowered into the water and Artimus took the lead in front of the Redemption, whose crew hoisted its anchor and slowly made its way through the canal.

At the very end of the canal on the west side was the Castillo de la Fuerza, and the docks were only a quarter mile away. Artimus knew he had to quickly get to the docks so he could give Willy time to set up in the canal. Willy came out onto the deck looking lavish in his new British attire.

"Lieutenant, splendid display of truth. You have my word that your family will not be harmed if you continue on in the manner in which you have conducted yourself to date. Are you familiar with the works of William Shakespeare?"

"I have heard of this man's popularity in plays," Claybourne replied.

"That is information that warms the heart because, Mr. Claybourne, you are indeed about to see one of the greatest plays in human history. Devereaux!" Willy called out.

"Just a moment, Sire. Men, keep the bays closed until the Captain gives the orders." Devereaux appeared from below deck.

"Is it ready, Mr. Devereaux?" Willy asked.

"Is what ready, Captain?" he said, looking most perplexed.

"Is my treat ready? You unpunctual, ungrateful…" said Willy.

"Ah yes, your treat. It will just be a few more minutes, Sire," said Devereaux. "I beg for your esteemed patience, Captain."

"That is splendid news. As you were," said Willy. Then he thought better of it, adding, "But hurry up about it." "What is this treat you speak of?" Prima asked.

"It is an ancient recipe I picked up from a few Aztec friends when I was held prisoner in the mines of Mexico City. Terribly depressing places, those mines. God knows how people can volunteer to work in them."

"It would be the coin, I expect," ventured Prima. "I doubt they *volunteer*, so much as preferring it to eating live, disease-bearing rats."

"Ah, there is that," admitted Willy with a laugh. "Anyway, my treat. I was telling you, not only is it delicious, but it is also even more enjoyable with a bit of entertainment, and I assure you, I will not disappoint."

The docks were fairly quiet, with a harbor master and a few guards running their early morning security routines. Artimus pulled up to one of the docks in front of the Castillo de la Fuerza—all the Spanish galleons and warships were also docked there. As his men threw the ropes over and laid the board from the ship to the dock, the harbor master ran down the dock.

"No tienes permiso aqui! No tienes permiso aqui!" he yelled.

Artimus stepped onto the dock with his hands up as if to slow the harbor master down.

"Calmese, calmese, me llamo First Officer Artimus P. Newhardt of the Royal British Navy."

"Hola Mr. Newhardt, me llamo Harbor Master Dominguez! What is your business here? You are not allowed to dock at these posts—no, not at these posts—these are specifically for Spanish naval vessels."

"Lo siento, lo siento. I am one of five ships sent by the financier Robert Perkins to support the

Spanish Navy in repelling an imminent attack by One-Eyed Willy and the Kinsman of the Tide."

"Solo cinqo barcos? Just five? Well, that is not many ships at all! We were expecting ten ships and not until noon this day," Dominguez replied.

"Si, Mr. Dominguez. However, Mr. Perkins, as intelligent as he is, decided it might be in the best interest of both crowns to have half of the fleet arrive ahead of schedule as a precautionary measure." He gave a beaming and self-assured smile.

"I assume Mr. Perkins, as generous as he is, hasn't forgotten about his old friend harbor master Dominguez?" Mr. Dominguez replied, his mouth almost salivating at the thought of gifts.

"Not in the least. We have rum, butter, honey, tobacco, ale and a bit of coin. Shall I have the men unload and spread the wealth amongst the ships as well?"

"Yes Mr. Newhardt, that sounds delightful," said Dominguez.

The men started unloading the barrels, each one with the tiniest of holes on the bottom so as not to be noticed by the harbor master or any of the guards.

As these barrels were rolled to their respective resting places, they left the smallest trail of gunpowder in their wake, and eventually, all the barrels were set up around the docks in front of every ship, cannon and defensive post.

"Dominguez, would you like any rum or tobacco for the guards? Would you like me to bring some to the Castillo?" Artimus asked. "Every man deserves a treat when working in the defense of his country and his fleet."

"Oh! Please, Senor Newhardt, and if you can keep it a secret, go ahead and put a few over by the guards' station where most of the men are. Oh, and Mr. Newhardt, I am going to need you to move your ship across the bay, since we are expecting two more galleons to arrive today."

"Consider it done. As soon as we have finished delivering these barrels, we will relocate the ship." The men rolled a few barrels over to the guard station, a few more at the gates to the Castillo, and then a few more was trundled across to each of the Spanish galleons.

After all the gunpowder was set up, the men retreated to the ship and left one barrel at the edge of the dock. They untied the ropes and slowly inched away from the docks.

Sebastian and Blackheart reached the tunnel and easily took out the two guards that were out in front. The thirty men quietly entered the tunnel of wretched foulness and one by one, each of the men climbed up the latrine. The stench of death, piss and feces was no match for these members of the crew, each one handpicked by Willy and Blackheart.

They were known because of their ferocity and lack of fear, and as none had a queasy gut.

Once inside the Castillo, they began to spread out and take out the guards in the jail, which was the fortress that protected the home to the Governor, inland on a hill.

There was a gate at the entrance to the rest of the Castillo, where Morgan would be located.

"Do you want the towers or the first floor?" Sebastian asked Blackheart.

"Which is easier for you?" Blackheart replied.

"Age before beauty, old man."

"Then I'll take the towers," Blackheart answered.

"I thought you would."

"Sebastian, don't be a hero. Do what needs to be done and get out. Follow the plan as your father has played it for you over and over," Blackheart replied.

"Yes, Uncle," Sebastian replied as he and his men journeyed to the first floor while Blackheart and the rest climbed up to the towers.

Each member of the crew knew the importance of the mission and that they had a responsibility and intended to complete the job whether it meant living or dying.

At the front gates of the Castillo, the drawbridge was raised.

"Wake the commander! It is Henry Morgan. I have come with an urgent message."

The drawbridge was lowered, and Lieutenant Commander Wallace was steadfast and swiftly walked across the bridge accompanied by one of his guards.

The guard then opened the gates for Morgan and three of his men.

"Mr. Morgan, good God! What message could be so urgent at this godawful hour in the morning? The cockerel has not yet crowed and the lamps are far from extinguished!"

"I have a message for the Governor. I must speak with him at once."

"What message? The Governor isn't in Havana. What message?" the commander asked.

"I've received word that Willy and the Kinsmen are going to attack the island and attempt to steal the treasure."

"That's impossible. As you can see, the Governor has reinforcements from Britain, a blockade of the canal and the bay, and doubled his regiments in and around the Castillo. You would have to be eager to die or absolutely insane to attempt such a feat."

As the Commander was speaking those words, Blackheart's men were removing the guards from their posts in the towers and their high positions around the Castillo. Sebastian and his men were gradually making their way down the halls of the first floor of the Castillo, taking out every guard they come across. They were using swords and knives as the element of surprise, for any gunshot might spoil the plan. Sebastian ran along the side of the wall until he reached the door to the drawbridge, then poked his head from behind it to give Morgan the signal.

Back on the Redemption, Willy yelled, "Devereaux, where is my treat? My treat, I say!"

"It's coming, Captain, just a few more moments." Devereaux took a few handfuls of corn kernels and threw them into a pot on the fire and covered it.

"When is this supposed thievery supposed to commence?" Commander Wallace then said to

Henry Morgan. "And do you think it will be punctual?"

Morgan pulled out a pistol and cried out, "It will be punctual, and it is—now!" He shot Wallace in the head, then quickly stabbed the other guard in the neck.

At that moment ,Willy yelled, "Come about!"

The Redemption came about and faced the canal and the Castillo de Morro.

"Fire," Willy yelled as the corn started popping in the pot. The sounds of fifty cannons roared as the cannonballs ripped through one of the ships at the entrance of the canal, turning brick and stone to dust as the cannonballs raged on, wreaking havoc on the walls of the Castillo.

Henry Morgan and his men raced across the drawbridge to meet Sebastian.

"What now, Mr. Morgan?" Sebastian said as twenty or more Spanish soldiers converged on their location.

"You go ahead to the vault and we will hold them off," Morgan insisted.

Sebastian and his men fought their way through and headed toward the vault.

Artimus was on his ship with a rifle aimed at the barrel he had left on the dock. He took a shot but missed his target. Dominguez noticed and started running toward the barrel to throw it into the bay. Artimus had another shot, and this time, hit the barrel on the edge of the dock.

It exploded, blasting pieces of Dominguez's body everywhere and igniting all the gunpowder trails on the dockside. Soon, the dock was ablaze.

One after the other, all the Spanish ships were soon engulfed with fire as they exploded, obliterating the once fortified docks of the Spanish Navy. Artimus's ship came about and began to unleash all the power in its artillery against the Castillo de la Punta.

The three ships out at sea also fired their cannons at both fortifications mercilessly.

The Spanish ships that made up the blockade were quickly sent to the depths of the Caribbean with Davey Jones.

After a bloody battle in the courtyard of the Castillo, Henry Morgan and his men arrived to join Sebastian and Blackheart as they formed a line.

The vault area was filled with smoke, and after taking a beating from Sebastian and his men, the Spanish soldiers and commander formed a line for what Morgan thought was the last defense between the crown's gold and Willy's henchmen.

Then, from behind, another group of Spanish soldiers began firing off muskets and pistols.

"We will hold them off. You go and get the gold," Morgan yelled to Sebastian, as if sending him off to buy vegetables from the market; he made it all sound so easy.

Sebastian yelled "fire!" as did the opposing commander and both sides charged at each other. Blackheart rolled a barrel of gunpowder down the corridor and it hit the door to the vault.

He then fired his pistol, causing an explosion, the blast sending everyone off their feet in different directions. As the smoke was starting to clear, Blackheart arrived to help Sebastian to his feet. With both men's ears ringing from the detonation, Blackheart said, "Are you alright lad?" Sebastian most likely was not alright.

He touched the top of his head and saw blood on his hand.

"I think I'll be alright," he replied. But he really was not sure.

There was a gigantic hole in the wall where the door to the vault used to be.

Sebastian hardly dared feel at his skull to check it did not also have a hole in it. But the fact he remained able to stand was a good sign.

Meanwhile, Blackheart's men were staving off what was left of the Spanish soldiers as he and Sebastian made their way into the vault.

Inside, to everyone's relief and astonishment, there had to be forty chests and enormous barrels filled with silver, diamonds, gold, rubies and emeralds.

As the men started carrying out the chests, Morgan and his men came back to help.

Sebastian signaled for two of his men to bring over a chest, and they brought one over and opened it, forcing open the heavy lid with a look of great greed and anticipation.

The very sight of all those jewels and all that gold put a smile on Morgan's face.

"We did it, Sebastian, we did it. We are rich," Morgan said.

"I don't know how we did it, but we did," Blackheart replied.

"We need to hurry, I'm sure there will be reinforcements arriving at any moment," Sebastian suggested.

"You look hurt, Sebastian? I'll take care of the chests and have them loaded onto my ship,"

Morgan replied. "See, there is much blood on your hair and face."

"Nonsense, Henry. We will stay and accompany you on your ship."

"Morgan is right, we should get you back to the ship to have a doctor look at that right away," Blackheart said.

"I agree with Blackheart, you've outdone yourself, Sebastian. You have already delivered more than the best. Your father will be proud. We wouldn't be carrying out this treasure if it wasn't for you. So please, extend my humble gratitude to your father for bringing me in on this adventure and we will see each other in Panama," Morgan replied.

"Very well, Henry," said Blackheart.

"We will leave some men to assist in loading the gold onto your ship," said Sebastian.

"Again, not necessary; kind, but not needed. Get your men to safety and we will split the gold in Panama. Take care of yourself."

"What shall I tell Willy?" Blackheart asked.

"Tell Willy to lead the way out of the bay and we will sail side by side to Panama." "Aye Henry, the Kinsmen will be most proud," said Blackheart.

"Aye, they will. We will all toast in Panama," said Morgan.

Morgan ordered his men to start loading the chests onto his ship—the only ship that was left in the bay, docked in front of the Castillo de la Fuerza. Morgan oversaw that every one of the chests was loaded. He yelled for the men to ready the cannons.

"And now, we are going to blow Willy and Artimus Drake out of the bay," Morgan said.

Just as Morgan and the Rum Rummer were just about to shove off, one of his men noticed someone on the hill waving a burning British flag.

"Morgan!" the man shouted.

Morgan rushed over and grabbed the scope to look—it was Blackheart.

He lowered the flag, which ignited something on the ground and the trail of gunpowder quickly started its intended route.

"Untie those ropes! Shove off, men! Now, now!" Morgan screamed.

It was too late, and within thirty seconds, the fire had reached the Rum Rummer, setting off the two barrels left on the dock by Artimus himself.

"Oh shit," Morgan yelled, and dived into the sea as his ship exploded from all the gunpowder on board. Willy, Artimus, Blackheart and Sebastian all broke out in celebration.

Morgan's ship went up in flames.

Devereaux ran, with the pot of corn all popped up, to One-Eyed Willy.

"Here you are Captain. Your treat. I'm sorry it took so long."

"Here you are Mr. Claybourne, try this recipe and enjoy the ending to the play," Willy said to the Lieutenant. Sebastian, Blackheart and the rest of the crew on land made their way through the jungle and back to the boats where Thomas and Sara were waiting.

"I can't believe it, they actually did it," Thomas said as he hugged Sara to his chest.

They both smiled as they watched the men bring all the chests and barrels filled with jewels and gold. Sara watched very closely, yet hadn't seen her brother.

"Has anyone seen Sebastian?"

None of the men answered and Sara started to think terrible things, then she noticed Sebastian at a distance holding his head, being held up by one of the other men.

Blackheart was a few hundred feet behind them.

She ran to him and gave him a hug like she'd never hugged anyone before.

"Sebastian, my dear brother, are you alright? I don't know what I would do if I lost you!" Thomas ran behind and put his head under Sebastian's other arm.

They walked him back to the boats.

"I say we load up the ship and make haste out of this cove as fast as the wind can take us. In order for that to happen, there's work that has to be done. What say you, men?" Blackheart shouted.

"Aye," the crew shouted back.

"First, we should gather a few supplies, fresh water being one of them," Blackheart said. Thomas picked up one of the empty barrels and went to fill it with water.

"Sebastian, I want you on the first boat back to the ship to see the doc. Sara, I want you to oversee the storage of all the gold on the ship, so I want you on that boat as well." "Yes, Uncle," said Sara and they all got to work.

Back on the King's Redemption, some of the men were eating popped corn and watching the Rum Runner, along with a dozen Spanish warships, burn and sink to the bottom of the bay and take their place in Davey Jones' Locker.

Artimus steered his ship alongside Willy's as Willy stood on the quarter deck.

"Listen up, lads. What we have done here today will echo through sands of time. Men and women all over the world will tell bedtime stories to their children about this day for centuries to come. You are all now richer than you could have ever imagined, and my gratitude to each and every one of you could not extend any further than it does today.

"We can all use some much-needed rest. Artimus Drake will lead us out of the bay and most importantly, what are all you lily-livered swine looking at? Back to work or I'll hang ya meself!" Artimus's men released the ropes from Willy's ship and shoved off toward the canal.

A quarter mile ahead of Willy and a few minutes later, the thump of two cannons roared, and without a moment's notice, two more.

All four cannonballs hit Artimus's ship, causing extensive damage.

The ship was going down and taking on water, when out of the smoke of the burning Spanish vessel in the canal, a dark gargantuan ship emerged. The ship had black sails, three masts, four rows of guns—it was the largest vessel anyone had ever seen.

There was more firing.

"Abandon ship!" Artimus shouted and his ship was ripped into shreds by two more cannonballs. The black ship sailed through the wreckage of Artimus's ship, coming to a stop next to the King's Redemption, almost belittling the largest vessel in the British navy.

Artimus and what men were left began to climb aboard the Redemption.

Jolly Rogers went to the side of the black ship and yelled, "Throw your ropes over and surrender or you'll suffer an even worse fate then they did."

Willy nodded his head to Devereaux to throw their ropes, and wildly waved the white flag.

"Intelligent choice gentlemen, very intelligent. Now where's One-Eyed Willy? I want my jewel?" Jolly Rogers said.

THE END

ABOUT THE AUTHOR

Growing up in a small suburb of New York City, Lawrence Phillip enjoyed writing music and lyrics. Translating his love of writing music to writing stories, he has aspirations of becoming a novelist. When not writing, he enjoys spending time with family and friends. *One Eyed Willy* is his first novel.

CPSIA information can be obtained
at www.ICGtesting.com
Printed in the USA
LVHW051034130122
708377LV00012B/552